BODY GUARD

A DEVLIN KIRK MYSTERY

VIKING
Mystery
Suspense

Also By Rex Burns

Rex Burns

BODYGUARD

A DEVLIN KIRK MYSTERY

Viking

VIKING
Published by the Penguin Group
Viking Penguin, a division of Penguin Books USA Inc.,
375 Hudson Street, New York, New York 10014, U.S.A.
Penguin Books Ltd, 27 Wrights Lane,
London W8 5TZ, England
Penguin Books Australia Ltd, Ringwood,
Victoria, Australia
Penguin Books Canada Ltd, 2801 John Street,
Markham, Ontario, Canada L3R 1B4
Penguin Books (N.Z.) Ltd, 182–190 Wairau Road,
Auckland 10, New Zealand

Penguin Books Ltd, Registered Offices:
Harmondsworth, Middlesex, England

First published in 1991 by Viking Penguin,
a division of Penguin Books USA Inc.

1 3 5 7 9 10 8 6 4 2

PUBLISHER'S NOTE
This is a work of fiction. Names, characters, places, and
incidents either are the product of the author's
imagination or are used fictitiously, and any resemblance
to actual persons, living or dead, events, or locales is
entirely coincidental.

LIBRARY OF CONGRESS CATALOGING IN PUBLICATION DATA
Burns, Rex.
Body guard / Rex Burns.
p.   cm.
"A Devlin Kirk mystery."
ISBN 0-670-83320-7
I. Title.
PS3552.U7325B63   1991
813'.54—dc20   91-50241

Printed in the United States of America
Set in Times Roman

To Audrey and Dusty

BODY GUARD

A DEVLIN KIRK MYSTERY

The Advantage case was Kirk and Associates' first big job in three months. Based on growing pilferage and theft, an increasing number of behavior problems, and especially a rapid climb in the accident rate—the classic indicators of substance abuse on the job—Advantage Corporation's management suspected that a worker in the warehouse or assembly area was peddling dope to the employees. Because Kirk and Associates was hungry, Devlin took a chance and put in the new kid, Chris Newman. Having come to Denver in search of bright lights and excitement, he'd wandered into Kirk's office looking for work. With his long hair and struggling mustache, Chris looked like a seventeen-year-old trying to act old enough to drink; and except for his lack of experience, he was a good choice. Unlike Bunchcroft or Kirk, he was new to Denver and passed easily as a young kid on his first job because that's just what he was. He'd recently moved from the Western Slope. Growing up on his parents' ranch near Creede, Colorado, he'd learned how to handle himself around heavy equipment as well as in the woods. Like farm kids everywhere, he knew a lot about tools and machinery. That made him a quick study for the various blue-collar jobs that provided cover for agents. It was a month or so later that Devlin told Reznick, the regional manager for

Advantage Corp., that, sure, Kirk and Associates could handle the case.

Like the rest of us in this racket, Chris got his training on the job. He started with the usual surveillance and paper serving which was routine and whose profits just about covered his salary. He did well. In fact, he found excitement and pleasure in the daily variation of assignments and the different people he ran across. It was, he told Bunch once, a lot like working on the ranch because no two chores were exactly the same. And a lot of times he was on his own to solve problems that came up. Bunch had told Chris when he was hired that he was getting a front-row seat at the greatest show on earth, and so far Chris thought the job lived up to its billing. But this was his first undercover work and his first solo, as well. Usually, Devlin said, he would have placed Chris on the job with an experienced operative so they could work together and Chris could pick up pointers. On this assignment, however, two new employees would stand out like a fart in church. But the job was too important for the agency to let it go by. Would he be interested?

Chris reckoned he would be.

If his inexperience worked against him, the fact that he looked like anything but an agent worked for him. Kirk told Bunch he thought the kid's skills with people and his native wit would get him through. Bunch told Chris that it was just a routine gig and he'd get used to it. All he was supposed to do was be a pair of eyes. No buys, no infiltration, no evidence gathering, no contact with suspects. Chris figured he could manage that much. Ten years ago, when he was thirteen, he'd started running cows alone up in the San Juans. The towering ice- and rock-capped mountains formed a wall around Creede and provided summer pasture for the ranch. There, the ability to look and listen meant survival, and that was no different from what he was supposed to do here in Denver. Besides, he hadn't yet met a townie who was as wild and mean as some of the drunk cowboys he'd tangled with as a high school kid. Not that he'd won any fights with those hot-eyed yahoos. But he had been able to talk his way out of most of them, and people were people all over. Just look and listen and phone in a report to Devlin once a day.

That's what Bunch and Devlin were waiting for that afternoon as the September sun stretched through the large arched window of their office and the grumble of casters rolled across the ceiling. For some reason, the sculptress in the room above moved her epoxy creations here and there about this time of day. The sound grated on Bunch's nerves like a knife blade over bone. Usually it didn't bother him, but he was still pissed that Kirk had given the undercover assignment to Chris instead of to him.

"I mean, for Christ's sake, Dev, it's been almost three weeks the kid's been in there. I know—so do you—that things are happening right under his nose and he doesn't even know what to look for."

The reason Chris rather than Bunch had been placed was because Bunch was too well known. And he was too big: he'd look like an elephant at a pony show. Average height, average looks, above-average intelligence—that's what you wanted in an undercover agent, and that's what they had with Chris. Bunch's real problem, besides being too tall, too ugly, and too dumb, Devlin said, was boredom. Bunch agreed with the boredom part of it: he was sick of sitting on insurance cases. That was half of Kirk and Associates' work nowadays—watching people who claimed disabilities or loss so insurance companies would make them rich. The other half was process serving and sitting around the office waiting for that magic call from someone who needed their specialty: industrial security.

"If you went into that factory, Bunch, you'd scare every suspect into hiding. It's tricky enough planting somebody who looks like Chris. If we tried it with you—or me—nothing would move."

Bunch understood that, but it didn't help much. One of the reasons he'd quit being a cop was because of the dull bureaucratic routines that kept stifling the excitement he felt on the streets. That, and the convolutions of the laws, which had made enforcing them seem like bailing water with a sieve.

"Besides," said Kirk, "he told me yesterday he has a suspect."

"Yeah. Somebody might be peddling baggies. Wowee."

"It's a lead. It might turn into something."

Bunch slapped his stomach and watched the flesh jiggle. "My gut's turning into fat. Sitting in goddamn cars all goddamn day."

Kirk filed one bill under "Wait for payment" and another under "Pay as soon as possible." The criterion was the shade of pink tinting the past-due column. "You want to do skip tracing? Or hunt straying husbands like Vinny Landrum does? That'll give you a little exercise."

"I saw that scumbag the other day. He said business was never better." Bunch heaved to his feet and wandered over to stare out the single large window. A glass panel had been cranked open in the hope of snagging a little stray air. All it gathered was diesel fumes from the trucks in Wazee Street a floor below. He spit through the opening and watched the fleck of white drift away and disappear. "Asked how we're doing."

"I hope you didn't tell him."

"I lied. I said we were doing great."

"Well, I'm glad you brightened his day."

"He didn't believe me."

What Vinny Landrum believed or didn't believe wasn't important in God's scheme of things or Kirk's. He didn't really think Bunch cared that much either. But it gave the big man something else to grouse about. "What's new on Zell and Truman?"

Those were the two latest insurance cases. Garth Zell suffered a back injury when he slipped on a supermarket's wet floor. The insurance company suspected it was a pratfall, but his lawyer claimed permanent disability. Zell couldn't hold any kind of job; his connubial bliss had flown. His settlement from a teary-eyed jury had been almost one and a half million dollars.

It was a type of injury and an amount that automatically called for an investigation—a point his lawyer had probably warned Zell about, because neither Kirk nor Bunch had yet seen anything suspicious. Truman's injury was a whiplash that, her lawyer told a jury, kept her in a neck brace twenty-four hours a day and gave her constant migraines. The insurance company's doctors testified that she didn't need to wear the brace, but they were the poorer liars. The result was a very nice piece of change to help cure the lady's alleged headache.

"Same thing. Same goddamned thing, Dev, and if I have to spend another week jammed in that Subaru with my knees up around my ears . . ." He almost said it. He almost told Dev that his string was fraying out, and by God if something better didn't come along, he'd find another job with a hell of a lot more excitement. But he didn't. For one thing, Dev wouldn't believe him. They'd been through this before. For another, he knew he couldn't find a job he liked better. It had its stretches of boredom—Christ knew it had those. But there was always the possibility it could change quickly. And even if it didn't, Bunch liked the freedom. It was the closest he'd come to being his own boss and still letting someone else worry about the payroll. The electronic wheedle of the telephone saved him from answering Kirk's raised eyebrows. Devlin picked up the receiver, expecting Chris Newman. But it wasn't a familiar voice. Instead, a hesitant male asked if Kirk and Associates provided personal security.

"Do you mean 'personnel'? Employee screenings, background searches?"

"No—personal. Like, ah, bodyguards."

Kirk glanced at Bunch, who was lounging on the rail that protected the lower part of the office window and staring out moodily. Across the flat roofs of the district's old warehouses, the mountains formed a ragged horizon west of town. Bodyguard work wasn't something Kirk and Associates listed on its letterhead, but it was a task Devlin was familiar with. It had been one of his principal responsibilities as a Secret Service agent. And it could offer a welcome change from surveillance.

"Sometimes we do. Would you care to tell us what you need? That way you can find out if we're the agency for you."

The receiver was silent.

"No obligation, Mr.—?"

"Uh, Humphries. Roland Humphries. It's after five, now. How late is your office open?"

It sounded as if the voice hoped Kirk would say they were closed. "If you want to come by, I can wait for you, Mr. Humphries."

"No—no . . . Maybe tomorrow. You're open in the morning?"

"Nine o'clock."

The voice said okay and verified the address in the Yellow Pages ad. Kirk told him about the free customer parking behind the building. When he hung up, Bunch looked back over his shoulder. "What was all that about?"

"Potential client."

"Not more goddamn surveillance work!"

In a way it was, but before Kirk could explain, the telephone tweedled again and this time it was Newman.

"Dev? I really think I've got something. But I'm not sure what it all means. I'd like to talk with you about it." His tense voice sounded worried. Kirk mentioned a couple places where they could meet without seeming conspicuous. Chris chose the bowling alley.

The sun-blistered bowling pin looked like a tilted exclamation mark against the darkening sky. Kirk scooted his Austin-Healey 3000 across oncoming traffic into the dusty gravel of an almost empty parking lot.

Chris sat at the four-stool bar beyond the white fluorescent glare of the rental shelves and sipped a beer. A few bowlers slid along the lanes. The evening crowd—if there was one—hadn't arrived yet, and the periodic rumble and crash echoed hollowly under the girders lacing the tin roof. He finally saw the two large men come in and turned away from them as they settled onto stools next to him. Devlin was big in a rangy sort of way, tall and slender. Chris hadn't been surprised to learn that he had been a rower at college. But Bunch reminded him of one of his father's prize Charolais bulls—the biggest ones, which moved with that stiff delicacy large animals have. Chris had seen one of those bulls pull up a tether stake with a shrug as if the seven-foot-long pole had been a rotten weed. He figured Bunch could do the same. Right now the bigger man was complaining about being cramped in the Healey's cockpit and asking Devlin why he would waste money to rebuild a piece of crap like that.

"Because it's the only sports car that fits me," said Devlin. He ordered two beers from the woman who wandered down from the rental shelves to ask them what they wanted.

"Well, it sure as hell doesn't fit the two of us," said Bunch.

"That's another reason."

Chris had a good start on size, but he knew he would never grow as big as either Bunch or Devlin. Still, he wondered if in time he could gain the kind of easy comfort they carried with them wherever they went. He'd seen it on a couple of people around Creede, weather-toughened men who knew they could handle themselves no matter what. Not that he felt himself awkward or inept—he wasn't, not in a lot of situations. But there were times and places around this city when he didn't quite feel he understood what was going on. He knew it was mostly a matter of time and that a man could do a lot worse than have Devlin and Bunch showing him the ropes. In fact, he'd found himself more than once in front of the long mirror on the bathroom door of that dumpy little apartment of his, standing the way he remembered Devlin standing, or turning with the whole upper body the way Bunch did.

The woman brought the two draft beers and took the money down to the cash register to ring up the sale. When she was out of hearing, Devlin's voice murmured, "What do you have for us, Chris?"

Keeping his face toward the bowlers, Chris scratched at the mustache he'd struggled to grow for this job. "I think I have a lead on a dealer. But I don't know if he's working alone or with somebody."

A question came back. "Name?"

"Dennis Porter. He's in assembly. I haven't seen him sell anything, but he hangs around his locker a lot—just what you told me to look for. And yesterday I heard a couple guys joke about going past the candy store."

Kirk drank deeply and wiped the foam from his lip with his thumb. "I'll check the company records tomorrow. What do you think his action is?"

The excitement of hunting a real-life dealer—of discovering one himself—was still in Chris's voice, though he tried to make it sound as if it was no big thrill. "I think it's pot. Maybe some pills. But like I say, I'm not sure. I didn't want to move too close without talking to you first."

"That's fine, Chris. You just keep playing it cool. Bunch or I will handle any contacts. Anything else?"

There was. He turned back to the bar and waited until a pair of bowlers passed in the aisle before answering. "I got this feeling about a couple other guys. That's why I wanted to talk to you."

Kirk knew that sometimes those feelings were truer than evidence. "Where do they work?"

"Over in shipping. Like I say, it's nothing I can pin down." Chris had been trying to define it himself, but couldn't. That was why he wanted to test his reaction against Devlin's opinion. "There're three guys always hanging around together. Warehouse crew, real standoffish. Everybody else, you know, they joke around, say 'How you doing.' Not these guys."

"Do they seem to be into anything?"

"Kind of. It's like they got some business going that they don't want anybody else to know about, so they're playing cool about it."

"Are they homos?"

Chris hadn't thought of that. "I don't think so. I don't think that's it." What he didn't add was that since coming to Denver, he had run across a couple. Their eager interest in him still made the flesh on his back crawl with embarrassment. But the men at the plant didn't have that about them.

"Have they done anything suspicious?"

"Well, last week during the lunch break I saw them in the warehouse—the receiving section."

"They're not supposed to be there?"

"Oh yeah, that's where they work. But it was lunch hour, and they went in and out three or four times, like they were busy at something."

"Was the supervisor around?"

"Not on lunch break."

"Carrying anything?"

"Nothing I could see. That's the problem." Newman ran a hand through his rat tail of long hair, another touch to his disguise. "You think they might be stealing stuff?"

"What's there to steal?"

That was another puzzle, because most of the units that came into receiving were in sealed canisters: large electronics components from the East Coast plant shipped here to be assembled with the components that came in from the West Coast. He explained that to Devlin.

Kirk was silent. He jotted a few words down in a small notebook. The woman pushed her folded arms off the glass top of the glowing rental shelf and came back to find out if they would like a refill. When she left again, Kirk asked Chris, "Any names?"

"Just the first names. Off their shirts: Eddie, Scott, and Johnny." He didn't have last names because it was hard to ask fellow workers a lot of questions about who this guy was or that one. Most of them would ask why the hell he wanted to know. Or else they'd shrug suspiciously and tell him to ask them himself. Unfriendly, yes, but more than that. Chris knew a lot of it was because he looked so young, and even more was the result of a clannishness the workers felt toward anyone who hadn't been there awhile. A lot of them, even if they weren't into pilfering or dealing, didn't like the idea of a company fink. "I got their locker numbers, though." He slid a scrap of paper down the bar and Devlin covered it with his elbow. "You want me to try and get close to them?"

"No. You just hang loose. You've been doing fine, Chris. Really good work. I'll get to Reznick with this and see how far he wants us to go. Check in tomorrow." Kirk folded the scrap into his jacket pocket and drank deeply. "Anything you need?"

"No." But he had to ask. "How much longer you want me on this?"

Kirk studied the light brown eyes behind the rimless glasses. The lenses were clear glass, he knew, another cosmetic touch to emphasize Newman's youth and apparent innocence. "It could be another three or four weeks. It's hard to say. But listen, if you want out, just tell me."

"No, no—nothing like that. I was just curious, you know."

And, Kirk thought, perhaps getting a little lonely, too. Even the experienced agents hit those times when the assumed life seemed to isolate them more and more from the world they were familiar with. Then a hunger for old normalities rose like an ache in the chest. "You're doing a fine job, Chris. Just don't take any chances, hear me?"

"Yeah. Hey, don't worry about me. There's nothing to this."

"And don't get too cocky," said Kirk. "That's when mistakes are made."

Chris sobered quickly. "All right, Dev. I hear you. I'll play it cool."

"Okay. Any hint of trouble, bail out and call me right away."

"Will do."

In the bar mirror, Kirk watched the young man drain his glass and, still apparently ignoring the two large men on the stools, stroll out the door.

Bunch asked, "How's he holding up?"

"He's a little nervous. But trying hard."

"Think he'll do?"

"Sure."

They spent another five minutes at the bar and then followed Chris out. Kirk didn't expect Newman to have a tail, but he didn't want to be too careless about the possibility either.

After a while in this business, Kirk knew, you discovered there really were people who lived by only one rule: what's in it for them. Any other rule, or person, that got in their way was expendable. It was something Bunch had known all his life, he told Devlin once. The only thing that surprised him was Devlin's not discovering it sooner. But then Bunch believed Kirk had led a sheltered life.

Crammed into the Healey and back in the flow of traffic, Bunch asked, "So what did he tell you?"

Kirk explained it and Bunch shifted restlessly on the narrow seat of the car. One of his shoulders and an arm hung over the door's padded lip. The other shoulder jammed against Kirk's and made it hard for him to shift. "If the only dope around is pot, Chris should be able to smell it," Bunch said.

"Unless they're smoking it outside in their cars or at the motor pool."

"I don't know, Dev. That crap sticks like a whore's perfume. You can smell it in people's clothes and hair." He added, "I still think I should have been the one to go in."

"Let's give him a chance, Bunch. He has to learn sooner or later."

"Sure, sure. I'm willing if Reznick is. He's the one paying the bill."

Which, Kirk knew, might be a problem. The regional manager for Advantage Corp. had urged haste in the investigation and hadn't been especially pleased to learn it might take four to six weeks. Now he had to be told it might take longer if there was an extensive network in the plant. Reznick was a decisive executive. He wanted things done and he wanted them done yesterday, by God. And, he made it clear, he didn't tolerate screwups. But in the long run, Kirk believed, it would be cheapest to do the job right, and that was what he intended to advise the man.

Mr. Humphries had been told nine o'clock. He was on time. Kirk wasn't. Humphries waited restlessly, feeling awkward and embarrassed to have everyone who passed on the second-floor landing glance at him and guess his business. The darkened glass of the door said only "Kirk and Associates," but Humphries felt people knew it was the office of a private investigator. And they knew he was in trouble. Probably scorned him for needing help, just as he had secretly scorned others for their weaknesses or illnesses. He glanced at his Rolex and promised himself three minutes more, max. Then he was out of here. This had been Mitsuko's idea in the first place, not his. She was the one who kept bringing up those worrisome what-ifs. She even seemed to enjoy it. It was a cultural thing, he knew—the Chrysanthemum and the Sword view of the world. At least he had to view it that way, because in other ways—so many of them—she was the woman who fulfilled his every dream. In fact, he could feel—just standing here and thinking about her— a gentle tightening between his legs, that strange clenching she knew so well how to stimulate. And then equally well how to relieve. Still, *she* wasn't standing here in public making a fool of herself.

Hurrying shoes ran up the iron stairway and echoed in the

atrium that formed the center of the remodeled warehouse. Mr. Humphries saw a tall man, younger than himself, take the stairs two at a time. It was, he guessed, the dilatory Mr. Kirk, and Humphries wasn't all that impressed with what he saw.

A bit late from the morning workout, Devlin sprinted up the stairs toward the man who stood tensely beside the office door. Bunch was still jogging on the Cherry Creek bike path and would reach the office in half an hour or so. With the kind of business Kirk and Associates catered to—industrial security was supposed to be their specialty—few clients came to the office. Most of the contacts came in over the telephone, and then either Bunch or Devlin would follow up with a visit to the prospective customer's office. Moreover, the phone answerer and fax machine stood watch twenty-four hours a day, so their sense of opening and closing was fairly casual. Which, Kirk supposed, had irritated the slender man in the expensive gray suit, because he let Kirk see him glance at his gold watch as he unlocked the door.

"Sorry I'm late, Mr. Humphries." He motioned to the only visitor's chair in the room and opened panels in the window to air out the overnight stuffiness. The red message light blinked on the recorder, and Kirk rewound the tape and turned it off as he sat down. "You say you need a bodyguard?"

Humphries was somewhere in his mid-thirties, possibly nearing forty. But he had one of those faces that aged well and appeared healthily free of wrinkles. Sandy, straight hair fell from a part designed to cover a thinning spot on his crown. He had blue eyes that bulged slightly, hinting of a possible thyroid problem. "First, I'd like to know a little about your qualifications. What guarantees can you offer for such work, Mr.—ah—Kirk?"

Kirk smiled. His face lost some of its lean wariness and made him look even younger than Humphries had assumed.

"As I mentioned yesterday, we don't often do such work. But if we can't help you, I'll recommend several agencies who might."

"If you can't do it, why did you tell me to come down here?" Humphries almost added, "And then make me stand waiting at your door."

"I said we don't often do it. It depends."

"On what?"

The young man ticked off the points on three fingers. "On the reasons you need protection. On the nature of the protection you need. On the range of commitment you're asking for." He leaned back and placed his fingers together just in front of his chin. Humphries had an intimation that despite his youthfulness, the man might be very capable indeed. Certainly he spoke like a gentleman and not out of the side of his mouth as he'd assumed private detectives usually did.

"Do you want to give me a little background?" Kirk watched Humphries think it over for a few seconds. The long fingers of the man's left hand twisted a ring on his right. The large wad of ornately carved gold bore Greek letters on its red stone. That, the suit, the supple leather of his shoes, all breathed money, and Kirk was glad the building's cleaning crew had made its rounds last night.

"I'm not sure how long we'll need—ah—protection. I'm not even sure I should be here. But my wife insisted." Kirk said nothing to help out and Humphries took a deep breath. "I think I'm being followed."

"Why, Mr. Humphries?"

"Well, I've seen this car repeatedly. A brown one. And I'm also sure there have been prowlers around my house."

Kirk was more specific. "Why would someone want to follow you?"

"I don't know. That's one of the things I want you to find out. But someone's watching me, and I'm worried. My wife and I are both worried."

"Have you gone to the police? It would save a lot of money and probably be very effective."

"I've talked to a policeman. An Officer Fredericks. He said there was nothing they could do. He said no crime had been committed yet." Humphries snorted angrily. "I guess I'm supposed to wait until after I've been attacked to file a complaint."

Devlin studied the man's pale eyes and wondered what he was hiding from him and why. It wouldn't be the first time a client held back the real reason he needed a private detective. "If we do take the assignment, Mr. Humphries, we'll need to know as much as you do about why someone might want to follow you."

"I just told you I don't know! I came here for help, not to be insulted." The man drew his feet under the chair as if to stand. Kirk said nothing. The moment teetered until Humphries sighed again and the stiffness went out of his shoulders. "If I knew—if I had any inkling—I would tell you." He added, "After all, I do have more than a passing interest in the matter."

"You say your wife insisted that you come here?"

"That I get protection." Humphries liked precision. "I was the one who selected your firm, based on the recommendation of someone you worked for previously."

"Oh? Who's that?"

"Owen McAllister." The name had weight, Humphries knew, and he borrowed some of it. "We were having drinks the other day and he happened to mention you."

"I'm grateful. What do you do, Mr. Humphries? Tell me about yourself."

The implied answer was that Humphries was rich enough to do nothing if he chose to. But since the men in his family had engaged in business or the professions for six generations, he had studied electrical engineering and moved from that into the proprietorship of a firm that had been bought by Sanyo for, as he said without modesty, an impressive sum. Now he was engaged in starting a new company to explore and develop the artificial-intelligence components that the next generation of computers would need. "Robotics is the new frontier in computer work. A-I is the road to that frontier."

His office was in the Meridian Office Park south of Denver. His home was farther south just across the line in Douglas

County. It was, Kirk knew, a semirural area of large lots and homes to match, scattered over broken prairie and pine-dotted foothills. A lot of professional and business people who commute up I-25 to the metro area settle there because of its isolation and beauty.

"Did the problem start before or after you began the new company?"

Humphries stared at Devlin. "I never thought of that."

"Is it possible?"

The man twisted the signet ring and frowned at the rug that covered part of the office's shiny wooden floor. "It's possible, I suppose. It's a highly competitive business, of course. But I can't believe that any of the people familiar with what I'm doing would stoop to . . ." He ended with a shrug.

"Names?"

"I can't make accusations like that, Mr. Kirk!"

"It's not an accusation. It's merely hypothetical."

"Still, this is very embarrassing. I mean, you will please keep this confidential, won't you? These people are my friends as well as competitors. In fact, 'competitors' is too harsh a word for—"

"We keep our mouths shut, Mr. Humphries." Kirk held a pencil ready. "Who might profit from a knowledge of your activities?"

"Well . . . Gunter. Gunter Schmidt—he's working in the same area. In fact, we exchange information occasionally. But it's a friendly rivalry."

"He's an engineer too?"

"Yes. He was recently promoted to head the A-I project at Reliable Electronics. I can't imagine him doing what you suggest. In fact, I've asked him more than once to work for me."

"But he hasn't."

"Not yet."

"Anyone else?"

"Michael Stratford. He's a vice president for research at Memory Technology. They're very active in A-I."

"And interested in what you're doing?"

"Of course. I'm interested in them, too."

"Do you think he could be the one?"

Humphries weighed that. "I don't like to think so. I really don't know the man that well, but . . ."

Devlin jotted the name down. "Anyone else who might possibly be interested?"

"Ned Liles. He was one of my research engineers in the old company. He elected not to stay on with Sanyo. He didn't want to work for the Japanese, he said."

"But he's now working in A-I?"

"Yes. His own company. Essentially a one-man, one-lab outfit. He doesn't have the capital to develop very far, or the patents to attract it."

"Was he upset when you sold out to Sanyo?"

"No more than anyone else, I believe. Everyone wondered how the new owners would treat them, of course. There was bound to be some anxiety. But I handled it pretty well."

"How's that?"

"Kept the acquisition secret until the last moment. That way, there was no time for rumors to spread and anxiety to increase. And Sanyo guaranteed all employee benefits and seniorities. It was a very quick and smooth transition."

"But Liles quit."

"It was something he'd been thinking about for some time. It was the right moment. In fact, he should be grateful—my decision gave him the impetus to do what he wanted to anyway."

"These are all the names you can think of?"

Humphries nodded. "I honestly don't think any of them would try to harm me."

"You think none of these men is the person following you?"

"No."

"You've had a good look at this person?"

"Well, no. As I say, there's this car—a brown one—that's

come by our home several times lately. And I began seeing it behind me when I drove to and from the office. I wouldn't have noticed if Mitsuko hadn't said anything." He added, "We live on a lane that doesn't get much traffic. You come to recognize the neighbors' cars."

"Mitsuko?"

"My wife. She's Japanese."

"Neither of you saw who was driving?"

"A man. That's all."

"What about the prowler?"

"Again, we haven't actually seen anyone. But I've noticed signs that someone's been on our property—gates left open, footprints, things moved about."

"What time of day?"

"Usually at night. I find the evidence in the mornings, the last few mornings especially. Before, I wasn't looking for anything. But since the car began following me I've begun to worry and started looking around."

"Exactly what would you want us to do, Mr. Humphries?"

"I suppose basically make the person stop. Whatever it takes to make that person leave us alone."

Kirk swiveled around to gaze out the window and talk to the dry, rocky crests of the distant mountain ranges. "If there is a prowler—if someone is following you—you've told me nothing to indicate that he constitutes a clear and present danger. However, if someone is planning to assault you, our merely watching over you might not remove that threat."

Humphries twisted the ring. "What do you mean?"

"Ultimately he would have to be identified, arrested, and brought to trial. It's a serious course of action."

Humphries leaned forward. The thin blue stripes of his shirt billowed up beneath the lapels of his coat. "Isn't it serious to be frightened for one's life?"

"Do you have any evidence that the prowler or the man following you is a threat to your life?"

"You sound like that damned policeman! If you can prove I'm mistaken, that's fine. If I'm not mistaken, I don't want to find out the hard way!"

"Twenty-four-hour-a-day bodyguards cost a lot. From us or from anyone else."

"My check won't bounce, if that's what's worrying you, Mr. Kirk."

"I'm sure it won't, Mr. Humphries. But in the absence of a definite threat, and given the legal ramifications of any action that might be taken, perhaps there are better options."

Humphries rubbed a hand across his chin. "Such as?"

"An investigation would probably cost less than providing round-the-clock security. That, and some coaching in basic survival techniques. Once the suspect's identified, we can decide the best way to handle him."

From the hallway outside came the heavy sound of familiar steps as Bunch ran up three stairs at a time in the final sprint. When he opened the door, almost filling it with his bulk, Kirk introduced him to Mr. Humphries and sketched the situation. "What do you think, Bunch?"

The big man wiped his face with the damp front of his sleeveless sweatshirt and shrugged. "Simple. What we do, we pick up this guy and convince him it's not nice to harass Mr. Humphries."

Devlin caught the "we." He turned to the man in the gray suit. "On defense, we have to wait for the opponent to make his move. On offense, we can dictate the action. My suggestion, Mr. Humphries, is that we go on the offensive. But the choice is yours."

Humphries looked at the large, sweaty figure, at the legs whose calves seemed almost as big as those massive thighs, at the torso whose muscle hung heavily defined. This was the ungrammatical one. But given what Humphries hadn't told Kirk, he was gratified to know he could hire this monster to be on his side. "All right."

"Then I think we can help you, Mr. Humphries. Here's what

I suggest." It wasn't the twenty-four-hour baby-sitting the man had first wanted, but it was effective. And, equally important, it left time for Devlin and Bunch to juggle the other cases as well.

The plan was all right with Bunch. He would stick with Humphries for a couple days to try and identify the suspicious figure and to familiarize himself with Humphries' routines and usual locations. He would also place security devices in Humphries' home and automobile. Meanwhile, Kirk would rehearse Humphries and his wife in personal security—how to avoid being approached in crowds, how to vary the routine patterns of life, how to stay visible to people around them. To avoid, in other words, making targets of themselves in areas that invited attack. These and other techniques that the Secret Service had drilled Kirk in would give Mr. and Mrs. Humphries a measure of self-protection for those times when they did not have a bodyguard.

"When we find out who the joker is," said Bunch, "we'll pick him up and talk with him." He cracked his knuckles for punctuation.

"We can keep this unobtrusive, can't we? I mean, if Schmidt or Stratford discover that I've mentioned their names . . . Well, we run in the same social circles. It would be extremely awkward."

"We'll be circumspect, Mr. Humphries." Kirk drew a standard contract from the drawer and filled in the blanks, adapting a paragraph or two to include the costs of installing security devices. "If what we've said makes sense and you want to proceed with it, I'll need your signature after you read over the contract. If you have any questions, please ask."

He didn't. When the pen stopped scratching, Devlin gave him a copy and nodded at Bunch. "Mr. Bunchcroft here can start right now."

That was what Bunch wanted to hear. This kind of job beat hell out of surveillance in that Subaru. Standing, he wiped his face. "Just call me Bunch, Mr. Humphries. We'll swing by my place and I'll clean up and then we'll be on our way."

Humphries nodded as Kirk folded his check and said good-bye. Going down the stairs, he eyed the wide back and shoulders of the sweaty man and hoped that Mitsuko was right. Kirk had bought the story. Now Humphries hoped the plan would give them the safety they sought.

CHAPTER 3

When the door closed behind them, Devlin read Humphries' check over one more time. Then he filed the contract in the "Active" drawer in its new manila folder labeled "Humphries." Opening a companion file on the computer, he typed in a code and brief synopsis of current information. On the time sheet, he noted the hour and day that Bunch started work. After running off a backup file, he turned to the telephone answerer for the messages that had come in while the office was empty.

The only one of interest was a report from Houston with the address and telephone number of a James Fackler. It cited the McQuiller Agency's costs of discovering the information: two hundred dollars. Right—it took McQuiller four hours and expenses to look through a telephone directory and then drive by to verify the suspect and address. Nevertheless, Kirk wrote out a check and put it in an envelope, noted the expense on the Fackler time sheet, and, in the World Association of Detectives directory, put a mark by McQuiller's name to remind him not to use that agency again. Most of the names in the directory were honest in their fees. But every now and then you ran across one that padded expenses.

Fackler was one of those insurance cases that had dragged

on because the principal had a tendency to move quickly and without a forwarding address, usually just ahead of angry creditors. But for some reason, the man never changed his name. Vanity perhaps, or an unconscious will to be caught. It happened that way occasionally. Kirk had chased the man from Colorado to Oklahoma, then out to California and back to Louisiana, wherever the oil companies set up operations. The last rumor led to Houston, and sure enough, he'd popped up there like a beer drinker's belch. Kirk faxed the information back to Security Underwriters in New York and flagged the computer file with the code number that meant *Wait for instructions.* Paperwork was a hassle, and most of it fell to Kirk because Bunch didn't like to do it. Besides, it was his agency and his responsibility. And making quick and careful records was the only way to keep facts and fees straight when working a number of cases. He didn't know any p.i. firms that had the luxury of working only one job the way they did on TV. Recording and filing taken care of, he scurried across town to meet with Reznick at the Advantage Corporation plant.

The regional manager was less than enthusiastic about bringing the police into the investigation. "No. Absolutely not! We deal in high-quality products—products whose name means reliability. And we ship that name all over the world. I'll be damned if I'm going to let a shitbird like Porter give our corporation a public black eye."

Kirk was hearing what he expected. Late-morning light filtered in through a wall of glass sliced by narrow vertical blinds and interrupted here and there by silhouetted sprouts of potted plants. Beyond the glass lay the parking lot and delivery bays where trucks from other corners of the far-flung Advantage empire brought in what they brought in, or carried away what they carried away for distribution to the company sales outlets. The Denver plant was the assembly hub because it was a convenient location between manufactories on the West Coast and in Florida. The same geography suited it for market distribution as well. "It's possible that Porter's working alone on a small scale," said Kirk. "If so, he can be handled quietly and easily."

"So handle him."

"But it's also possible he may not be working alone. His supply could be coming from outside the plant or inside it. We don't know yet."

"Kirk. It's been—what?—two, three weeks already. You've had a man looking at this guy Porter for three weeks now, and you're not sure if he's working alone?"

"He's been looking *for* Porter for three weeks. He found him only a couple days ago."

The telephone on Reznick's desk buzzed softly. Irritably, he jabbed the talk button without giving his secretary a chance to speak. "I'm in conference!" He switched the telephone off and leaned across the desk toward Devlin. "You know there was a guy last week, Montoya, caught his arm in a scissor lift? Was so goddamned stoned he didn't even know it—goddamn doctor said he didn't have to give him any anesthetic, he was so stoned. Was afraid to give him any, as a matter of fact, because it might have blown his goddamn heart away. And now you're telling me we got to let this Porter go about his business while we just keep an eye on him?"

"If he's part of a network, you won't get rid of the problem by firing one man. You'll just chase it somewhere else in the plant."

Reznick shoved his fingers through stiff, curly hair that had a touch of gray at the temples. With all the headaches that had come up in the past month, the last thing he needed was a goddamn dope problem in the factory. Not that it wasn't expected. Despite Stewart's high-sounding rhetoric at each monthly executive conference, Reznick and everybody else knew that a good percent of the labor force wasn't Just Saying No to drugs. They snorted, smoked, dropped, or shot up assorted chemicals whenever they had the chance. It was one of the givens of running a factory in the late twentieth century and of the goddamn commie-liberal erosion of American virtues so the goddamn Japs could take over American industry. What wasn't a given—and what lay behind Stewart's rhetoric—was letting the habits affect the bottom line. And now this tall son of a bitch was sitting across his desk calmly telling him that the problem in his plant—his goddamn plant—could be far more extensive than he'd at first believed. Reznick could understand why bearers of ill tidings tended to be executed. "All right. But no cops. I want this investigation to be kept absolutely confidential. All reports come to me—my eyes only—and you don't make a move without my authorization. Understand?"

To Kirk, Reznick seemed a little too young to have those gray patches at his temples. He wondered if it was a touch of dye to give a bit more weight to the man's office. "Of course. Speaking of moves, I'd like to search these lockers." He handed Reznick a slip with 105, 112, and 207 penciled on it. "I'll need your authorization to make the search legal."

"Are they involved with Porter?"

"It's possible. We're not sure."

"Well, I don't see why my own security people can't make the search. They have the right to do that kind of thing."

"They can. If you want everyone in the plant to know about it."

It took him a minute. "Oh. You mean leaks. I see." Then, "Well, all right. When you want to do this?"

"Soon. Perhaps this evening."

"All right." He made a cryptic note on the paper and pushed it back to Kirk. "Do what you have to. But I want this plant cleaned up and I want it done fast. Understand me?"

Kirk understood. He understood too that Reznick was reaching the point where he was beginning to worry about the cost of the investigation in relation to what it was accomplishing. And how that ratio would look on his section's profit and loss sheet. You had to balance the ideal investigation against the willingness of a customer to keep paying. And when Chris called in after work for his daily report, Kirk asked him if they could go through the lockers that night.

"I guess so—sure. Where should we meet?"

"I'll pick you up in front of your apartment in half an hour."

Chris waited in the shadows of the deep porch that ran across the entire front of the old-fashioned house, half listening to someone's music thump through the open window of one of the first-floor apartments. Having expected to feel excitement about going on his first search, he was a bit surprised at its absence. Maybe it was because the locker room was so familiar to him that it would be like searching his own closet. Or maybe he was finally getting used to this business of snooping and saw it as a job. Then again, he thought as Devlin's Austin-Healey throbbed to the curb, maybe there wasn't any reason to feel all that excited. Shaking down an empty locker room wasn't the most thrilling chore in the world.

After six, the traffic was a bit lighter and they made it across town quickly. The wind around the cockpit and the rap of the twin exhausts blended with the noise of surrounding cars to make it hard to talk, so they rode mostly in silence. There wasn't, Chris reflected, much to say anyway. And Devlin seemed to have things on his mind that he didn't want to share. Chris directed Kirk around the company's perimeter fence to a locked rear entry. Gate 6 was at the end of the wire where it was anchored by rusty bolts to the concrete block of warehouse 3.

"Any rent-a-cops on this side?" Kirk asked.

The guards hadn't been told about the investigation, of course. Sad but true, a lot of private security agents—underpaid, ill trained, and quickly recruited—are easy targets for the extra cash they can pick up by turning their eyes away from a dealer's operation or the activities of a theft ring. Besides, not many of them put their responsibility to a company above their responsibility to their skins. They aren't paid enough to take that kind of risk. That's where Kirk and Associates come in.

"Shouldn't be," said Chris. He held up a jingling key ring. "I've got a key for this gate. The trash hauler comes in this way. So no problem."

He pointed them across the almost empty parking lot. Kirk drove toward a scarred concrete loading dock banded by a yellow and black steel lip. Sections of old tires made a series of vertical bumpers on the steel. He parked the Healey on a patch of gravel that held enough delivery trucks and private cars to make it look as if it belonged there. Then Chris unlocked a steel-faced door in the blank wall and relocked it behind them.

"Down this way." He led Kirk along a narrow alley between palleted crates stacked almost as high as the unlit bulbs nesting behind metal grilles. Devlin smelled the oily-chemical odor of new electrical components. From somewhere in the echoing gloom came the tinny, distant sound of television voices.

"Where's the inside man?"

"He's over going through the administration wing. I checked out his routine: Starts over there because people work late sometimes. Then he makes a round of the assembly and warehouse areas after that." Chris paused to listen. "That's his office television. Turns it up when he's gone so a burglar might think somebody's around." He laughed quietly. "Sitcoms—the first line of defense."

They pushed through a pair of swinging doors. The locker room was lined with narrow gray metal doors and anchored benches like the dressing room of a high school gym. Some had penciled slips of paper in the name slots, as company policy called for. Most were blank.

Kirk started with 105, closest to the door. Chris stood guard. He breathed shallowly and lightly, listening for the sound of footsteps echoing across the concrete floors. A ripple of excitement started along the back of his neck. There shouldn't be any footsteps, he knew. The guard's routine should be the same. But there was always that chance, and in the silence and vastness of the warehouse with its alleys between towering stacks of canisters, he could imagine someone's shape. If not the security guard, maybe another of the janitorial crew. Or a worker who'd forgotten something and talked his way past the gate to return to the locker room. Suddenly the locker room wasn't as familiar anymore, and the silence that should have been comforting held a vague threat.

Devlin eased a pick into the tumbler of the cheap lock. Using a filed-down Allen wrench for torsion, he nudged the lock's pistons up into their seats with the rippled blade. Then he swung the handle down to open the door. A flash of something tiny dropped to the floor. It was the stub of a paper match knocked loose when the door moved. "This guy's worried about something."

Newman stared at him. "Why?"

Devlin held up the stem. "The old paper-match-on-the-door trick."

"So he's got something to hide?"

"We'll find out."

Exactly what the match stem was guarding was unclear. A pair of grimy overalls hung on a hook to breathe the odor of stale sweat and grease. The embroidered red thread over the pocket spelled *Eddie*. Heavy work shoes worn at the heels filled the bottom shelf. On the top shelf was a construction hat apparently issued by the company but never worn. The stenciled name Visser was still shiny across the back. There were several pairs of worn cotton work gloves, a couple of tightly rolled black plastic garbage bags, unused, and a well-thumbed copy of *Hustler* magazine that showed a blonde smiling with as many orifices as the camera could find. Both shelves were coated with a film of dust that had scrape tracks from a lunch pail and the boots. Kirk ran his finger across it and felt its smooth, talclike glide. Using a cotton swab, he picked up a sample and corked it into a plastic container. Then he relocked the door and placed the match stem back on guard, hoping it was near the place it fell from.

Chris had been watching closely. "You find anything?"

"I'm not sure." He moved to the next two lockers, discovering just about the same things, including the balanced match stem and the dust. Number 112 belonged to a Johnny Atencio, number 207 to Scott Martin. Labeling the containers by locker number, he stowed the dust samples in his jacket pocket and worked on Porter's locker, number 223. There was no dust in this one and it didn't have any tricks outside. But it did have one inside. "Look at this, Chris."

He gazed over Devlin's shoulder. "Look at what?"

Kirk nudged the locker's back panel with a knuckle; the thin metal sheet bent easily. "Hidden passages and secret compartments. A veritable Otranto of lockerdom."

"A what?"

"He's hiding something."

In a one-inch space behind the false back rested a tier of baggies carefully sealed and stacked. Lifting one out, Devlin untied it and sniffed a pinch of the dark tangle. "Quarter-ounce package. Pretty good stuff." He held it for Newman to get a whiff.

"Whew—makes me want to sneeze. We going to take them?"

Kirk was already retying the baggie. He set it back in place and half closed the door so the number was visible. Then he took a couple of flash photographs with a small camera. "Not yet." He replaced the panel and closed the locker. "I'd like to find out if he's working alone or not."

Chris thought about that. "Yeah. If Porter's busted, Eddie Visser and those other two will climb the walls."

"If they have a reason, they will." Devlin was pleased to see that Newman was thinking like a detective.

"Well, we know they're already nervous about something."

"And we want to find out what. Can you get close to them at all?"

"Maybe. I'm not sure. I've tried a little. But like I say, they don't want anything to do with me or anybody else." He reminded Kirk, "And you told me not to push."

"That's right. Just keep an eye on them, and I'll have the lab check out these powder traces. Then we'll see what Reznick wants us to do."

He hadn't changed his mind. "I don't care how much pot you found. I don't want the police called in." He tossed the photographs back to Kirk. "Keep Porter under surveillance, and when you find out if he's working with anybody, we'll can the lot of them."

"The trouble is, we ran a check on the lockers of some other people my agent has suspicions about. The lab tests on the dust samples came back positive. It's cocaine dust." Kirk handed him the slips from ProLabs, the private laboratories they used.

Reznick stared at the pink report forms. "Jesus." The question was in his eyes before he asked it. "Do we have a legal obligation to tell the police?"

"A trace isn't enough evidence for a charge. And we haven't seen them actually dealing. But if the case develops, we'll have to tell them." Kirk added, "And if we stop the investigation now, you'll have no idea how extensive their infiltration is or who else may be involved."

"How many goddamn suspects do you have?"

"Three, plus Porter."

"Jesus."

"The best way we can convict—the way the police will want it handed to them—is with a possession charge."

"Jesus. Jesus." Reznick shoved back from the expanse of gleaming desk and wandered over to the window to look down at the roof of a slowly moving semi. Now this. Just what the fuck he needed. What a can of worms he'd opened up, and he knew what Stewart would ask: Why did Reznick let it get out of hand? Well, by God, he had an answer for that. The answer was that he acted as soon as he had suspicions. And he acted decisively and with circumspection. Stewart couldn't fault him on that, by God. Nobody could. He acted with the best interests of the company in mind. Besides, despite what this know-it-all son of a bitch was telling him, Reznick himself would be the one to decide whether the cops were brought in. "You say if the case develops."

Kirk knew that Reznick's picture of himself was as a decisive, take-charge kind of guy. Paid to make the tough choices, he wanted people to know he was willing to stand behind those choices. And once they were made, it was on to the next problem without looking back. That attitude had, apparently, brought him a long way in a short time, and he wasn't about to slow down now. Still, Kirk wanted Reznick to know the ramifications of this decision before he jumped. "If we do turn up a substantial cocaine ring, and if you do not go to the police at least eventually, Kirk and Associates will have to withdraw from the case."

Reznick turned from the window. "You'll what?"

"It's a felony substance."

He eyed the man lounging in the padded chair. His long legs stretched out to cross at the ankles like the bastard was in his own living room. "And you have a responsibility to report felonies, that it?"

Not only a responsibility, a legal obligation. All citizens did. But Kirk didn't bother with his reasons. Reznick wasn't interested in reasons. "That's right."

"I hired you, by God! I hired you for a job!"

"You hired my skills and I'm using them." He didn't add that Reznick hadn't hired his conscience. Despite any truth in it, that sounded pompous and self-righteous—two of the major headings in Kirk's book of venialities. He gazed back levelly into Reznick's brown eyes and waited for the man to make up his mind to govern his temper or surrender to it.

"You said 'eventually.' "

"All we have right now is a suspicion and a trace. Neither is admissible in court. The police would be interested. They'd take a report, but there's nothing they could do with that little."

"I see." What Reznick saw was Kirk willing to shrug off the case and go his merry way. Leave him dangling with only bits of information to act on, and to act on without guidance. Unless he brought in some other snoop, who would probably tell him the same thing. "All right. Let's leave your man in there and let him come up with something." He couldn't help adding, "I suppose it is all right with you if we don't report the marijuana right away?"

"Even Supreme Court nominees use a little pot now and then. Besides, if Porter is turned in, the other three will suspect an agent in place. I suggest we continue to keep an eye on him while we develop the others. When the time comes, we can get them all."

"You think they're working together?"

"I'm not sure of that. Porter apparently doesn't hang around with Visser and the others, at least not at the plant. We can find out what he does after work."

"That scissor lift operator, the one who was so stoned— what's his name, Montoya. He almost lost his goddamn arm. We can't afford another round of accidents."

Reznick meant that literally, Kirk knew. The investigation had been started because the increasing medical claims were nearing the red line. If Advantage Corp. went over it, the premiums would jump dramatically. The union contract required the company to provide full accident coverage for every employee, and insurance companies never took losses. On top of that were the company disability payments to victims who hadn't been tested for drugs following their accidents. "We'll work as fast as practicable."

"Well, I hope so, Kirk." Reznick smiled. "Otherwise you won't have to worry about Kirk and Associates withdrawing from the case."

CHAPTER 4

Chris, Bunch, and Devlin met at the Silver Spur Lounge to talk it over. The bar was one of those with a lot of Naugahyde and gilded swag lamps. It had live music instead of television sets turned to sports events. The music was country swing, heavy on piano and electric guitar, and featured a man and woman who liked to sing with their heads together in front of one microphone. It was the kind of place Chris's fellow workers would call "nice" and feel right about dropping in with girl-friends or wives. It wasn't likely they'd be there just after work.

Bunch was pleased about Reznick's decision to stay with the surveillance. For one thing, it meant steady income. For another, it gave him more time with Humphries. He'd followed the man through his routines and for two days had seen nothing of the brown car or anyone suspicious. The man had insisted on having security devices installed on his automobile and in his home. Bunch had also placed a mobile telephone in Humphries' car in case the suspect showed up. His wife, slender and smiling and one very good-looking woman, had seemed less nervous than her husband. Though she made Bunch double-check the home alarm system, it seemed less out of fear than from the practical habit of getting what she paid for.

Now it was a matter of waiting to see what happened, if

anything. That, and once more sitting in the goddamn Subaru to keep an eye on Zell and Truman.

Chris, too, was pleased to keep the assignment. He figured it meant he was doing a good job. "You think it might turn into a big case, Dev?"

"It's possible. But let's not worry about that now. Let's just figure a way for you to get closer to them."

Bunch sipped his beer. "Chris could try the old let's-sell-them-dope scam."

"Do what?" asked Chris.

Devlin explained. "Tip them that you're a seller, not a buyer. Tell them you've got some coke for sale."

"It could be heroin," said Bunch. "But coke would be better. Direct competition."

"What about the—ah—I mean, isn't that illegal?"

"It is if you actually sell them anything. It's not if you just talk about it," said Kirk.

"Oh." Newman thought it over, uneasy at the idea. "What if they want proof? I mean, what happens if they want a sample or something? What do I do then?"

"No problem. You give it to them," said Bunch. "We can get a few lines for ol' Chris, can't we, Dev?"

It wasn't all that easy, but it could be done. Devlin studied the young man's face. "It's up to you, Chris. You don't have to do it if you don't want to."

"Hey, that's all right. It's just I hadn't thought about it. And it's a little different from surveillance."

"Nah," said Bunch. "We wouldn't ask you if we thought you couldn't handle it. Right, Dev?"

Kirk nodded. "What you do is set me up as your supplier. Just make the initial contact and tell them you can get as much as they want. When they bite, turn them onto me."

Chris felt a little disappointment. He'd had a vision of himself handling the sale like a big-time dealer. Still, Devlin was right; he'd never done anything like this before. "You really think they'll believe me?"

"Hey, let's have a little more enthusiasm," Bunch said. "All you have to do is make three ugly people think you're going to take over their dope business."

"I'm not saying I won't, Bunch. I think I can do it. I just want to be sure you guys think I can."

"Aw, yeah!" Bunch wrapped a large hand around the back of the young man's neck and wagged it gently. "Listen, first time I went on a buy and bust I was scared shitless. And I'd already been a cop on the street three years. All you got to remember is this: They're just as nervous as you. They're worried you might be a cop, they're worried you might rip them off, they're worried you might be competition. Most of all, they're worried about how they're going to save their own ass if something goes wrong. Not about how they're going to stomp yours."

"Hey, I said I can do it. I just . . . well, I just don't want to screw up the whole case. I mean, it's my first time, right? You guys know better than I do what I'm getting into. If you think I can do it, fine."

"Just make them think you're the middleman. You don't handle the stuff, see? What you tell them is you drum up customers for a percentage but you don't sell. Somebody else takes the money and delivers. Tell them the action's divided up that way for security reasons. They'll believe you. Dealers are paranoid about security. Besides, they won't be interested in you. They'll be after Devlin here."

Devlin agreed. "That's how it will work."

"No problem then," said Chris. "But why you?"

"If they're in the business, they'll want to protect their territory and they'll want to go as high up our line of people as they can."

"Right," said Bunch. "All you do is tell them you've got a pipeline to Colombia. You can get any amount of coke real cheap." He leaned back and grinned over his beer. "That way they'll want to find out as much as they can about your operation before they unscrew your head."

"Thanks a hell of a lot."

It was finally worked out. Chris would make the offer in the next couple days. Bunch and Devlin would be ready to back him up with a meeting and a sample of goods. In the meantime, since Bunch was tied up protecting Mr. and Mrs. Humphries, Devlin would tail Porter to learn what he could.

"You want some help with that, Dev? I haven't had much practice tailing people yet."

Kirk saw Chris's excitement at his expanded role, and that was healthy. "He might recognize you, Chris. You just concentrate on your end of things. Everything depends on how well you handle that. Bunch and I'll take care of the rest."

"Yeah." Bunch added, "Remember, it's a business and you're an old hand at it. Just play it straight—no tough act, nothing phony, nothing like the movies. It's just like selling bubble gum, okay?"

They watched the young man leave the bar ahead of them as they finished their glasses. From the far end of the lounge on the tiny stage came some early twangs of an electric bass warming up as the band began to gather. Bunch watched a long-haired blonde swing past on her way to the ladies' room. "Old Chris is getting a little cocky about all this, Dev. Did you explain Kirk and Associates' generous hospitalization plan to the lad?"

"Old Chris hasn't been in a position where he had to think seriously about it."

"Ah, he'll be all right. It's not that big a deal anyway. And he can handle himself."

Kirk eyed Bunch. Since the Humphries case started, no more gripes about being bored. And he believed Bunch was right despite a mild twinge of worry about Newman. He hadn't wanted to show it—no sense making the kid feel any more nervous than he'd be naturally.

But agents do face some danger. Any time you make a living by sticking your nose in other people's business, you stand a chance of getting it remodeled. Chris understood that, and to his credit it was the excitement of a little danger that had brought him into the game and kept him here. But heretofore he had only been used as a pair of eyes or as backup. And when he'd been planted in the warehouse, it was with the understanding that he would only observe. Any sniff of trouble and he was to pull out. Now Kirk had him doing contact work. And with some characters who seemed to know a lot about what they were into.

But, as Bunch said, Newman was over twenty-one, though not by much. And the stakes on this deal weren't high enough for anyone to risk a murder rap. If things fell apart, they would try to scare him off with at most a beating. Though something as innocuous as that could rearrange his face, Kirk knew. And sometimes the brain as well.

Bunch glanced at Kirk's watch and finished his beer. "I got to check in with Humphries. I told him I'd sweep the neighborhood and drop by tonight."

"Keeping a good record of your time?"

He tapped the vest pocket of his shirt where a small notebook rode. "Every billable minute. Christ only knows how long he's going to pay for this crap. Me, I think it's a waste of time and money."

"You don't think anyone's following him?"

"Not from what I've seen. It's only been a couple days, though. Oh yeah, I told him you'd coach him in evasion techniques tomorrow afternoon. Him and the wife both." He added another item that had puzzled him. "I can't see a woman like that going for somebody like Humphries. The guy's a toad, Dev. I bet he croaks when he hops in bed." Then, "She's a lot younger than he is, too."

"Jealous?"

"Me? Naw. But I have to admit Mitsuko-san's a nice-looking piece. A little shy in the tit department, but it all goes together pretty well. Nice compact Jap model. And even if she's young, she seems to have been around enough to know what she's talking about. I just can't see her going for a fish like Humphries."

Devlin knew what he meant. Humphries struck him, too, as a cautious and calculating man, one more likely to fall in love with a balance account than a woman. But he was rich, and that made up for a lot. Especially if Mitsuko, like a lot of women, saw marriage as a polite form of prostitution. "No accounting for people's tastes, Bunch."

"Ah, the inscrutable Orient."

"When do I meet with them?"

"Tomorrow after five."

The two men paid the tab and paused by their cars in the parking lot. Bunch asked, "How do you want to handle this setup with Chris?"

"Think Miller can help us out?" Bunch's ex-partner from his days on the Denver police was now a detective in Vice and Narcotics. Sometimes he did favors for old times' sake. As well as the resulting credit for any arrests.

Bunch thought he would. They hadn't called on him for over a year now. The ill-defined but precise balance of obligation had been left tilted in their favor, and what the hell was that Christmas bottle of Laphroaig for anyway? "I'll give him a call in the morning."

On the street beyond the strip of worn grass with its fringe of litter, hot traffic rushed past in a blur of glinting metal and glass. "Reznick wants to keep the police out, remember. He doesn't want the company to lose face."

"Miller'll go along with that—for a while anyway." Bunch waved goodbye.

CHAPTER 5

The days were moving into one of those routines when a lot went on but little seemed to happen. Devlin drove down to Douglas County and found Humphries' home—as he expected, large and well appointed. Set far off the unpaved county road, it was, despite its size, invisible among the pine and juniper that covered the rolling hills. Humphries' wife seemed to be in her early twenties and was as attractive as Bunch had said. She was also very interested in the personal security techniques Devlin explained to the two of them. Humphries, while paying attention and occasionally asking a question, seemed less worried about avoiding attack in his home than on his way to work. "That's when I'm vulnerable, Kirk—in the car. All he has to do is run me off the road and I'm trapped."

Which was why Bunch installed a cellular phone in the man's Mercedes. "Have you noticed anyone following you in the last few days?"

He shook his head and Mrs. Humphries smiled. "Not since Mr. Bunchcroft came. He is so big!"

"That doesn't mean it's safe," said Humphries. "That man could just be waiting."

Bunch had run quick checks on Stratford, Schmidt, and Liles.

The first two men lived south of Denver in an area of impressive new housing developments that had followed completion of that quadrant of the beltway. Liles had recently sold his large home, apparently to get capital for his new business, and moved to a smaller house in southwest Denver. None of them owned a brown car. That didn't preclude one of them from hiring someone who did. But under the aegis of Kirk and Associates Loan Company, Devlin had surveyed the printouts of their last three months' bank statements and found no unusual jump in withdrawals—the size, for instance, of a retainer. Of course, Liles could be paying through the company funds, but they had no access to that account through their credit service. Kirk asked, "Is there anyone who might have a grudge against you? Or any other reason someone might wish you harm?"

Humphries let out a disgusted sigh and looked around the large living room, with its displays of Oriental prints on the walls and its carefully placed carvings. One was a gaunt Buddha in ivory old enough to have turned brown; another had the deep translucent green of fine jade. The prints, too, looked antique, though Devlin couldn't read the red and black characters at their borders.

"Mr. Bunchcroft has already asked that question in half a dozen different ways, and I'm getting tired of answering it."

"He even," said Mitsuko softly, "asked if someone might wish to harm me." She made a comically sad face and glided her long fingernails down the curves beneath thin sweater and tight slacks. "Who would want to harm little me?"

Kirk caught a hint of challenge in her black eyes and focused on the printed sheet of tips for personal security that he'd copied for them. Humphries, whether he knew it or not, had his hands full with this young lady. "Can you give me a list of your acquaintances, Mrs. Humphries? We should check out that possibility, too."

"But I have so few! Our household help—Mr. and Mrs. Lucero. The hairdresser at the A La Mode Salon, the butcher at

Safeway, the mechanic at the Texaco station near I-25 . . ."

"I meant more personal acquaintances—social friends, for example."

Humphries broke in. "Mitsuko has the same friends I do. She's only been in America a couple years, and in this area only a few months."

"Are you newly wed?"

She laughed. "Very!"

"I thought you were American—you speak English so well."

"Thank you. I've studied the language since elementary school. And," she added, "been fascinated by things American."

Kirk stifled a grin. "And now you have an American thing."

Her laugh was a tiny silver bell that tinkled up an octave in delight. "And Roland, who loves things Japanese, has his Japanese thing!"

"My wife has made no enemies here," said Humphries primly. "That's a foolish hypothesis."

Foolish or not, it was an item Humphries hadn't shared when Kirk asked for recent changes in his life, and Kirk passed the information on to Bunch. But so far, it had led to nothing. The big man's reports on the office recorder fell into a routine like the days: "No problem with Humphries so far, Dev. I'll swing by Zell's house this afternoon and see what our boy's up to."

Chris, too, made his daily reports on the telephone. But their monotony was relieved by small victories. "Dev, I ate lunch with one of Visser's pals, Johnny Atencio. Nothing came up, but I think he's going to be a good lead. You might check him out."

Devlin had already done that, between tailing Porter when he left work in the evenings and juggling surveillance on Truman and Zell.

Security Underwriters had assigned Truman and Zell to Kirk and Associates. They were a New York outfit that took over suspicious claims and got paid a percentage of anything they saved the insurance companies. Out of that they paid Kirk and

Associates a share. A small share, but it was more than nothing and so far had been steady because Devlin did good work. Fortunately, Truman and Zell weren't very demanding. They called for a videocam and still camera with telephoto lenses, and a random pattern of surveillance. As well as a white Subaru which Bunch hated but which Kirk used because it was the world's most unobtrusive car. Thus far neither Devlin nor Bunch had been lucky enough to see them do anything that clearly showed a lack of physical limitations. But it was, they were convinced, only a matter of time before the suspects got careless.

You know the feeling you get about people who are ripping off an insurance settlement: a kind of certainty that you haven't any facts to support, but you know sooner or later it will prove true. That's what they both felt about Zell and Truman.

Porter was something else. A nervous little man with a fringe of black hair around a shiny pate, he was always worried about being followed and took a lot of precautions when he left the Advantage plant. Unfortunately for him, those precautions ran into a pattern. On Mondays he turned left out of the gate and took I-225 south to Mississippi and then back west to his apartment, a sort of Tudor military barracks just off that main thoroughfare. On Tuesdays he turned right to Havana and drove south from there. Wednesdays had a little variation—sometimes south on Peoria, sometimes as far west as Monaco before circling back. Thursdays were I-225 days again, and on Fridays he tended to use Quebec. Occasionally it varied, but Kirk could usually pick him up as he approached the straight rows of fake-beam-and-plaster apartment houses and cruised a couple times around the parking lot before settling into a space one or two buildings away from his own address.

The man's night trips were equally challenging for Devlin. He went to three bars. Two were in Aurora. A municipality bordering on Denver's eastern edge, it had spread rapidly in the last twenty years since Denver had been prohibited from annexing any more of its suburbs but Aurora had not. It had, in fact, grown faster than its services—including police—could keep up with. The result was a migration of certain types from Denver across the city line to the neighboring town. Two of the bars were in a string of dives and strip joints on East Colfax, and Porter spent a lot of time there. The third was south on Leetsdale Drive in Glendale, another section surrounded by Denver. Glendale had its own jurisdiction and a reputation as the home of the single swingers. This bar's ferns had been replaced by television sets locked on sporting events and by video games poked at by howling males and shrieking females. A table against the back wall near the rear exit, a visit only long enough to leave a half-finished drink, and Porter would be off again, headed home with his weekly kilo to carve up into nickel baggies. None of the faces he talked to matched the company ID photographs of Visser and his buddies. It was, however, information to hand over to Bunch's friend Miller. Even though Glendale was out of the Denver policeman's jurisdiction, the information would be useful. Those were the little favors Kirk and Associates did to keep the balance sheet even.

Reznick called Devlin a couple times the first week and more frequently afterward. Kirk told the regional manager that the two—Visser and Porter—didn't seem to be working together, and that it looked as if Porter was a loner. But he urged Reznick to let things ride until Chris made contact with the trio. Reluctantly, Reznick agreed, and it wasn't too hard for Kirk to see that his patience was wearing as thin as a mother-in-law's smile. So it was a relief when Chris finally called, excited, and said he'd made the offer. And Atencio had bitten.

"He was cool about it, Dev. I mean, you could tell he was really interested, but he tried to act like it was no big deal." In memory's eye, Chris could still see the stiffening of Atencio's face, with its flattened nose and the two white scars chopped into his left eyebrow.

"Have you talked to the others yet?"

"No. Just Johnny. He said he might be interested but he'll let me know." The sudden rumble and bang of loud music from a jukebox made Chris burrow deeper into the shelter of the phone hood. "But you can tell the guy means business. He's just afraid to say anything without talking to Visser first."

"Did you tell him about me?"

"I just said I had people behind me." And it had been surprisingly easy. Sure, his throat had been dry and his palms wet when he brought it up. But Atencio hadn't noticed; he'd been listening too hard with a blankness that told Chris he was both very interested and very wary. In fact, thinking back, it was kind of fun. And he'd done as Bunch instructed: just treated it like it was no big deal. A chat between friends. Take it or leave it, Johnny, but I can get you all the coke you want, and at a good price.

"When's Atencio getting back to you?"

"He said maybe tomorrow."

It wasn't. It was a long two days later. Apparently they didn't want to seem too eager. But when at last Chris called in, it was with good news.

"I talked to Eddie Visser today, Dev. He wants a meet."

"When?"

"He said tomorrow night. I said I had to talk to you and see if that was okay. Was that right?"

"Just right. Tomorrow, tell him I want to talk to my people before I meet with anybody. Tell him I'm cautious and that's why I haven't been busted. Tell him you should hear from me in a few days."

Chris wondered about that. Eddie had a quick, decisive way about him, rapid talk and sharp gestures that nailed down his words. In fact, if things hadn't happened so fast, Newman would have been far more worried about talking to Visser than he had been with Atencio. But it had come as a surprise. The wiry, intense man appeared out of nowhere just after lunch break and said, "Newman—let's talk." Now Chris asked, "You think that's a good idea, Dev?"

"Why not?"

"Visser's a pretty tough character. Johnny told me he spent time in Canon City or someplace." And he had the caution of an ex-con, the surface politeness that so obviously kept at a distance people he didn't know.

"Then he'll expect these moves, Chris. If we come on too heavy, he'll think cops and we'll lose him. Remember, we're supposed to be bad guys too—we're worried about cops and we don't know much about Visser. He might be a cop."

"Okay—I guess you know best. I'll tell him."

"One thing more: You've got their attention. They'll be watching you. So be careful with security, hear?"

"I hear."

When Bunch learned about the contact, he grinned. "What'd we tell ol' Chris, Dev? Hook, line, and sinker."

"It means we have to come up with something for me to show those people. Any word from Miller?"

"I talked to him. He's willing to go along if."

"If what?"

"If we keep exact records of the stuff. If we return the exact amount he checks out to us. And—the most important—if he gets called in for the busts."

"He wants the exact amount back?" That would be difficult. There was always a little shaving for samples, even sometimes for a bribe or two.

"We'll worry about that when the time comes." Bunch pulled a small package from his jacket pocket. Narrow and flat and designed to fit unobtrusively against the body, it was wrapped in thick, clear plastic. "Five ounces, ninety percent."

"Right." Devlin locked it in the heavy, old-fashioned Mosler anchored to one of the pillars that formed part of the office wall. A decade or so ago, the safe had been obsolete. But as with many skilled professions, the ranks of safecrackers had been thinned by attrition. Besides, following an aborted attempt to strip it a year or so ago, Bunch had modernized this one with a few electronic touches in addition to the tumbler system. "Let's go see what Zell and Truman are up to."

CHAPTER 6

Over the next few days, Bunch followed Humphries periodically to be certain no one stalked the man. He accompanied him or Mitsuko on the necessary trips to the supermarket and even down to Colorado Springs for a three-day company retreat. The man's wife went along because Humphries said he would be worried about leaving her alone. She said she would be all right at home—provided Bunch looked after her. But Humphries insisted, so she shrugged and smiled and they packed.

When he had delivered them to the Broadmoor, Bunch turned around and came back the seventy miles to Denver. He had already screened the Luceros; they were a hardworking pair who had been with Humphries for four years before Mitsuko came. The man took care of the house and grounds; his wife did the cleaning and cooked the noon meal. Sometimes she prepared supper as well, but mostly Mitsuko did that or Humphries and his bride ate out. There was no reason, Bunch figured, for the Luceros to have Humphries followed—anything they wanted to know, they could find out where they worked. But Bunch wanted to follow up on Mrs. Humphries' other contacts: mechanic, butcher, hairdresser. The first two knew her only as "that Japanese woman." To the butcher she was the one who was very picky about fresh fish—"I think she eats it raw." The mechanic knew her as the Jeep Wagoneer that belonged to Mr. Humphries. They both said she showed up five, maybe six weeks ago and seemed to be a very nice lady. The hairdresser knew her as Miss Watanabe.

Bunch eyed the man's face, with its full beard brushed out from his chin like an orange ruff. He had long, highlighted hair pulled back into a severe braid. "She uses her maiden name?"

"Well, I certainly don't know if it's her maiden name. That's the name she gave when she called for her first appointment. And that's what I've called her ever since. She doesn't seem to object."

Mitsuko Watanabe had been coming into the A La Mode once a week for a shampoo, manicure, and facial. Occasionally she had a razor trim. Her thick, black hair—"Really beautiful! I love working on Oriental women, they have such fabulous body to their hair"—grew rapidly, and she liked it shaped around her face. "Plumes, I call them. Feathered in an almost casual way to accentuate the high cheekbones and wide mouth." And she was a very valuable customer who always tipped well. "I hope this information isn't going to cause her embarrassment. I mean, if I hadn't seen you chauffeuring her around, I wouldn't be speaking to you like this, you know." The twenty-dollar bill Bunch had handed the man flickered like a lizard's tongue between his fingers and disappeared.

"She won't hear anything from me. Has anyone else come around asking about her?"

It was the same question he put to the other two, and the answer was the same: no one. Bunch sighed and glanced at the small LED clock glued to his car's dash. Chris had set up the meet with Visser for later tonight, and that left time to swing by Jean Truman's house. All the hours he'd invested in watching that place made Bunch hungry to catch the woman. Even if irregular and sporadic surveillance was a long shot, there was still the chance he might spot her doing handstands on the front lawn.

Devlin, too, had been traveling. He made a quick flight down to Houston on behalf of Security Underwriters. Apparently Fackler used the three hundred thousand dollars of his disability settlement to set up business as a refurbisher of secondhand oil well equipment. Security wanted Devlin to file a lien on the man's property and have the local police hold him under arrest for fraud until their lawyer could get there. The legal paperwork had taken a full day, and it was late by the time Devlin got back to Denver. He had the satisfaction of closing Fackler's file and sending the bill to Security on the U-250 fax machine. It would be sitting in Schute's machine when he arrived at work in the morning. If the man was his usual prompt self, they should have his check deposited within five days, which would help that pile of bills in the "Pay as soon as possible" stack.

Bunch and Chris got to the office around eleven. They had a cup of coffee as they went over the plan one more time.

Chris was nervous and tried to hide it with chatter. "You were right, Dev. Visser's been all over me—trying to pump me about who my supplier is and where the stuff comes from."

"What'd you tell him?"

"Just what you said to. That you were my contact and that you made trips to Phoenix. That's all."

Bunch gathered up the keys to the rented Lincoln Continental that was part of tonight's charade. "Is Visser worried?"

"He's thinking narc, that's for sure. You could tell by some of the questions he was asking me: Where'd I work before I came here? How old was I really? He's been around, so he's acting real cagey."

"Chris told me he's an ex-con," Kirk added.

"Well, that's what Atencio said. He does seem kind of . . . guarded, you know? Like he thinks somebody's watching him all the time."

"I let Reznick know about the meet. He's happy something's finally going down."

Bunch was glad Devlin was the one to deal with guys like Reznick. "Screw him. If he knew his ass from a teakettle, he'd know how tricky this kind of work is."

Devlin didn't feed the big man's disgust. "What about Martin, Chris? What's he like?"

"Doesn't say much at all. Mostly stays in the background. Johnny's an ex-boxer—Golden Gloves, I think. And like I say, Visser's been around a lot. But Martin just seems to follow along." He tried to recall anything telling that Martin had done. But the only picture he could bring up was of the man's brown eyes watching over cupped fingers that pinched a cigarette.

Devlin checked his regulation .38 and Bunch pulled his Python magnum from the safe. Both were licensed to carry, but seldom did. Bunch did have a strap holster riveted under the dash of his Bronco where the Python sometimes rode. But neither man wanted to use a gun except as a last resort.

Chris eyed the long barrel of the Python, and the shadows in the corner of the office suddenly grew darker. "You think you'll need those?"

Kirk shook his head. "They're just for show."

Bunch tucked the weapon in his belt and draped his jacket over it. "Visser'll expect us to come armed. No sense disappointing him."

The time had been set for one o'clock in the morning. The place was the north end of the railroad yards, which weren't too far from the office. There was plenty of visibility in all directions against the night lights of the city and the traffic glare from I-25. Any approaching vehicle would be either cops or criminals, and could be seen a long way off. Yawning wide enough to crack his jaws, Bunch guided the fat tires of the Lincoln through the gravel and broken glass and searched the level darkness for the outline of Chris's van.

The procedure, agreed to by both parties, was that Chris would guide Visser's car to the meet early. As a main pusher, Devlin wasn't about to tell some stranger where he'd be waiting. Bunch had told Chris to take a roundabout way, doubling back as if checking for tails, and generally convince Visser that Devlin wasn't eager to make his presence known, and that he wasn't about to take Visser's word for anything just because he seemed like such a nice guy.

Kirk peered through the scattering of red and green gleams that untangled the snarl of tracks for those who knew what the lights meant. The weeds rose knee-high, thick in some places, thin in others. Here and there jumbled shadows marked piles of old railroad ties, dumped as high as a team of men could toss them. "Is that them?"

Bunch shaded his eyes against the city's glow, then turned the heavy car toward the dim shape of a van. It was the one Kirk and Associates had leased for Chris, and behind it was another car. A head and shoulders were dimly silhouetted in the second car. Two figures huddled out of the cold breeze against the van's side. Bunch flicked off the lights and coasted the Lincoln to a spongy halt. Devlin gave it a long minute before getting out—a little drama never hurt your entry—and the figures pushed away from the shelter of the van. One snubbed out a cigarette.

There were no handshakes. "This is the guy I told you about," Chris said to Kirk.

"Kept us waiting fucking long enough." Visser was a bit under six feet and built like a swizzle stick. He bent and jabbed a finger toward the Lincoln. "Who's in the car?"

"My driver." Kirk nodded to the other sedan where the blur of a face aimed at them. "Your driver, right?"

"Call him that." Visser stared at the Lincoln again, trying to see where Bunch's hands were and if they were empty. "You got a piece?" he asked Kirk. "If you got a gun, lay it on the hood of the car."

Devlin glanced at Chris.

"I checked him out," said Newman. "He's not carrying."

Kirk lifted his weapon from its shoulder holster and set it on the Lincoln's long hood.

"All right," said Visser. "Let's go on the other side of the truck." He motioned to Chris. "You stay here."

Kirk followed the jumpy man out of Bunch's sight. "You wanted a meet. Let's get to business."

"How do I know you're not wired?"

Kirk raised his hands, and Visser's fingers brushed knowledgeably across those places where a weapon or body transmitter might be taped. Then he started to lift Devlin's wallet from his pocket.

"What the hell you think you're doing?"

"Hey, man, chill out. I'm going to check you over, okay? I don't know you, do I?"

Visser paused and, when Kirk didn't answer, tugged the wallet out gently. Tilting the driver's license to the sky glow, he squinted through the dimness to read it. Kirk knew what it said: Bernard DiAngelo and an address in Phoenix. The address was a motel whose manager was a friend of his uncle Wyn. The DiAngelo name wasn't unknown to the Phoenix police as well as to certain Las Vegas figures who had low profiles and high insurance premiums.

"Since when do narcs sell stuff?" Kirk asked.

"Shit happens, man."

He took his wallet back. "Don't it. Now it's your turn. Man." He patted Visser down, finding a slender switchblade tucked in his belt at the back of his pants. "You think you're going to use this?"

"No, man. It's just I always carry it."

He tossed the knife back to Visser. "You can try to use it right now if you want."

Visser dropped it into a pocket and shook his head. "Like I said, I just carry it around. I forgot it was there. No offense, okay?"

"Right." Kirk took his time leafing through the man's wallet. It didn't tell him anything he didn't already know from the company personnel file. "Okay." Kirk pretended to relax. "It looks like we can do business."

"I want to find out a little more, first. Like where you get your stuff."

"I'm going to tell you that?" Kirk snorted. "Man, if you want to do business, fine. But we ought to act like gentlemen about this. You understand what I'm saying?"

"I understand, sure. But it's, you know, important we trust each other. We know a little bit more about each other, we trust each other, you know?"

"It's good stuff. You can check it out. Good and consistent."

"The kid says you're up from Phoenix."

"The kid's right."

"You know Mike Turley down there?"

"It's a big town. I don't know everybody. You in the market or not?"

"Take it easy, man. What's your going rate?"

Devlin told him. "The kid give you a taste?"

"Yeah. It's okay."

"It's more than okay. It's prime. Ninety percent." Devlin looked at his watch. "I got other business, man, so if you're interested . . ."

Visser, suddenly more nervous, backed off a step or two. His hand edged toward his pocket. "Listen, man, I don't want to buy. Sorry about that. I'm here to give you a message is all."

"What kind of shit is this?"

"The message is, find yourself another place to peddle. That factory's our turf."

"Bullshit."

"Our territory, man. We see that kid reach out a hand, he's pulling back a stump."

"That the way it is?"

"That's the way it is."

"No. I'll tell you how it is. We're moving in. We've got prime stuff and we can undersell you for the next five years if we have to. So here's your message: Either move out or split the territory with us. You tell your boss that—half of something or all of nothing."

"I'm the boss."

"Like hell you are, pimp. You tell him this is chickenshit

crap he's pulling. He wants war, he's got one. He wants to work together, we can do that, too." Kirk smiled. "We're not greedy. But we're building outlets in Denver. Like we've got them in Dallas and Kansas City." He let that sink in. Nothing moved in either city without the mob's okay. Even the Kansas City Haitians had to buy their territory from the mob.

"You're full of shit."

"Three days. You run back and tell your boss you got three days. Then we do what we have to." Kirk backed into the view of Bunch and Chris, and Visser followed, frowning.

"You're asking for trouble, man."

"The kid's like my ambassador. You talk with him. Understand?"

"You're so full of shit. You guys are really full of shit, you know?" Visser turned and walked away with the stiff haste of anger, fear, and bravado. His car started before he reached it, and Devlin quickly picked up his pistol from the Lincoln's hood. But the sedan only wheeled sharply across the rattle of tracks to become another cold gleam moving through lights made brittle by the chill silence of early morning.

The three met back at the office. Chris was still wiping sweat from his forehead with a large yellow bandanna. All he'd had to do was stand there and hear the murmur of voices tossed on the wind. But he felt as if he'd been running full speed for the whole ten minutes. "Wow—do you ever get used to that? My pulse is still about two hundred rpm."

Bunch pressed the coffeepot down on the hot plate to make it boil faster. "Sure you do. Matter of fact, I was about asleep there before Dev and the toothpick came back."

"Really?"

He yawned widely and nodded. "Just another night at the office, Chris." He poured a cup and handed it to Devlin. "Did he buy it?"

"Enough to check out my name and address." Which would be all right. Oscar, Uncle Wyn's buddy at the Phoenix motel, knew what to tell anyone who called to ask about Bernard DiAngelo. "But I don't know how convincing I was as a Mafia lieutenant."

"Not very—you ain't a wop. But that wimp wouldn't know mob from Girl Scouts."

"You think they're going to roll over and play dead?" Newman took a cup from Bunch and sipped gingerly at the hot coffee. It seemed a lot like the times when he was a kid and stayed up to listen while the cowboys drank coffee and told tall tales around the fire.

"If they're nickel-and-dimers, they will," said Devlin. "If they don't, that means they've got muscle behind them somewhere." He saw Newman's look and added, "If we find that out, we'll pull you and let them have their laugh."

"I can handle it—you don't have to pull me out of it."

"It's not a question of whether you can handle it. It's a question of wasting Reznick's money."

"Yeah," grunted Bunch. "If it falls through, we go after them some other way."

"What do we do now?"

Kirk shrugged. "My guess is Visser'll go back to his boss and tell him what he learned. They'll want to check out DiAngelo, maybe have a council."

"You really don't think Visser's the boss?"

Kirk shook his head. "He has to be getting his stuff from somewhere. Either inside or outside the plant. Dope dealing's a distribution system—his boss is whoever delivers to him to sell." He remembered something. "Did you recognize the one driving Visser's car?"

Newman shook his head. "I couldn't see him too well, but it wasn't Johnny or Scott. I'd have recognized them."

Bunch stretched, his chair creaking and popping. "This is the toughest part—waiting." He drained his cup. "Back to the sack for me. I got to get up early and baby-sit."

CHAPTER 7

Despite assurances that no one was following him, Humphries still wanted protection. His check to that end was waiting in the mail when Devlin got to the office late the next morning. He'd found it was best to bill certain clients by the week unless they were a big enough corporation to stand the shock of a grand total at the end of a job. Moreover, a little working capital was always welcome. Devlin walked the check down to the bank to deposit it. He'd also discovered it was good to find out early if a man's paper was really rubber.

His midday was spent down the street from Zell's house. It was a split level in a neighborhood of similar designs and located on the kind of curving avenue that a million other suburbs had. The lawn was getting shaggy, and Zell might discover enough physical ability to mow it one of these days. Armed with the cameras and lenses and a book to skim between snoops, Kirk slid the Subaru into a parking space just in sight of the yard and waited for something to happen. It seldom did, and today was no different. The lawn still hadn't been mowed, and the hedge running down the property line from the street to the back fence was growing leggy and ragged. The afternoon sun slid toward the mountains and filled the car with drowsy warmth, and he could feel the drag of last night's late hours pull at his eyelids. Yawning, struggling against sleep, Kirk finally gave up; it was time to move on. He wouldn't do anyone any good dozing off when he should be watching.

The office telephone answerer gave its familiar red wink for *Message waiting,* and far down the tape Kirk found a raspy voice that identified itself as Oscar: "Some guy called me to talk to Bernard DiAngelo, Dev. I give him what you told me—you know, DiAngelo's out of town but I could hold his messages. This guy didn't have no message. Thought you'd want to know." And that reminded Devlin to check out Eddie Visser's police record.

Sergeant Lewellen preferred to do favors for Bunch—they had gone through police training together and shared a squad car for almost a year. But he condescended to help Devlin because he was Bunch's partner, because Devlin wasn't asking for much, and possibly because of the expensive Christmas gifts Kirk and Associates provided each year. "Hang on, Kirk. I'll see what I can punch up."

In the background, Devlin could hear a blather of voices and an occasional telephone bell, the routine sounds of a squad room. "Okay, here we are: Visser, Edward Leonard . . . two felony raps and a misdemeanor sheet going back to juvenile. Spent time in Buena Vista . . . was a guest in Canon City . . . rape and assault with a deadly. Off parole last year. Looks like your everyday scumbag, Kirk. But right now he's a rehabilitated citizen with all the rights and privileges thereof. What's going down?"

"We have a security problem in the plant where he works. I'm checking out everybody in his section."

"I'd say you found your problem. And if it's on private property, I don't want to hear any more about it. We're understaffed and we got shit up to our ears."

"How about Scott Martin and John Atencio?" He added quickly, "Then I won't bother you anymore."

"Hang on." An audible sigh and more background noises. "I got two Scott or Scotty Martins, one in Canon City right now and one with a couple knocks for dealing. Nothing big locally, but he did a stretch in Illinois for burglary. No cross-reference to Visser in the known-associates file. Atencio I can't help you with unless you got a birth date or his Social Security number. I got maybe fifteen John or Juan Atencios."

Kirk could get that information from the man's personnel file and call back. "Thanks, Sergeant. I owe you a bottle."

"Make it Johnny Walker. Black label."

Kirk would, and on the Advantage expense account. The electric clock on the wall—placed there for Bunch's convenience because his wrist was too big to wear a watch—marked ten after three. Though Kirk was eager to find out what Chris Newman had learned at work today, it was best not to call him at the plant. For one thing, it was against company policy for workers to get personal calls. Worse, it would draw attention to him. Kirk would have to be patient until five-thirty, when Chris was due to telephone his daily report. And since Bunch wouldn't be back in the office until later, that left Kirk a block of time for a much needed sweat at the a.c.

Bunch was sweating too. The afternoon sun fell through the windshield of the cramped Subaru and burned across his lap. Zell had another half hour and that was it. Bunch had promised to convoy Humphries back from Colorado Springs, and the ride down to the Broadmoor would take an hour and a half. In fact, he should have started fifteen minutes ago, but Devlin wanted an eye kept on Zell's house. He had a theory that the man would be out mowing his goddamn grass one of these days. That the lawn was ratty was true enough. What wasn't true was that Zell would mow it himself. Bunch didn't think the man was that stupid; he wasn't going to show the neighbors how healthy he was. No, what he'd do was hire a kid to mow it, and all this extra surveillance would turn out to be one more goddamn waste of time.

Bunch swigged at the thermos of stale coffee and shifted to find a different cramp for his jammed legs. Fifteen minutes more. That's all. Whether or not Dev got here in time to relieve him. Fifteen minutes.

Bunch shifted again, forcing his heavy eyelids to stay open against the day's heat and the long night. He consoled himself with the idea that he was probably doing just as much good here as anywhere else, and the fact that he'd be driving his Bronco to the Springs made him feel better. That led to a consideration of what kind of game Humphries might be playing. He and Dev had talked things over and done some basic background on the man, but it hadn't turned up much. There was no marriage license in their names issued in Colorado. But that left only forty-nine other states and the rest of the world where they could have been married. Humphries' credit rating, as expected, was excellent, and the list of references he used on his home loan application would make an investment counselor salivate. No criminal record. No loans other than the tax-deductible mortgage. His credit card purchases showed fairly routine entries: a number of restaurant bills, clothes, travel expenses. He traveled a lot, but given his business, that was to be expected. The only odd thing was an absence of any charges in the name of Mitsuko Humphries. Apparently she paid cash.

But the man's check was good, and as long as he was willing to pay the bill, Bunch was willing to give him his fill. Though that would be a hell of a lot more fun with Mitsuko-san. And wasn't she the little tease? Bunch knew the commandments of p.i.-dom, the first of which was: Thou shalt not sleep with the clients. Devlin had forgotten that once, and it cost them both a lot. Still, it was hard to watch that saucy little tail switch around the room without having visions of romps on the futon dance through his head. He sighed and scratched at his sun-warmed groin. It was no surprise the woman flirted with him—big, handsome, gum-chewing stud that he was. A few people had it, a lot didn't; Bunch knew he was among the select few. And he'd run across plenty of women, newly married or not, who agreed enough to want to find out. That's how he read Mitsuko: knowledgeable about the world of men and sex, yet still eager and excited to learn more. To compare men, perhaps. And already bored with Humphries. Just as she would be bored after she sampled Bunch. Which was okay with him: a quick roll in the hay and a "heigh-ho Silver" was all he wanted anyway.

He glanced at the dash clock and was about to start the car when a movement caught his eye. The garage door was opening to show the rear of a new Ford Taurus—another benefit of Zell's claim. A few seconds later, the man himself worked a lawn mower past the car's gleaming chrome and bent to start the machine. Goddamn Devlin was right again. Bunch grabbed the camcorder and aimed as Zell pulled the rope several times, until the mower bucked with a puff of blue smoke. Like a distant insect, it began to hum. Bunch taped a series showing the man push against the handle as the blades churned through the high, thick grass. When the mower jammed, the camera followed as Zell bent to free something from the blades and restart the engine; when it reached the end of a row and had to be swung in a different direction, Zell's body heaved against the mower and Bunch caught that, too. For a man whose back had made him a permanent invalid, he was pretty spry. After the lawn was scalped, Bunch cruised past with the camera braced across his arm to get a close-up of the man's face. Then, satisfied, he quickly headed back downtown to drop the film off at the photo lab that did Kirk and Associates' work. Devlin would be pleased to express the videotape to New York. Bunch was pleased too—one less suspect to watch from the cramped front seat of the Subaru.

Devlin made it back to the office about a quarter after five. Comfortably loose from the stretching and lifting, he felt more awake than if he'd slept for a few hours. There were times when working out seemed like too much of a burden and he'd be tempted to let it go for a day or two. Tell himself that he'd make up for it with a real sweat when he finally got over to the gym. His self would answer that he'd better go now even if he didn't feel like it, because it was an investment in his line of work. The day might come when he'd have to bench-press a malefactor. But the real reason he would groan and heave himself to his feet to face the gleaming machines and the running track was because he knew he would feel better after it was over.

This afternoon was no different, and his sense of well-being was added to by the good news waiting on the answering machine in Bunch's voice. The Zell case was close to payoff. All in all, it was a very satisfactory day. That satisfaction was in his voice when, at exactly five-thirty, he answered the telephone. Hurriedly, Chris told him Atencio said that Visser was pissed and worried, that the man had come to work angry and thoughtful, and that he—Atencio—wasn't sure what it was all about. But Visser wanted Atencio to tell him every word Chris had ever said to him.

"Did Visser make any threats?"

"No." Chris poured himself a beer from the small refrigerator. It sat on a shelf in the kitchen alcove that wasn't much bigger than the machine. "I hardly saw him all morning. I wanted to eat lunch with Johnny and he said we better not. That's when he told me about Visser. But get this." He paused and waited until Devlin asked what. "Visser came up to me just before quitting time and said he wants another meet with you."

It was strange not just because Chris wasn't expecting it after what Devlin said last night but also because Visser seemed almost happy. He even smiled and smacked a hand on Chris's shoulder like they were the best of buddies.

"Where and when?" asked Kirk.

"He said he'd let me know in a day or two."

Kirk wasn't sure what it meant either. "All right. As soon as you hear, call in."

Kirk spent the next morning watching Truman's house. Maybe their luck with Zell would spill over. After an early breakfast, he cut across town before the six A.M. traffic began to build into a rush hour. He figured Truman might be one of those people who got out of the house before the rest of the world was awake, since she never seemed to come out during normal hours. In the gray of dawn, the condominium was silent and dark. He parked in the street, facing away from the house, and adjusted the rearview mirror. Slowly, the neighborhood came to life. A milk truck made its stops to let the driver run clunking up and down the long sidewalks linking the clusters of four- and six-unit condos across green widths of carefully tended lawns. Shortly after the blue and white milk van pulled out of sight, the first of the day's workers backed from garages and parking slots to turn into the gleam of rising sun. Then the pulse of the neighborhood picked up with the main migration of cars leaving the condominiums. After that, traffic slowed to the occasional school bus, followed by housewives, salesmen, and delivery vans. And a few people—like Kirk—who seemed to have no reason for being there. No Jean Truman this morning. He pulled out into the small increase of traffic that came with noon. The street wound through the trimmed common areas and past privacy fences that marked each unit's own attached patio. He found an Arby's restaurant and dawdled over the hot bread and beef with his legs fully stretched out. Then he drove back to sit again and wait for Truman to do something.

That kind of waiting makes for long days, and it was with relief that as the return migration of evening began to peak he headed back to the office. He'd be back later this evening. Maybe those drapes would open enough to show her walking without the brace. Maybe she'd put on her dancing shoes and trip the light fantastic down the sidewalk. She was attractive in a dark and intense way, and Kirk had seen a blond man visit the address occasionally. Woman does not live by neck brace alone. But how long it would be before she slipped up, Kirk couldn't say. Still, that possibility—like an angler's faith in a fish's hunger—was what made surveillance bearable.

———

Chris, too, had found the day a long one despite the extra janitorial work caused whenever a large shipment of components came in. Visser hadn't called last night, and today neither Visser nor Johnny Atencio said a word to him. In fact, they avoided him. If they saw him coming, they headed suddenly in another direction down a warehouse aisle. It was puzzling—especially Johnny, who had seemed like a nice enough guy and who enjoyed telling Chris about his amateur boxing career. Chris stripped off his sweaty wool socks and padded barefoot to his bathroom to splash cool water across his face. He was due to make his daily report in fifteen minutes and he'd ask Devlin about it. He was half undressed for a shower when a knock rattled his door.

Through the peephole, he saw Scotty Martin on the landing, half smiling at the little fisheye of glass. Surprised to see the man at his door, Chris quickly unlatched the security chain. This was it—the contact.

He started to say hello to Martin when a large figure, as big as Devlin, moved quickly from the wall to the doorway. It was a face Chris thought he recognized—maybe the one in the car the other night. Up close, the face was chiseled with hard lines around the eyes and mouth, and it was dark with heavy tan. Chris looked at Scotty half hidden behind the big man's shoulder. Scotty looked back at him with distant, expressionless eyes. It was the same look Chris had seen on cowboys at branding time when they threw a calf and, hooked castrating knife clutched in a fist, approached the bawling and helpless animal.

CHAPTER  8

An accident somewhere up near the Mousetrap had turned the rush hour Valley Highway into a miles-long parking lot. Devlin and the Subaru, caught between exits, crept and braked while the cheery babble of a radio talk-show host kept telling commuters how bad the traffic jam was. By the time he could pull off the interstate and work his way along crowded side streets through downtown, the hour for Chris's report was long past. He finally reached the office and dialed the young man's home number, but there was no answer.

It didn't mean anything—Chris often called in from wherever he happened to be. And maybe what he had to say, he hadn't wanted to leave on the office's telephone answerer. Kirk walked from his office over to Larimer Square for an early dinner while Josephina's Restaurant was still uncrowded, then came back half expecting something on the answerer. But there was nothing. He settled down to the paperwork that had piled up, bringing expense sheets up to date, answering correspondence that required reply, filing those letters that didn't. Sometime later, he turned on the desk lamp and tried Chris's home number again. Still no answer, and Kirk felt a twinge of irritation: Chris was over two hours late in making his report. Kirk called the telephone answerer at his own home, but a playback of messages held nothing. He was finishing up the last routine office chores and a cup of coffee when Bunch came dragging in. His afternoon had been spent wandering around Humphries' half acre, and then the three of them went out to dinner. Humphries and wife enjoyed a menu that unfolded stiffly to four large pages of ornate hand-lettering and had a flocked maroon cover with a gold tassel. Bunch ate McDonalds in the Bronco.

"Humphries swore he heard something in the bushes next to the house after I left last night, so I made a tour around the place."

"Any sign of a prowler?"

"Hell no. Nothing anywhere. The ground was soft too in a lot of places. My guess is it was a skunk or raccoon." He yawned widely. "Christ, I'm still tired from yesterday."

Humphries was beginning to sound like the kind of case Kirk and Associates tried to avoid—one whose demands interfered with what they should be doing in industrial security. If there had been enough to do in industrial security. "We might have to bring somebody in temporarily."

"Something heating up with Advantage?"

Devlin told him about Visser's request for another meeting. Bunch sipped at his steaming cup while he thought about it. "Why would he want to talk with us so soon?"

It wasn't expected. Normally there would be delays for conferences and blustering, time spent to check out the opposition's strengths and weaknesses before war councils were held and decisions made. "Maybe they believed me when I gave them three days," said Devlin.

"And maybe they didn't. What's the latest from Chris?"

"I haven't heard from him today."

"He didn't report in?"

"Not yet. I tried getting him earlier, but no answer."

Bunch drained his cup. "Maybe we better go by."

It was almost nine by the time Bunch's Bronco found a slot along the curb a block from Chris's apartment building. A stately red stone mansion in Queen Anne style, it had been sliced into half a dozen living units. Tenants and guests had to sniff out their parking on streets lined with the cars of other lodgers. Two blocks to the north, Colfax Avenue glittered with a steady rush of traffic. To the south, the street fell away downhill to offer a distant glimpse of quiet residential blocks that stretched to Governor's Park. This late in the evening, the September air tingled with a hint of coming winter, and yellowing leaves covered the sidewalks and crackled underfoot with a sound that promised cozy warmth around the fireplace.

A short walk led to the front door, which was flanked by panels of varicolored beveled glass. Chris's apartment was on the second floor, front, and the wide stairs creaked with age and perhaps indignation as the two large men climbed through the musty smell of an ancient carpet.

"Why's the kid live in a dump like this?" asked Bunch.

"You want me to say it's because I don't pay him enough, right?"

"Hey, you don't have to tell me."

"He also thinks it's better cover."

Besides, it wasn't that bad a place. The carved dark wood was still unscarred and impressive, and the leaded glass shades over the bulbs and chandeliers showed that the owner cared about the property. It was old and worn but clean, and the compartmentalization had been done right, so the house was a quiet one. Even the music, turned up loudly somewhere, was muffled and dim in the hallway, and the outside street sounds faded into silence. It was less like an apartment house than the large private home it had once been, and here in the common area of atrium and stairwell, Devlin felt a sense of hushed intrusion. As they reached the second floor the music grew louder. It came from behind the heavy door of Chris's apartment, and they could feel more than hear the weighty thump of a bass speaker tremble the banister rail.

Bunch rapped his knuckles on the dark wood and they waited.

The heavy rock beat dimly against the other side of the thick door.

"Try again," said Kirk. "Maybe he didn't hear us over that noise."

Bunch did, louder this time. Then he turned the knob. "Uh oh." It was unlocked.

Easing the door open, Bunch peered first through the crack at the door's hinge and then down the wall to the right. He stepped in cautiously. "Chris? Hey, Chris?"

Devlin slipped past Bunch into the living room with its small tiled fireplace. A lamp burned on an end table beside a worn sofa. The doors leading out of the room were closed. Against the wall, the stack of sound components—amplifier, turntable, CD player, tuner, and even a twin-reel tape deck—glowed with digital signals, and the large speakers thudded heavily in the small room. Kirk turned it off and in the sudden silence his voice seemed loud. "Chris? You here?"

The alcove that served as a kitchen was empty too. A light in the stove hood showed only the small gas range and a half-size refrigerator facing the sink. Devlin pressed open the door leading to the dark bathroom. The only sound was the steady tink of a slow drip into the stained washbasin. Bunch opened the door to the bedroom. Wadded covers looked for a moment like a man lying still, but the bed was vacant.

"Any idea where he went, Dev?"

"No." The irritation Kirk had felt was turning into worry.

"Dev."

He looked. Bunch pointed to the floor. From beneath the closet door a small, dark stain had swelled on the pale floorboards and spilled into a crack to run an inch or two before clotting.

Bunch opened the closet door.

The clothes bar had been cleared by jamming the clothes and coat hangers to one end. A white bag—a large laundry sack, lumpy and soggy with blood—hung heavily. The closet floor and a half dozen street and tennis shoes were thick with pooled blood. Its odor, a faint mustiness like an exhaled, stale breath, floated through the open door.

"Lift the bag, Bunch. I'll cut him down."

"You can't do that, Dev. It's a crime scene. Homicide'll want it untouched."

"Lift the goddamned bag!"

He did, grasping it at the top. Kirk sawed with a pocketknife at the cotton rope lashed around the closet bar.

"Leave the knots tied, Dev. That's evidence."

The canvas bag settled heavily onto the shoes and floor. Kirk sliced an opening through the cloth. Chris's face—what was left of it—was tilted up open-eyed. Beneath the handkerchief wadded and tied over his mouth with a torn shirtsleeve, Devlin could see the effort to scream frozen in the stiffened flesh of his cheeks. The dead eyes, still bloodshot from pain, stared at him and through him and into some agony that he could only imagine. Chris's arms, tied in front where he could see them, ended in ragged cuts of flesh where the hands had been severed from the wrists. Farther down, in a darkness caused by blood and the shadows of tightly bound and folded legs, Kirk saw the glimmer of drained and curled fingers. Somewhere behind him, he heard Bunch calling the police.

The final paperwork was finished around three in the morning. Kirk inked his initials at the bottom of each page of his statement, along with those of the homicide investigator who witnessed the signing. Bunch, who had been treated with a bit less suspicion because he was an ex-cop, waited in a separate office and visited with a couple old buddies who were now in Vice and Narcotics. And who didn't hide their belief that the murder was drug-related. "It looks like a revenge thing, Bunch." Dave Miller propped a shoe on the corner of his desk and stretched. "Do you know if the victim was dealing? Maybe ripped somebody off?"

The preliminary investigation was being wrapped up by Sergeant Kiefer, who was irritated because he thought Bunch and

Devlin weren't telling him all they knew about the motives for Newman's death. And he was right. They had talked it over quickly before the police arrived to separate them and prevent them from talking things over. They knew who was behind the murder, if not who did it, and they didn't want cops getting their hands on the suspects yet. Visser's remark about pulling back a stump had been demonstrated. They also knew Visser would have an airtight alibi in case his name did get handed to the police. So both Bunch and Devlin decided to stay in the game as players—especially with the stakes upped in blood. They owed Chris that much. They told Kiefer a lot of the truth but not all of it; they kept their mouths shut about Visser. Yes, the victim was working for Kirk and Associates. Yes, the death could be related to the case, but Kirk didn't think so. It was a routine investigation of a small-time industrial security problem, the same one Devlin had asked Officer Lewellen for information about two days ago. Give Lewellen a call, ask him. No, Devlin had no idea who might have done it, but if anything turned up, yes, he'd call immediately. He'd appreciate the same favor from Kiefer.

Then, once more, he'd described how he and Bunch happened to drop by to talk over the case with Chris and how they found his body hanging in the sack and cut him down.

"You knew that was a crime scene, Kirk. You shouldn't have cut him down."

"I didn't know at the time he was dead. I wasn't going to leave him hanging there if he was alive." He wasn't going to leave Chris there if he was dead, either, but Kiefer didn't need to know about that. The cop was already tired and short on patience and unhappy with the gaps in Kirk's and Bunch's stories.

The detective rubbed ink-stained fingers into the loose dark skin beneath his eyes. "All right, all right. Put it down in a statement. Use your own words and initial the bottom of each page. Here, use this desk over here."

The cause of death may have been something other than loss

of blood, but the autopsy would determine that for certain. When the forensics people had carefully peeled away the wet canvas from the cramped and bound body, Kiefer looked at Chris's face and shook his head. He said something about torture. The cut wounds on Chris's chest and stomach and the blisters of burned flesh on armpits and genitals testified to what he went through before he died. Devlin was sure he'd told Visser's people who he really was and what Kirk and Associates was up to. Devlin was sure he himself would have told anybody anything. But that hadn't been enough. To make the message clear, they cut off his hands while he watched and stuffed him into a bag to finish dying. The forensics team said the bathroom had been recently and thoroughly scrubbed, and their guess was that the torture and butchering had taken place in the old claw-footed bathtub. The only fingerprints they found on the apartment's likely surfaces were Bunch's and Devlin's. The absence of Chris's prints indicated that the killers had wiped the place down just before they left. Kiefer would tell Devlin or Bunch all about the rest of it when the autopsy was completed sometime tomorrow.

"You finished yet, Dev?" Bunch, showing the weariness of the hour and his anguish, leaned through the doorway.

"Yeah. Let's go."

Kiefer looked up from his pile of reports and diagrams. "If you gentlemen do come up with something, you will tell me immediately, right?"

"Right." Bunch nodded. "Have you called Newman's family?"

"We haven't. The sheriff's office over in Mineral County—they'll handle it. Unless you want to."

Kirk had never met Chris's parents. He only knew that the young man was raised on a ranch near Creede and had left the mountains for Denver to find some excitement. But Devlin had their address on the employment form—next of kin—and their telephone number for emergencies. "Any idea when the sheriff will give notification?"

Kiefer shrugged. "First thing this morning, probably."

"Let him do it, then. They'll need their rest." And Kirk had a lot to do in the next couple hours.

Bunch was silent until they were in the Bronco. He glanced at Devlin's face and had a pretty good idea what was going through his mind, because he was thinking the same thing. "You sleepy, Dev?"

"Hell no."

The empty streets with their flashing yellow traffic lights had the hardness that comes when the dust of the day's business hasn't yet been stirred, and the cold, high air holds a breath of moisture. Soon it would congeal as dew, but right now it was still in the atmosphere and sharpened the nip of the predawn chill.

"We can't let this slide, Dev."

"Tell me something I don't already know."

"You think Visser's all snug in his bed?"

"I think we go find out."

One of the basics of Secret Service training is to move fast and decisively—to use the element of surprise if you are attacking, to take it away by quick, almost reflexive response if you are attacked. Visser might have learned that Chris was a detective rather than a mob representative. But Dev's guess was that the man didn't know how much they knew about the three scumbags. And Kirk also guessed that Visser shared the arrogance of so many murderers—an arrogance that not only judged the life of others worthless but also made them believe they were invulnerable to those they scorned.

Bunch groped under the dash for the strap holster that held the .357 Python with its box of Super Vel cartridges. He had filled its quick-load cylinders with an assortment of slugs—ball, cupped, hollow, Teflon-coated. It provided a variety of solutions to different problems that might come up. So far, all the jobs with the magnum had been on the firing range. He asked Devlin to unscrew the Hutson pistol scope from the weapon. "You armed?"

Kirk shook his head. He owned the standard-issue .38 special with two-inch barrel and hooded hammer. But he seldom carried it since he left the Service. The tiny .32 Seecamp that he preferred was at home in a desk drawer with its ankle holster.

"I just hope that son of a bitch is," said Bunch. "I just hope he reaches for a weapon."

CHAPTER 9

The Advantage Corporation records had noted that Visser lived out near Commerce City in the 3500 block of Beekman Place. It was a small frame house set back in a littered yard with a high wire fence and a large sign warning people to beware of the dog. They cruised past the darkened windows in a row of equally small houses and turned to make a slow loop around the block. No alley led behind the homes. Where Beekman came to an end, a crumbling brick warehouse looked black and vacant. A railroad track—rusty from disuse—led off toward the industrial sites just beyond the city boundary.

"What do you want to do about the dog?" asked Devlin.

Bunch rustled in the gym bag behind his seat and then hefted a can of dog spray which he gave to Kirk and a snare of piano wire. It was rigged through two wooden blocks to make a running loop. "We do what we have to."

The name stenciled on the rusty mailbox nailed to the top of a fence post said "E. L. Visser." Kirk squirted WD-40 on the hinges and then gently lifted the metal catch to swing the faintly creaking gate. They skirted the low front porch, with its single board step leading to the screened door. Silently, they picked their way along the building's side. Bunch pointed to a tricycle and a scatter of digging toys that marked a kid's favorite corner in the sandy yard. That was something they hadn't counted on: Visser with kids.

They eased past the rear corner and toward the back porch, a screened addition tacked onto the house. Bunch was testing the lock on the door when the skitter of clawed feet and an angry, deep growl pulled Kirk around. A charging police dog, its teeth a ragged whiteness, rushed out of the dark, eyes green with the hunger to kill.

"Bunch!"

"Son-of-a-bitching dogs!"

Devlin sprayed the cayenne mixture into the lunging mouth and eyes and dived aside. The dog coughed a startled bark and whipped around to slash blindly toward Kirk's throat. Bunch's hands were a blurred motion and the dog, blinking and slinging saliva and straining for Kirk, was yanked straight in midair. As splayed feet scrabbled in the dirt its weight and drive tightened the piano wire around its throat. The flailing tongue whipped in agony against the bulging eyes. Bunch lifted the kicking dog off the ground again. It twisted and flapped from side to side like a broken fish. Its frenzy was all the more intense for the muffled, strangled noise it made while it died. When the animal finally hung motionless, Bunch eased it down, then slipped the blood-wet piano wire through the blocks and wiped it on the dog's coat. Then he dragged a hand along his damp forehead. "God, I hate dogs. Son of a bitch must weigh over a hundred pounds. Hear anything?"

Devlin stepped over the dog and leaned an ear toward the dark house. Silence. From somewhere in the tangle of streets to the south came the ringing whine of heavy tires on the elevated spans of I-70. Beyond that, a train gave a long, sad moan as it headed out of Denver and into the black prairies. "It's quiet." He slipped a knife blade under the latch on the screen door and eased it off. The porch boards groaned beneath their feet, and the main door clicked loudly as Bunch slipped a thumb lock with a plastic card. He opened it with a slow creak.

They stepped into a kitchen warm with a mixture of odors:

the rancid tinge of ill-concealed garbage, a chemical odor from the box of soap sitting open by the sink, the pungent tang of a poorly ventilated water heater in the tiny bathroom just off the kitchen.

The rooms were built in a row. It was the kind of arrangement Devlin's uncle Wyn called a shotgun house. The room next to the kitchen was crowded with a pair of bunk beds and a crib. Adenoidal breathing came from the small shadows humped under light blankets and half visible in the thin glow of a night-light. The next room held two sleeping forms in a double bed. Beyond could be seen the living room with its television set and litter of toys across the carpet. The largest sleeping form had straight blond hair that tangled on the pillow and across her gapped mouth. The other was Visser. His mouth, too, was open in loud, sour breathing. The steady noise turned into a muffled snort under Bunch's wide palm.

Bunch held the long-barreled pistol so that light from the window caught it. Visser's eyes widened over the side of Bunch's hand. His body, starting in surprise, froze. Devlin motioned for the man to keep quiet and to get up. Bunch followed Visser's careful movements with the revolver jammed into the flesh under his chin. Pinched, white skin rolled over the barrel's muzzle. They went out the way they came in, past the sleeping children and the smelly kitchen and into the icy air of the silent backyard. Visser, in his underwear, shivered.

"You see that?" Bunch whispered.

Visser stared at the dark form of the dog and then made a little jerk against Kirk's hand.

"One fucking sound out of you and we kill you and your ugly kids and fat wife like we killed your dog." Bunch wagged the wire and blocks. "Hear me?"

The man's head jerked yes.

Bracing him between them, they half carried Visser around to the Bronco. Bunch sat holding the revolver against Visser's ribs while Devlin drove.

"What you guys want?"

"We found the kid," said Bunch.

"What kid? What's that mean?"

"The kid you people tortured and killed."

"Killed? Man, I never killed nobody! I never even heard about nobody being killed!"

"Right," said Kirk.

"I mean that, man! I don't know what you people are talking about. I was shooting pool all goddamn night. A lot of people seen me, man—I can prove it!"

Bunch clicked the hammer back on the revolver. It made an oily, efficient sound. "We're not cops, Visser. We don't have to worry about due process. Your alibi don't mean shit to us, so shut the fuck up."

The streets seemed a bit grayer with the thinning of night, and the widely spaced streetlights were growing feeble. Devlin turned onto Brighton Road and then off again at a dirt track. It followed a chain-link fence around sprawling and ill-lit acres that held piles of heavy equipment, rusty oil rigging, stacks of wire cables and wooden spools. Then it bounced toward the fringe of weeds and scrub that marked the banks of the South Platte. Here the forgotten river was a shallow expanse oily with waste and clots of yellowing chemical spume that floated on the almost stagnant water.

"You guys listen—whatever happened, I didn't have nothing to do with it!"

"With what, Eddie?"

"You know. What you told me about. The kid."

Kirk halted the truck beside the fence. A tall stack of steel construction frames hid them from the view of distant I-270. An early jet whistled in from the north as it glided toward Stapleton Airport. In the south against the lightening sky, a tall plume of dark steam and smoke rose from the Public Service generating plant. The nearby Conoco refinery made the cold air smell thick and heavy with its flaring burn-off.

"You hear me? I don't know nothing about it!"

Bunch gestured for the man to get out.

"No! I don't want to!"

Devlin grabbed him by the nape and hauled him writhing from the Bronco. Shaking too hard to support him, his legs collapsed against the vehicle. He slid down until his bony knees pressed against his chest, and his hands splayed outward to hold off the two men who leaned over him.

Bunch took the wooden blocks from his truck and ran the loop of piano wire through the holes. It made a high-pitched, sizzling noise.

"Uh hunh—no . . ."

Bunch yanked Visser's head back. Dropping the wire around his neck, he cinched the blocks, and the wire bit into flesh. Visser made strangling sounds and dug his fingernails at the wire as his face turned blue. Then Bunch slacked the blocks. He drove a fist into the gagging man's stomach. Visser doubled over to vomit and scrabble in the dirt in a mindless effort to crawl under the truck's high running board. Bunch again yanked the wire taut, and planted a shoe on Visser's back. "You keep wiggling, you sorry son of a bitch, I'll slice your head off just like that fucking dog."

Kirk dragged him from beneath the aluminum running board, with its little piles of gravel and dust collected in the corners. "Maybe I should break his knees so he'll stay put."

"No. . . . Don't . . ."

They leaned against the vehicle and watched Visser slowly stop retching and shuddering.

"I'm puking blood. . . . You busted something inside—I'm puking blood!"

"Enjoy it while you can, Eddie," said Kirk. "You're going to hurt a lot more."

"No!"

"Oh, yeah." Bunch smiled.

"But I tell you what. We won't start until you finish talking. How's that for Christian charity?"

"What you want to know? Goddamn—what you want to know?"

"Who did it."

Eddie named Scotty Martin and someone called Tony. Martin had told them that Tony was from out of town—back east somewhere. "I never saw him before the other night when I met with you guys. He come in just for that meeting. I swear I don't know nothing about him. That was the first time I ever saw him, honest to God. Scotty, he's the guy set all this up, I swear! I don't even know that much about it, man. Scotty asked me if I wanted to help out—we're all on the same shift in the warehouse, so we all had to be in it. That's all I know about anything, I swear!" He told why Martin and Tony killed Chris. "They wanted to keep you people out of the factory. Nobody brings no shit in, you know?"

"Why?"

Eddie sighed and looked around at the gray dirt of the road, the chain-link fence with its scrolled crest of gleaming razor wire, the empty tangle of weeds and brush at the riverbank. The only humans in sight were the two big men who stared at him as if he were something on a shoe to be wiped away. "We got a thing going there. I really don't know that much about it. All I know is, every now and then Scotty says there's a shipment, and me and Johnny Atencio help him move the stuff."

It took a while. Every time Eddie slowed down, Bunch tapped the piano wire against his neck. That made the words come again. Once or twice each month, Martin, Atencio, and Visser would gather in a corner of the warehouse to unpack a shipping canister and find several kilos of cocaine hidden in the Styrofoam bracing around a molded plastic unit. Visser had no idea how Martin knew which container held the shipment, and he wasn't about to ask. "It's not my business to know, man. Me and Johnny, we're just the mules in this, you know?" They took their shares and stored the rest in their lockers for a few days. "Scotty's got a touch in with the security people—somebody tips him if there's going to be a locker shakedown. If there is, we take the stuff out. Take it to one of these storage rentals. It gets broken down into smaller wraps—usually four, sometimes five or six. Scotty tells us how many it's supposed to be. But I don't know who tells him."

"What do you do with it?"

"Ship it out in some other canisters. Scotty takes care of that. He knows what canisters are going where. He tapes the load into the Styrofoam packing and off it goes."

"Where to?"

"I don't know, man. Really. Scotty's the only one who knows. It goes to the company's wholesale outlets, but which ones I don't know."

"You make a good piece of change off this?" Bunch asked.

"We get a cut. When a shipment comes in, Scotty divvies it up and we take ours before we repack it. But no selling in the factory, Scotty says. We got our own customers away from the factory. That's the rule. He don't want management to think they got to run searches for dope all the time. You know: lockers, cars, whatever. . . . That's why he got so uptight when he heard about you people wanting to sell in the plant. That, and it's his territory."

"His and Tony's?"

"Yeah. I guess. It's a big operation, you know? But I swear to God—I swear on my mother's soul—I didn't know what Scotty and Tony were going to do to that kid. He said him and Tony was going to ask him about you people. That's all he told me. He didn't even want me to come along. Just him and this guy Tony."

Visser told them a little more about Martin—where the man lived, where he liked to drink, who he hung out with. "We don't pal around a lot, you know? Me and Johnny are on the same crew, so he had to take us in. You can't handle them canisters by yourself, you know?"

"You never meet outside the plant?"

"Just a drink now and then to unwind. Scotty, he don't let people get close to him." He added, "And if we have to take stuff out to a storage locker."

"Where's this Tony from?"

"I told you—back east somewhere. That's all I know. I swear. I only saw him a couple times."

"When?"

"At the meet with you guys. He drove. And . . ." He chewed his lip.

"When?"

"Day before yesterday. He wanted me to talk to the kid."

"To set him up."

"I didn't know what they were going to do!"

"What about Porter?" Devlin asked.

"Who?"

"Porter—the fork lift operator. Where does he fit in?"

"Christ, I don't know. I never heard of the guy."

"He's selling pot."

"A pothead? Scotty wouldn't bring in a guy like that. Me and Johnny, we don't use. That was part of the arrangement— no snorting on the job. Hell, we don't even deal the streets, you know? We sell our stuff through a couple middlemen. Scotty told us to do it that way."

"You've never heard of Porter?"

"No. I swear. We kind of keep to ourselves—if he ain't part of the warehouse crew, I don't know him."

Visser crouched against the running board with his arms wrapped tightly around his shivering, naked legs. He looked up at the two men. The red glare of the dawning sun brought a palpable warmth to the air but Visser didn't feel it. "Man, I told it all. You know everything I know."

"Then I guess it's time," said Bunch.

"Aw, man, don't do it. Please don't do it."

"How fast can you pack your ass out of town and stay out?" Devlin asked.

"Now, man. I mean right now."

"It's a mistake, Dev. We should wad this little fucker up and flush him."

"Don't do it, man. I can go. Nothing to keep me here, man."

They loaded him up and Devlin drove to a telephone at the corner of a closed 7-Eleven. Visser stood in the phone hood, his pale underwear streaked with dirt and bagging against the puckered flesh of his blue thighs. He talked to his wife. "I don't care what you got to leave behind—fuck the house! It ain't ours anyway. We're getting out, hear me? Now! Pack everything in the goddamn car and get up here. Now! We're going and we're gonna keep going!" He hung up and stared at Devlin, eyes wide and round above the pinched chill of his cheeks. "Fucking women! Want to know everything before they'll do anything."

"Dev, this son of a bitch is going to drop a dime on us as soon as he gets out of town. I think we ought to box him up."

"No, man—I won't do that. I promise. I been thinking of quitting anyway. Really! I got a stash saved up and I don't owe Scotty nothing. I won't do that—I swear!"

"There's only one way to make sure he won't, Dev." Bunch patted the bulge of the Python's barrel inside his jacket. "Nobody's around to see it. He'd be just another turd lying in the gutter."

"Hey, my wife and kids . . ."

"You're not a good influence, Eddie," said Kirk. "They might be better off without you. Ever think of that?"

"Come on, guys—I swear!"

"We need insurance," said Bunch. "The best insurance is to waste this little fucker."

"Guys . . ."

Devlin scratched around in the Bronco's glove box for a pen and paper. "You write down what you told us about Tony and Scotty."

"A statement for the cops?"

"No. For us to give to Martin if we find out you called him."

"I said I wouldn't!"

"Yeah. Honest Abe Visser. Write."

He did, in a sprawling, shaky hand. He signed and dated it where Devlin told him to.

Kirk leaned over the man and gazed deep into the staring black of his pupils. "We can find you, Eddie. Anywhere you run, we can find you if we have to. And so can Tony. Understand?"

He nodded. A white, powdery tongue dragged across blue lips.

They left the man in his underwear, crouched against the wall of the closed grocery store and shifting from foot to foot with nervousness and cold.

Bunch twisted back around on the passenger seat after watching the figure disappear behind them. "He's going to call Martin. I know how shit like that thinks—he's going to call to get even with us and then haul ass out of town."

Devlin tapped the statement folded in his pocket. "He might not. Besides, what can he tell Martin that Chris didn't?"

"You think Newman spilled?"

"I would have. Wouldn't you?"

Bunch thought that over. "Probably." He wiped the Python down with a lightly oiled rag and began dropping large cartridges into the empty chambers. "I could have blown that shithead away so easy. Let's go find Martin."

"Suppose we do. What then?"

"We shoot the son of a bitch."

Devlin felt that way too. Martin had cut off not only Newman's hands but any claim to humanity as well. But without delving into the philosophical niceties of lynch law or the ironies of duty as a curb to justice, he reminded Bunch that they had taken money from the Advantage Corporation.

"You're telling me we solve the dope case before we step on Martin?"

"That's right."

"That's bullshit, is what that is. Next you'll tell me that's what Chris would have wanted. And then tell me to win this one for the Gipper."

"I think the only thing Chris wanted was to be out of pain. And maybe to live."

"That's what I want to see in that fucker's eyes just before I pull the trigger."

"But we took the Advantage paycheck, Bunch. We promised we'd do a job. And Martin's our only lead to Tony, isn't he?"

That's what Kirk told Reznick, too, a couple hours later.

"You mean some workers are moving cocaine through the company shipping system?" He stared at the tall man whose face, despite a fresh shave that left dots of crusty blood in a line along his jaw, was pale with weariness and puffy and unhealthy. In fact, if it weren't for the man's cold eyes, Reznick would wonder if Kirk had been on a three-day drunk. "You sure you know what the hell you're talking about?"

"Some kind of network has been set up within the company, Mr. Reznick. How much is shipped and from what points, I'm not sure. Obviously, since it comes in and goes out of here, at least two other locations are involved."

The plant manager ran a hand across his cropped, curly hair. Kirk had told him that the agent, whose name he'd never known, was dead. That was bad enough, but the news that really shook him was of the illegal operation in his own plant. It was big and it was professionally organized, and if the newspapers ever got wind of it . . . Reznick had wanted to arrest Martin and Atencio immediately. When Kirk told him there wasn't enough evidence to do that, he wanted them fired. Kirk talked him out of that, too, on the grounds that Martin wasn't working alone and probably wasn't the organizer. He was at the middle of the distribution system, not at the head of it.

"But you said they know we're onto them. You said that young man—Newman?—probably confessed he was an undercover agent."

"They're worried. That's one of the reasons they killed Chris. The other is that they're making enough money to risk killing someone. That much cocaine, assuming it's pure, means a hell of a lot of profit." Especially in the Denver area, where a shortage of cocaine had generated a spate of murders and gang squabbles. "Mr. Reznick, they're not going to run from a setup like this. They killed to protect the trade as well as themselves. They'll lay low for a while and if things stay quiet, they'll be back. Just like flies on puke."

"It comes in from one of our supply plants and then they distribute it to our regional wholesalers? How does the gang know what containers have the cocaine?"

"I don't know. Nor am I certain that Martin's is the only ring here."

"What's that mean?"

"There could be another just like his operating in your plant, each one ignorant of the other." Devlin nodded toward the window that overlooked the sprawl of metal roofs and loading docks. "You ship a lot of goods and you hire a lot of people."

"But it definitely involves more than my plant?"

"Definitely."

A thought worked behind the man's dark eyes, and Devlin could see the relief it brought. If the ring involved more than one Advantage Corporation site, that meant Reznick didn't shoulder the blame all by himself. In fact, if he worked it right, he could make some take-charge points with the board of directors by clearing up the mess.

"You don't think we should bring in the police right away, do you?"

"We could. But the ring touches a lot of jurisdictions—local, state, and federal. You would lose control of the operation."

Reznick stared through the vertical blinds over the windows. "But what about your man's death? Isn't there some sort of accessory risk if we don't tell the police about the dope ring's involvement?"

"They've been told enough to avoid that. Besides, the evidence of Martin's role in the murder isn't admissible in court."

"Why the hell not?"

"It was extorted by force."

"Oh. . . . Oh, I see." He eyed Kirk a bit oddly and then pushed back in his swivel chair. "I see." Then, "What do you recommend next?"

"We put in another agent."

"Who in God's name would take that risk?"

Bunch and Devlin had asked that too, and had come up with an answer. "He'll have to be paid enough." Kirk told Reznick how much was enough and the man blinked, but he didn't say no.

"Will he do it?"

"I'm sure he will. Don't you have to hire people to replace Newman and Visser?"

"Yes, I guess we do."

"It would help if a couple other vacancies could be filled at the same time. The larger number of new employees is better cover."

"I see—yes. Yes, I can arrange that with Personnel."

"Just make certain our man is the one who takes Visser's place on the warehouse crew. If they want to keep the operation going, they'll have to bring him in."

"Why?"

"It takes more than one person to handle the canisters. And they can't take the chance that somebody who's not in on it will discover what's going on."

"He'd better be a good actor. Convince them he's no better than they are."

"They'll believe that, all right."

———

The name Bunch and Devlin had both come up with was Vinny Landrum. He was on the telephone by the time Devlin got back to the office.

"What's this crap you got a job for me, Kirk? Get into something you and Homer can't handle?"

"I need somebody who's a natural sleazeball, Vinny. You're the first name I thought of."

"Yeah. I get wet dreams about you too. So what is it and how much does it pay?"

"Come over and we'll talk about it."

"When I can work it in, Kirk. Maybe this afternoon, if I'm not too tied up. Maybe tomorrow morning, if I feel like it."

Bunch, red-eyed and yawning before he started his day's work looking after Humphries and the Japanese-American Princess, had shaken his head at the name. "I hate that asshole, Dev. I wish we'd started with him instead of Chris."

"We didn't."

"I don't like him and I don't trust him. That bastard would sell out his own mother."

"He never had a mother. And we'll just have to keep him honest, won't we? We'll just have to do a better job for him than we did for Chris, won't we?"

Bunch had looked at Devlin. The gray morning light from the arched window made the bags under his eyes look puffy and etched. "Newman understood it was a dangerous business."

"No. He was told it was a dangerous business. But he didn't understand it. He didn't have a chance to understand it."

"Hey, we didn't do it to him, Dev. Martin and that scumbag Tony did it. They're the ones, not us."

"We—I—put him in over his head. And he went under."

"You want to blame yourself, go ahead. But I'm not taking any part of it. And you're a damn fool if you do." He added, "And maybe just a little bit phony." Bunch paused in the doorway before starting on the day's official work. " 'Luxuriate in self-pity'—that what you sensitive types like to do? Does it make you feel better to think you helped kill the guy? Bullshit.

The ones I'm going after are the ones who did it. I'm sure as hell not going after myself!"

No, Kirk thought, it didn't make him feel better to think he helped kill Chris. In fact, he'd like to be able to dismiss that thought entirely. But despite Bunch's scorn it still nagged. Sometime after Vinny called, Kirk finally reached for the telephone.

He'd wanted to give the sheriff's officer time to bring the bad news, because he wasn't sure he had the courage to do it. The voice that answered after a number of rings told Kirk that they knew: a teenager's voice, it had the stuffy, cramped sound of grief. When Devlin identified himself, there was a long pause before the youth said, "Just a minute. I'll get my dad."

Mr. Newman's voice wasn't deep, but you could tell it had lost some strength. "We appreciate your calling, Mr. Kirk. Chris liked working for you. He told us that when we talked to him last . . . last Thursday night, it was."

"He was a fine young man, Mr. Newman. The police—and we—will do everything we can to catch the people who did it."

"I appreciate that. Any—ah—information yet on how he died? All the sheriff told us was he was killed. Stabbed."

"Yes. In his apartment."

"Did . . . Was it sudden, Mr. Kirk? Did my son hurt?"

"I haven't seen the autopsy report, Mr. Newman." That was the most Kirk could say. "As soon as I have information, I'll send it on to you."

"I appreciate that."

There were a few more words, but it was the sound more than the content that had any meaning at all—another human voice that spoke their son's name in a way that a small bit of their grief was shared. After Devlin had hung up and sat in silence for a long time, he made a second call, this one to a florist. Then he tried to bury his thoughts in the routines of work.

Vinny Landrum came in sometime around midafternoon. In cold weather, he liked to wear a trench coat, apparently because that's what detectives did on television. But on this warm afternoon he had on lime-green slacks and white patent leather belt and shoes. An orange sport shirt open at the neck showed the glitter of gold chains: power dressing *Miami Vice* style.

"Vinny—you give new meaning to the phrase 'a sight for sore eyes.' "

"I'm surprised you know taste when you see it, Kirk. I figured yours was all in your mouth." He looked around the office and then sat to flick something off his cuff. "Where's that big asshole Bunchcroft?"

"Out on a job."

"Good thing one of you is working. It's starting to look a little seedy around here."

"The cleaning crew's due in tonight."

"Yeah. Sure. You said you got business, Kirk." Vinny glanced at his watch. "I'm pretty busy, so let's get to it, right?"

"Process serving or skip tracing?"

"Hey, I make a living, right? It's a hell of a lot better than you people been doing lately." He tapped a filter cigarette from the box to his mouth and torched it with a butane lighter. "I hear about you people: no divorce cases, no debt collection. Maybe your shit don't stink like everybody else's or something."

"I might have some work for you, Vinny. The kind that pays a little bit. But if you're too tied up right now . . ."

"Hey, don't get cute, Kirk. I'm here, right? Just tell me the deal."

"Undercover." Devlin explained as much as Landrum would need to know and a bit more than he should be trusted with: a big local company, suspected narcotics, the need for an inside plant who could be convincing in a short time.

"What's the pay?"

Devlin told him. The lowest figure anyway.

"Shit. I make more than that skip tracing. And I'm my own boss."

"There's also a hazardous-duty bonus."

He squinted at Kirk through a puff of smoke. Behind him,

vague figures moved across the frosted glass panel of the door, looking for one of the other offices in the building. "What kind of hazard and what kind of bonus?"

"We had an agent in there. He was killed last night."

"Well shit! I'm not going in—they'll be looking for another one! How goddamn dumb do you think I am, Kirk?"

"Five new people are going to be hired at the same time. Only one's the plant. You'll go through the regular employment procedure for cover. There's no way they'll know you're an agent."

"I bet that's what you told the last sucker! I'm not going through any employment procedure. You just wasted my fucking afternoon." He mashed out his cigarette and started to rise.

Devlin told him what the bonus was. "Besides, you'll be right at home with these slimeballs, Vinny. They'll never spot you for a plant."

"How much did you say?"

He told him again. The shorter man chewed his lip. Overhead, the sculptress began rolling something heavy across the floor. Then he shook his head. "Not enough, Kirk."

He upped the amount.

"Oh?" His eyes narrowed and he tried to read Kirk's face, tried to find the balance between demanding too little and losing it all. "It's my ass, Kirk. And I don't notice you or Homer all that eager to do it."

"They might know us. Besides, you have a talent for undercover work, Vinny. You're always getting under the covers with some client or other."

"Five hundred a week more, you son of a bitch, and just leave my personal life out of this!"

"Two hundred, Vinny. And that's it. I can get anybody else in town for less than that."

It was true and he knew it. The man nodded and tried to hide the greedy triumph in his eyes. "All right. What's the deal?"

Devlin filled him in on where to apply for the job and the

people he'd need to keep an eye on. "They'll advertise tomorrow morning. Be at the employment window before seven so you're first in line. You apply for the warehouse job." They worked out a cover identity: Vincent Landscomb. Vinny wasn't all that imaginative, which, given Devlin's memory of Chris's body, was probably a good thing. And Kirk set up the communications schedule as well as a couple of basic emergency routines. The latter brought a frown.

"You and jumbo turd Homer gonna cover me, right? I mean none of this out-to-lunch shit if I push the panic button, right?"

"You're a valuable property now." Devlin smiled. "For once you're worth more alive than dead."

"Yeah? Well, you remember that, hear? And remember this, too: You're my contact. I mean, if that two-ton blivet is my only backup, I don't care how much you pay. You can shove this up your nose."

"I'm your contact," Devlin said, and gave Vinny a quick quiz on the information they'd gone over. After Devlin listened to the white patent shoes trip lightly down the iron stairs, he turned his chair to the window and gazed across the flat roofs of the neighboring warehouses toward the mountains. A couple hundred miles beyond that silhouette of the Front Range were the San Juan Mountains and, in a high valley whose surrounding peaks dwarfed the problems and purposes of those who lived there, the ranch where Chris grew up.

Kirk called the office answering machine when he pried himself
out of bed late the next morning. Bunch's voice told the recorder he was on his way up to Broomfield to answer a company's inquiry about debugging their offices and telephone lines
to qualify for bidding on secret government work. Sergeant
Kiefer told it he had a copy of the forensics report on Chris
Newman, and a muffled voice said cryptically, "I got the job.
I start today." Kirk and Associates' newest agent was in place.

As Devlin headed for his garage, Mrs. Ottoboni, who owned
the other half of the Victorian duplex, waved good morning
over the low fence that separated the two backyards. Hers was
a series of billowing colors—the result of a long summer's feed-
ing and watering and the flowers' last efforts to draw life before
the late-September sun dropped any lower. Devlin's patch of
yard was easy-care weed that merely needed an occasional trim
to retain a touch of respectability. A few bare patches of dirt
were the remnants of last spring's planting fever. Only the pe-
tunias that had been a gift from his neighbor flooded a sunny
corner of the small yard near the garage. Devlin thought Mrs.
Ottoboni sneaked over to care for her orphaned seedlings.

"There was a man around yesterday asking about you, Mr.
Kirk."

"Oh?" Since a couple years ago, when Mrs. Ottoboni had witnessed a small fracas in his backyard and probably saved his life by calling the cops, she'd had a kind of proprietary interest in his health and welfare. Anything out of the ordinary—the milkman coming late, a new mailman on the route, someone asking questions—might be a clue for one of her neighbor's cases. So Devlin received a constant nattering of Neighborhood Watch reports and newspaper clippings that she judged might be of help in his work. Exactly what she thought was his work, he never could be certain. When he tried to explain that it was usually tedious detail wrapped in boring repetition, she only smiled knowingly and nodded agreement with a detective's need for circumspection in discussing such topics.

"He said he was doing a background check on you for security reasons. Asked all sorts of things about you."

That was possible. One of the many types of jobs Kirk and Associates bid was to upgrade the mechanical security devices of companies that did classified work for the government. In fact, that's what Bunch was doing in Broomfield this morning. "Did he show any identification?"

"Oh my, yes! A whole string of cards down to here! But they didn't mean a thing to me—I wouldn't know a real one from a counterfeit. He asked about your habits and if you had loud parties or if a lot of strangers went in and out. What your routine was like. If you'd ever been arrested or owed money."

"Did he ask whether you would trust me with national secrets?"

"He did! And I told him I certainly would! Not that I know any national secrets. In fact, the whole idea of a national secret seems to me a contradiction in terms, and I told him that. He didn't think it was very funny. A very serious young man—as tall as you are, but no sense of humor."

"Did he say he'd be back?"

"No. I watched him, though. He went down this side of the street asking questions and then back up the other. I'm not sure what the Fettapaldis told him." The gray head bobbed at the frame house across a narrow walk from her fence. "They're likely to say anything if it can cause harm to somebody."

"Sounds like a routine clearance check, Mrs. Ottoboni. Thanks for telling me." And for indirectly letting him know that Kirk and Associates was still in the running for at least one of the bids they'd placed.

It was always hard to find a parking place near the police administration building during working hours. Devlin finally had to settle for a pay lot a couple blocks away. By the time he reached the homicide offices, most of the detectives were on their way to lunch. Kiefer, shrugging into his neatly pressed sport coat, paused long enough to toss a brown envelope Kirk's way before heading for the elevators.

"I thought you were in a hurry for this, Dev."

"I got held up." He glanced at the Xeroxed pages. "Anything unexpected here?"

"Unexpected? No. But you might be interested in the cause of death."

"Why's that?"

"Doc says he bled to death. I kind of guessed that when there wasn't much lividity."

"You're saying he was alive when they cut off his hands."

"That's what I'm saying. He could watch the whole thing. Maybe he passed out first. I like to think he passed out."

Two uniformed officers entered the elevator on the second floor, and Kiefer and Devlin were silent until they were in the lobby. Kirk handed his visitor's badge to the desk sergeant. He didn't think Chris had passed out. His eyes were open and staring when he was found, and they still held the remnants of his knowledge of a new and unimaginable agony.

"You got anything to tell me yet?" Kiefer's voice broke into Devlin's thoughts.

"No. If I find out anything, I'll let you know."

Kiefer got back on the elevator for a ride down to the underground parking garage. "Ah. Well, I hope you do that, Dev. I sincerely hope you do. See, I really want the son of a bitch who would do something like that. My guess is, it's not the bastard's first time. And my guess is, if I don't get him, it won't be his last. So you be sure you tell me anything you find out. Hear?"

Nodding, Kirk watched the elevator slide across the detective's stiff face. Even if Kiefer didn't get him, it was going to be the killer's last time.

He finished reading through the pages of the forensics report on Chris and tried to frame words into a letter to his parents—words that would give some idea of their son's death, yet hide the worst and offer what sympathy could be offered. Every sentence he put down seemed like a cliché, and none of the words said what he really wanted them to. "Dear Mr. and Mrs. Newman—Your son was working for me in a dangerous job and a killer tortured him and cut off his hands and threw him in a sack to blced to death. I'm sorry." Sometimes you had to go around the edges of things instead of speaking clearly. That's what, Uncle Wyn occasionally reminded Devlin, a college education was all about. And a man who had a year of law school shouldn't have any trouble at all bending words. Uncle Wyn said that, too.

Finally he wrestled something into a rough draft and read it over a couple times to change a word here or rearrange a sentence there. He had a pretty good idea what would happen to this letter—the Newmans would place it in some paper mausoleum along with the other documents relating to their son's death. Devlin still had the telegram notifying him of his father's death. That, and the police reports and news articles. Why, he didn't know, except that somehow all that stuff was a thread, admittedly tenuous, that kept the dead in memory and gave if not meaning at least an understandable cause for their destruction. So he knew that his words would be kept and read again and again. That knowledge made him prod them gingerly and with care. And copy the letter in longhand off the computer screen instead of printing it out.

The latter part of the day was spent peering at Jean Truman's house. Her curtains were pulled open this time, and occasionally a dim figure moved past the windows with that busyness which foreshadows some kind of social activity. But there was no concealed avenue of approach to the condo's window. The landscaping was designed to foil prowlers, and it kept him from moving closer with the camera. He hoped she was getting ready to come out, but she didn't. Instead, a silver Chrysler convertible pulled to the curb and the blond man strode up the sidewalk that arced past the entries of Truman's unit. In his late twenties, heavyset and with glistening hair that curled down behind his ears, the man rapped briefly and stood gazing around the neighborhood as he waited for an answer. Kirk had the camera ready when the door opened. But the woman stayed back in the shadows and the door closed quickly, and the click of the shutter was wasted film.

In about an hour, Kirk saw the pale blue smoke of a barbecue rise above the patio fence. If he listened hard enough, he could make out the tinkle of piano music from a stereo. But neither Devlin nor the camera's telephoto lens could see a thing. As the evening drew toward that time when streetlights began to grow bright, a string of colored lights glowed softly under the arbor that covered part of the small patio. Later, the lights still glowing, curtains were pulled quickly over a dark window upstairs and a light shone briefly and then went out. Kirk gave it some more time, but the window remained dark and the tinkle of the piano continued. When he left, the Chrysler was still at the curb. It looked like Ms. Truman had found a cure for her migraines.

CHAPTER 12

On his way back from the Broomfield interview, Bunch had been called to Humphries' home. The man's tense voice had rattled the car phone as he demanded protection.

"We had another prowler last night."

"Did you see anyone?"

"No. But I heard one. I did what Kirk told us to do—turned on lights, let him know we were awake. It must have scared him off. But I want additional protection—I want additional sensors and I want them now!"

Bunch drove slowly up the dirt lane that led to the ranch-style home at the crest of the gentle hill. Below, the shallow valley formed against the Front Range by Plum Creek was filled with sunlight and wind. Here and there groves of flickering cottonwoods or Lombardies marked clusters of buildings where executives played at ranching.

It wasn't Mrs. Lucero but Mitsuko who waited for him at the door. "I heard your car."

Bunch nodded hello to the smiling woman. She was braless, as usual, and the tight cloth of her slacks showed no furrow of underwear. He sighed. His rule was absolute: no involvement with the clients. "Your husband told me there was a prowler last night."

"We think so." She explained with exaggerated gestures that after they had turned off the television set and gotten ready for bed, Roland thought he heard noises behind the house. He turned on the back light and looked, but they saw nothing. Then he turned on the perimeter lights, as Mr. Kirk had instructed them to do, and crept around the windows trying to see if anyone was out there. "Roland was very brave. He told me where to hide and he went by himself to look through the windows."

"Nothing?"

"He didn't see anything. Actually, I didn't hear anything, either, but Roland was certain he did." She lit a cigarette which looked incongruous against the young smoothness of her face. "At about three in the morning, he jumped out of bed again, saying he heard more noises." She shrugged. "I still heard nothing."

"The perimeter lights were still on?"

"Of course. I'm sure the electricity bill will be very high."

"If anyone tried to get in," Bunch told her, "the alarms would go off. There's no sign anyone tampered with the alarm feed."

"As I said, I heard nothing. Roland hears things, but I usually sleep too well."

"He said something about installing more sensors?"

"Yes. At the property line. He doesn't like the idea of anyone walking all the way up to the house before an alarm goes off."

Bunch looked out the window at the wooded acres surrounding the rambling building. "That's a pretty expensive job, Mrs. Humphries." He glanced at her. "That is your name, isn't it? Mrs. Humphries?"

The cigarette paused. "Why?"

"I understand you're also known as Miss Watanabe."

"You've been detecting!" She clapped her hands and laughed. Bunch could almost count the silver notes that rose to the ceiling. "I am Miss Watanabe!"

"Not Mrs. Humphries?"

"Not officially." She drew a last puff on the long cigarette and stubbed it out. "Perhaps not ever." She held the door open for him to slide past her outthrust body. "Now, about those sensors . . ."

Bunch could take a hint. He started a tour around the house, eyeing the windowsills and doorframes for tool marks, the soft earth at the house foundation for fresh footprints. The woman followed him, her glossy black hair cascading smoothly down her back to end just above the taut swell of rounded flesh.

"Is Mr. Lucero here today?"

"No. Just his wife. Do you need to talk to her?"

Bunch shook his head. Lucero would be the one to notice if anything around the grounds was disturbed.

"Do you know I'm only a little taller than your elbow?" She posed beside him to show the level of her head. The softness of hip and shoulder pressed against his side in two warm spots.

"How did you and Mr. Humphries meet?"

"In Japan. He was at an electronics conference that my father also attended. I saw him there."

"Your father's name's Watanabe?"

"Hiroge Watanabe. A very wealthy and important man."

"So you came with Humphries to America?"

"Oh no! My father gave me a trip to America when I graduated from the university. I applied to graduate school at Columbia, was accepted, and spent a year in New York. Roland and I saw each other there occasionally."

"How did you get here?"

She shrugged. "Roland asked me to come. I said, 'Why not?' I'd never been to Colorado." She tossed her long hair and looked around at the vista across the shallow valley to the Front Range. It rose in a series of blue-green ridges against the clear sky. From somewhere in the house came a rattle of dishes and the muted ranchera music that Mrs. Lucero liked. "It's very pretty. But frankly, it's boring. I expected to see Indians and cowboys."

"They all got trampled by roaming buffalo. Humphries calls you his wife."

Mitsuko shrugged again and looked away. "It's what he thinks he wants. And it doesn't bother me."

"Thinks?"

"He doesn't really know. Sometimes I believe that if I said I would marry him, he wouldn't want me anymore." Her black eyes glanced at him. "This way, I'm like a toy he's borrowed and knows he has to give up someday." She sighed, smiling again. "I don't know why things have to get so complicated. Do you?"

Bunch didn't. "How long do you plan to stay with him?"

She leaned back against the stretch of blouse and slacks, and that little tingle was in the air. "Why?"

"Just a professional question, Watanabe-san." He led the way back to the front door, satisfied that no one had tried to force entry into the home. "Maybe somebody's jealous of Humphries' good luck. Maybe somebody wants to get rid of him so they can have you."

"How romantic! But who could it be? I don't know anyone in Colorado except Roland and Mr. and Mrs. Lucero. And Mr. Kirk and you."

"Somebody from New York? Any possibility of someone following you out here?"

She shook her head, seeing that Bunch was serious. "I don't think so. I had an affair or two back there, but it was nothing. Uncomplicated, you know?"

Bunch knew. "Maybe I'd better check it out anyway. Want to give me the names?"

She hesitated. It was the first time he'd seen caution in the woman's dark eyes. "Is it really necessary? Roland doesn't know about them."

"If they haven't followed you out here, he doesn't have to learn about them."

"And if someone has?"

"I thought you weren't planning on a long-term relationship?"

The shrug was quicker this time, irritable. "What I don't

want to do is cause any unnecessary complications. Roland would be very upset if he learned about those others." The irritation disappeared in a bright smile. "He is not as mature as I think you are, Mr. Bunch. Besides, I'm certain neither of them followed me out here. Neither had any reason to."

"But it should be checked out." Bunch could be equally stubborn.

Her expression doubted the necessity of it, but with a slow nod of acquiescence she gave him the names. He verified the spelling and jotted them in a small notebook.

"You're leaving already?"

"Humphries wants his sensor field installed as soon as possible. I've got to get the equipment."

In the Bronco's rearview mirror, he saw her lean against the doorframe as he bounced down the drive. Until the road turned and pinched the house out of sight between stands of pine trees, the isolated flicker of white stood motionless and staring after him.

"They're not married?" Devlin looked up from the letter that had just come in over the fax machine. Allen Schute from Security Underwriters had not been overwhelmed by the videotape of Zell mowing his lawn. It would make a stronger case for the jury, he wrote, if Kirk got pictures of the man using his back more strenuously. Devlin had an idea, but it involved breaking and entering, which meant illegally obtained evidence. He had been reluctant to try it, but they'd wasted enough time on Zell.

Bunch rummaged through the large closet that had been fitted up with shelving and a worktable and served as the storage room for his electronic equipment. "Mitsuko Watanabe, not Mrs. Roland Humphries. And probably never Mrs. Roland Humphries."

"Why not?"

"I think she wants him to marry her, but she knows he's not

going to." He shrugged. "I can't put my finger on it, but there's a lot going on they haven't told us, Dev."

That was Kirk's reading too. "Could their relationship have anything to do with the prowler?"

Bunch told him about Mitsuko's New York flings. "Think Percy can find out if one of them's been out here recently?"

Percy was an ex-Secret Service agent who had his own p.i. business in New York City. He and Devlin did favors for each other. But lately the balance had been against Kirk and Associates, and Devlin was reluctant to tip it any further.

"Hey." Bunch poked his head out the closet door. "It'll take him, what, a couple phone calls to find out if these guys took any time off from work? Christ, it can't cost that much. Put it on Humphries' bill—I can cover it in the cost of setting up the electronics."

"Why not just list it?"

"She doesn't want Humphries to find out about these guys. Says it'll just cause problems." He stacked sensors and electronic eyes on the floor and started coiling wire. "So I promised her I'd keep it quiet."

Devlin picked up the telephone. As usual, Percy wasn't at either his office or his home. A recording at his pager number said to leave a message and if it was vital, a representative from the Percy Ahern Agency would call back within the hour; if the message wasn't vital, the representative would return the call as soon as possible. Thank you.

Devlin waited for the beep. "Percy, Devlin Kirk and it's about seven P.M. our time. Please check two names for us to see if they've come to Denver in the last three weeks: Daniel Chaney and Lawrence Kosman. I'll fax the information to you now." He hung up and fed the papers with names and last known addresses, compliments Miss Watanabe, into the machine, which peeped its gratitude.

"Somebody else I'd like to call while we're at it, Dev."

"What's this 'we' shit?"

"Okay—'you.' Call Yoshi. See what he can find out about Watanabe and her old man. He's supposed to be a big bowl of rice in Tokyo—Hiroge Watanabe."

Devlin considered that. Every now and then Bunch came up with a good idea. "How much can you cover in that electronics bill?"

"Hey, Humphries wants the best. If it doesn't cost enough, he'll be disappointed."

Kirk hoped Yoshi Kamakura wouldn't charge Tokyo prices for his time. With the exchange rate, even Humphries couldn't afford much of that. Devlin wouldn't call, though. He'd use the fax machine. On the other side of the world, Yoshi would be sleeping—or at least out of his office.

By the time Devlin drafted the inquiry and sent it beeping on its way, Bunch had lugged a pair of oversize gym bags out of the closet. "I got another good idea, Dev. You know how we're falling behind on electronics? How the state of the art is moving away from us?"

Devlin didn't know that. "What are you trying to say?"

"There's a new nonlinear junction detector out. Top-of-the-line stuff. It's something we should have if we're going to bid seriously for security sweeps."

"How much?"

"About twenty-five."

"Hundred? Maybe after Reznick's next check—"

"Thousand. But that's with all the extras."

"Twenty-five thousand? Jesus Christ, Bunch!"

"Hey, we can cover it on the bid or hold off on some of the extras."

"We try to keep bids down so we win them, Bunch. And we can hold off on the whole damned thing! What's wrong with the junction detector you have now?"

"Nothing yet. That I know of. But listen, I warned you we'd have to update every few years. Listening devices get more sophisticated, detectors have to get more sophisticated too."

Kirk tapped the pile of mail that had fluttered through the

door slot earlier in the afternoon. "You know what's in these envelopes, Bunch? Any idea what's in these envelopes?"

"I know—I know. But think of it as an investment, Dev. You want to be the best in industrial security, you got to have the best detection equipment. You know that."

"And I know a lot of these new electronics features are cosmetic! Just tell me honestly, Bunch—honestly, now: Will the equipment you now have do the job? Because if it won't, I'm not going to bother writing up that Broomfield bid." He added, "We do not have twenty-five thousand dollars for some new nonlinear whosis, especially if we don't really need the damn thing."

"Well, yeah, I guess I can do a good sweep with the one we got. It'll take a little longer, that's all."

"Then take longer. I'll figure the bid with you taking longer. I'll be goddamned if I'm borrowing twenty-five thousand when we don't really need it."

"We don't need it yet. But you better figure it in the budget, because it won't be long before the opposition finds a way around the stuff we do have." Bunch shook his head as he closed the door. "Some of the things the Japs are coming up with now . . ."

It was close to four in the morning when Devlin coasted the Subaru to a halt near Zell's house and sat listening to the night sounds of the quiet housing development. Beyond the high wooden fence of a neighbor, a dog barked persistently, an unending and dull-minded yap that rapped like a small hammer into the darkness. Past the ridge of lightless houses, the thin traffic on a freeway rushed with a hiss of running water, and, floating on the cold night air, came a thread of sound—fragmented, pointless—the grunt of a chugging engine somewhere distant.

Bunch had spent the rest of the evening placing a network of sensors, trying—as he explained in detail to Devlin later—to set the beams just high enough to miss animals such as raccoons and skunks which came out to prowl at night. "I couldn't do a thing about the deer, though. I warned Humphries that he's going to be up half the night if the deer start setting off alarms."

"He was still acting worried?"

"Yeah. Eyes look like two piss holes in the snow. He's not getting much sleep."

Whatever it was that worried the man was still worth the salary he was paying Kirk and Associates for protection. And as long as his checks didn't bounce, Devlin and Bunch stood guard. But professional curiosity made Kirk itch to know the truth of what the man was protecting himself from. That, and the knowledge that he and Bunch could do a better job if Humphries was willing to be honest with them.

Easing the car door open, Kirk slid out into the cold and across the lawns toward Zell's home. The shadow of the eaves darkened the driveway close to the garage door and he crouched, testing the locked handle and poised for any sound from inside the house. Silence. Devlin slipped the blade of his lockpick into the keyhole and a few minutes later turned the handle open. The twanging groan of heavy springs sounded loud in the night and he hesitated, listening again. Warm, oily-smelling air pushed into the cold. He ducked under the partially lifted door and stood in the dark. No creak of cautious footsteps from the room beyond the far door; no skitter of animal paws— dog or cat—alarming the sleepers. Quickly, Devlin gouged at the tread of the car's tire with an ice pick. A moment later, a loud spurt of hissing air jetted across his knuckles. He eased the garage door shut and walked quickly back to the Subaru. Engine off and coasting in neutral, his car glided back down the curving lane to a halt and Kirk settled to catch a short nap before dawn.

The tiny chime of his watch alarm woke him at five-thirty. He rubbed grainy eyes to see the faint red of sunrise streak low along the eastern sky. The coffee in the thermos was still warm and served as breakfast, and he tried not to think of the pressure that had begun to push on his bladder. Lengthy stakeouts called for the long-necked portable urinal with its tight lid. But Kirk didn't plan to be stuck in the car for that amount of time.

At seven-fifteen, as Kirk expected, Zell's garage door lifted and a wisp of exhaust laid a pale haze over the driveway. Then the car started backing out. It paused and backed again, easing toward the street. Zell's wife was off to her job as a bookkeeper and secretary in a wholesale plumbing supply house over on South Broadway. The car swung into the street heading away from Devlin, and as it started forward the brake lights flashed and it stopped. The woman opened her door and leaned out to look down at the rear tire. Then she turned off the engine and got out of the car and walked back to stare at the flat. Kirk saw her shoulders rise and fall, and she glanced at her wrist and walked quickly into the house. A few minutes later, Zell, tucking a shirt into his pants and stepping gingerly in bare feet, came out to stare at the tire too.

Devlin balanced his videocamera on the dash and waited, watching the man's face through the circle of magnified light.

The wife said something and Zell's mouth moved in answer. She held up her forearm and pointed to her watch; his lips said a single word—"Shit"—and he grabbed the keys from the steering column. Opening the trunk, he started lifting out the spare tire and tools as Devlin's camera whirred. When the car settled back on its spare, Zell folded up the jack and slammed the trunk shut. The woman gave him a quick kiss on the cheek and he picked his way barefooted across the dewy lawn, wiping his hands on a grimy rag. Devlin started his own car and swung around, headed for downtown and the photo lab.

Percy Ahern had a report for Devlin late that afternoon. The flat, nasal voice bounced with the energy and rush that typified everything the man did. "Devlin, lad, you've brought to my attention two angels—two saints on earth—two citizens who stand pillarlike in upholding the virtues of hard work, patriotism, and love of one's gray-haired mother. These lads, Devlin, have caused not the slightest harm to the smallest fly in Christendom, and I hope it's not in your heart to bring unto them woe and misery."

"You're telling me they're clean."

"As the newly driven snow. As a babe's sweet breath. As a virgin's thoughts of love. Speaking of which, one is shacked up with the daughter of a state representative of the borough of Queens, and has been for the last six months. What higher recommendation could there be? The lad is finishing his law studies at Columbia and apparently has a brilliant career in politics ahead of him. At least one might say he's laying the foundation for it. Vice presidential material, certainly."

"Which one's that?"

"Chaney. Kosman's no less ambitious and equally pristine, being, as he is, eminent among the energetic and thoroughly honest young traders on the floor of the mighty New York Stock Exchange. Not a captain, perhaps, but certainly a shavetail of industry, with promise of greatness to come."

"Neither one's been to Denver lately?"

"As far as I could find out, neither one's ever been west of New Jersey. Nor do they want to be. In fact, I don't think they even know where Denver is—a fairly common affliction in the Steinberg geography of New York."

"Thanks, Perce. Send me a bill and I'll get a check by return mail."

"Knowing you, I should ask for a money order. But I'll trust you this once for old times' sake—and may the gods grin on your every endeavor."

Vinny Landrum did not have a report. In fact, the last Devlin heard from him was the cryptic message on the answering tape stating that he'd gotten the job. Devlin waited until an hour or so after work and then called the man's apartment. "Vinny, I expected to hear from you yesterday."

"If I got something to report, Kirk, I'll report. That's how I operate. Listen, if you don't like it, you can always bring in somebody else, you know."

"For what you're being paid, that'd be easy to do. What about Martin and Atencio? What have they been doing?"

"They've been working. I haven't made contact with those guys yet, Kirk, and I'm not about to push it. I fucking well told you when this caper started: it's my ass, and I'll go at my own speed."

"I asked how they're behaving. Do they seem nervous? Are they looking over their shoulders?"

"From what I seen, no. They show up for work on time, do their jobs, go home without rattling any cages. I mean for Christ's sake, it's only been two days—give me a chance to do my job! That all right with you?"

"They don't act like people who've just killed a man?"

"No. They act like citizens with clean consciences, and I think that's how they're going to act until things cool down. No shipments coming in, no panic, no nothing. Just wait and see if things blow over before making any moves. That's what they act like."

Kirk didn't think Martin and Atencio—or Vinny, for that matter—knew a damn thing about clean consciences. "I want you to call in, Vinny. I don't give a fart if you've got nothing to report. I want to enjoy the sound of your dulcet voice every day. Hear me?"

"You can enjoy my dulcet dick is what you can enjoy, Kirk. I call in when I got something to tell you. Otherwise, leave me the hell alone—I don't want my cover shot to hell by some tight-ass like you."

"Vinny—"

"Yeah, 'Vinny.' You let me do this my way. If you knew how to do it right the first place, you wouldn't need to bring me in. Now don't call me—I'll call you. Got it?"

CHAPTER 13

A week later, Humphries came in to pay his bill and tell Devlin there was no need for any further protection. To Kirk, the man didn't look happy about it. And in fact, Humphries wasn't happy about much at all, and there was no reason he should be. Mitsi had asked for the detectives in the first place, telling him that her father's man had somehow learned where she was, and that they had to protect themselves against whoever her father might send after her. Now, for some damned reason, she was just as anxious to have the detectives gone. She wouldn't tell him why—just the smile and the caress and the insistence that they didn't need to spend any more money on Kirk and Associates. Which, by God, was a point he could agree with—like everyone else, once these people had their hooks into you, they took you for all they could! Still, he felt that nagging worry; even if her father hadn't been heard from—and no one threatening had showed up in the past weeks—there was the possibility it could yet happen.

"If I—ah—need to get in touch with you in a hurry, can I do it?"

Devlin handed him a business card with a penciled telephone

number on the back. "This is my beeper number. Twenty-four hours a day."

"I mean, it may not be necessary, you understand? I just don't know yet."

Humphries had a fair foundation for the safety of self and home—a quick course in escape and evasion techniques, the electronic barriers and alerts installed by Bunch, his car fitted with an underhood fire suppressant system and tailpipe protection. But he was still spooked by whatever it was he didn't trust Kirk to know. "If we're not on retainer, Mr. Humphries, I can't guarantee that we won't be tied up on a case." Kirk shrugged. "We have to make a living, you see. But if you need help, call that number. If neither Mr. Bunchcroft nor I can come, we'll find someone who can."

The man nodded and stood to shake hands. "I'll rely on that."

"Of course," Devlin said, smiling. But if that call did come, Humphries would have to be a hell of a lot more honest about the reason for it than he had been in the past. And there would be no more nonsense about alleged prowlers or brown cars.

After the Humphries file was closed, the Advantage case and the Truman surveillance took most of their time, which was good, because those were the only two cases they had. Vinny's report sang the same song over and over. In fact, his reports tended toward the monosyllabic: "Nothing, Kirk. Will you quit the fuck bugging me?" There was still no word on their bids outstanding, and the periodic stakeouts at Jean Truman's condominium were equally profitable. A disgusted Bunch tossed the keys onto the desk and blew wearily as he groped for the coffeepot. "That broad's a hell of a lot smarter than Zell. I tried your flat tire trick. All she did was call Triple A and didn't even come out of the house to watch."

"Allen Schute was happy with the videotape of Zell." Devlin waved a pink check with its New York address. "He paid us."

"That's good. What about Reznick? What did he tell you?"

Devlin had gone to Advantage Corporation to make what

could laughingly be called a progress report. "He's not happy. It's been almost two weeks, he says, and Vinny's costing him a lot of money. He thinks we're giving him damn little back for it."

"If he knew Vinny, he wouldn't expect much."

"He's beginning to feel that way about Kirk and Associates."

Both Bunch and Devlin had been making periodic surveys of Atencio and Martin—picking up their cars at work and following one or the other home, cruising in the dark past their driveways at odd hours to note any activity, tailing Vinny after work to ensure that no one was following Kirk and Associates' newest agent. Vinny wouldn't be thrilled to learn of their interest, but after what happened to Chris, neither Kirk nor Bunchcroft wanted to take chances. Not even with Vinny. Not yet anyway. But his hours of surveillance and the days of his labor brought nothing. Atencio and Martin were lying low, and as a member of the warehouse crew, Vinny could swear that no dope was being shipped through the plant.

Bunch glanced at the wall clock. "I think we ought to squeeze Vinny a little. After two weeks, even that maggot should have something besides the clap." He drained his cup. "Let's pick him up after work again."

Bunch and Devlin parked down the street from the factory's main gate and waited until they saw Vinny's beat-up Chevy pull out of the company parking lot. Then they followed. Devlin drove the Subaru, and Bunch, his seat jammed back against the stops, sucked the last of a can of beer and surveyed the heavy traffic for anyone following the Chevy.

"Little bastard's not going home this time," said Bunch.

Vinny's apartment was near downtown in the Capitol Hill area, but his car turned east from the parking lot to I-70 and the Peoria interchange. Then it headed south past Fitzsimmons Army Medical Center.

"A girlfriend?"

Bunch shorted. "Vinny? Naw, he keeps his love life in hand."

The Chevy turned on Seventeenth Avenue and went a dozen blocks to a small, almost treeless park, where it pulled to the vacant curb and waited. Kirk drove past without changing speed, face angled from the park, and pulled over when Vinny's car became a tiny dot in the rearview mirror. From a long block away, they watched Vinny get out and walk to a concrete bench set away from the kiddie playground that glittered hotly in the late-afternoon sun. A man was already seated there, staring across the empty slide and jungle gym.

"It's some kind of meet," said Bunch. He studied the distant figure through the telephoto lens of his camera. "Guy's about thirty-five, brown hair, mustache. Glasses—the shooter's kind. You know: wire frames and big yellow lenses. No scars or marks that I can see." The camera started a series of clicks and whirs.

"Are they talking?"

"Yeah. Mostly Vinny. Now the other guy's saying something and Vinny's listening. And picking his goddamn nose with his thumb. I bet he looks at it."

"Want me to back up?"

"No. They'd spot us sure as hell. No, the son of a bitch didn't look at it—he's wiping his goddamn thumb on his pants leg. . . . Now he's talking. He's picking again—he's being couth this time, Dev. Wiping his goddamn finger inside his shirt pocket. . . . They're talking some more. . . . That's it; Vinny's up and going. The other guy's up and headed across the park the other way."

"Can you see his car?"

"Naw. Swing around. Maybe we can spot it."

Devlin pulled left around the block, squealing the tires in a fast turn.

"If we had one of those high-powered shotgun mikes I want, we could have picked up what they said."

"If we bought one of those high-powered shotgun mikes, we'd be out of business."

"Just a suggestion, Dev. Don't get defensive about being cheap."

The neatly spaced homes with their square patches of lawn and picture windows blurred as the Subaru swayed onto Sixteenth. Down the almost vacant avenue, a metallic-blue BMW pulled away from the curb. Devlin accelerated to move closer.

"Don't push the yuppiemobile, Dev—I can shoot him from here."

Kirk eased up and Bunch clicked the camera several times as the blue car picked up speed. "Okay. Now all we need's party and plate. Let's get back to good ol' Vinny."

They caught up with him on Havana, going north to turn on Colfax. The familiar rusted roof surged through the remains of rush-hour traffic in a long but straight run toward Capitol Hill. The commercial highway passed crowds of small signs for mom-and-pop businesses and low-budget chain stores. Among the assorted shops was a sprinkling of high-class restaurants and low-class motels that rented rooms by the hour. Apparently, Vinny was headed home now, but Devlin stayed with him just in case. The late-afternoon traffic clogged the lanes and shimmered with its own heat and that of the dry early-October sun. A couple blocks from his neighborhood, Vinny suddenly veered into a side street and pulled to the curb. He locked the car and stood waiting in tree shade as Kirk and Bunch nosed in behind him.

"You people couldn't tail a blind man without him spotting you."

"Hello, Vinny. Strange to see you moving around in daylight."

"You're as funny as dead babies, Homer. I been working all day at that fucking factory. I'm hot, I'm going in for a beer. You people want to talk to me, you're buying."

He turned on his heel and strode toward the Rocky Mountain Lounge, a small bar that had served a neighborhood when there was a neighborhood to serve. Now it was just another of the faceless pickup joints along Colfax.

They made their way through the sudden gloom to one of the high-backed booths away from the door. In the rear of the dark and smoky room, a pool table clattered as players wordlessly circled the brightly lit green to study the glinting colors.

"Bring a pitcher, Larry—this big dude's paying." Vinny pointed to Bunch.

Devlin waited until Vinny's glass had been filled and emptied and filled again. "What do you have for us?"

"Same thing I told you day before yesterday—not much."

"It's over a week. Our client's spending a lot of money on you. This isn't government work, Vinny. You're supposed to produce."

"Hey, what is this? What the hell can I do if the fucking suspects just sit on their thumbs?"

"Have they made you?"

"Shit, no! I'm no amateur."

"Do you have any contacts with them?"

"Eight fucking hours on the job, sure." Vinny wagged his head once and buried his upper lip in foam. "But they're not going to invite me to have fun and games with them, Kirk. They're still nervous. That turkey you put in before, he really screwed things up."

"What'd they say about him?" asked Devlin.

"Nothing. Just a few things they let drop."

"So drop them."

The head wagged again. "They know somebody was running an investigation." He held up the empty pitcher and called to Larry for a refill. "You people ain't thirsty?"

"What did they say, Vinny?" asked Bunch.

"Nothing. They were too busy laughing at you clowns. Giving them some shit about being Mafia types or whatever— they were laughing at you, Kirk. Laughing about bringing in some dude who scared the living shit out of you." He drank. "Serves you right, pulling that kind of amateur crap."

"Did they say anything about Chris?"

Vinny glanced at Kirk's face and shut up. "No. I just overheard them talking, is all."

"What about Eddie Visser?" asked Bunch. "Have they heard from him?"

"I don't know. Nobody's said the name around me."

A rattle of pool balls came from the table. "Who'd you meet in the park?" asked Bunch.

"What park? Where?"

"In Aurora just now. The guy with the sunglasses. Who was it?"

"Oh, him! You people were on me from there?"

"Who was it?"

"Hey, it was business, all right? I got a private business of my own I got to look after too."

"What kind of private business?"

"Listen, I'm not your fucking slave! I do my job for you, you don't tell me what to do on my own time."

"You don't have any time of your own. We're buying your time—all of it. What kind of private business?"

"I don't have to tell you shit!"

Bunch put both large hands on the table in front of Vinny. "You can tell us here. Or we can go to your place and I'll squeeze it out of you." The hands slowly folded into fists. "Like a goddamn tube of toothpaste."

The man stared at the meaty fists for a long moment, his Adam's apple bobbing. "He—ah—he's a dude I met. Before I took this job. Wants me to—ah . . . He's worried about his wife. I told him I'd check her out."

Devlin shook his head. "No other jobs, Vinny. You're full-time on this one. That was the deal."

"Yeah—I told him I was on a case. I said I'd check her out in a couple of weeks when I get off this job."

Bunch slid out of the booth and Devlin stood too. "Time's getting short, Vinny. Make your move on those people."

"I'm doing my best!"

"That's what we're afraid of. You'll want to do better than that."

As they left, Vinny's voice followed. "Jesus, you people not even going to leave the tip?"

Allen Schute wasn't overjoyed that the Truman case was taking so long. But he was happy enough with the video of Zell to send Kirk and Associates another job. The morning telephone call was about an insurance company's longtime customer who had been burglarized and who filed a claim of almost a hundred thousand dollars for missing household property. Since filing the claim, Mr. Ralph Eckles had taken another job and moved out of the Denver area. But the claims representative who handled the case hadn't felt right about it. The value of the items listed as stolen seemed inflated, and the burglars had been erratic in what they took.

"And the claimant, he seemed almost too eager to help. You know what I mean?"

Devlin nodded, his pen busy jotting down items that the young black claims rep told him. The plastic nameplate on the desk said Clarence Hines. Though Devlin hadn't worked with the man before, the small, almost bare office, the bulging briefcase at the wall, the filing cabinet, and the color-coordinated jacket and tie Hines wore all seemed familiar. Many insurance companies enforced a dress code for their field men, and all the claims reps were schooled to report any quiver of suspicion, especially with major claims. Insurance crime ranked second among violations involving fraud. First was tax evasion, but the feds didn't need help from Kirk and Associates. "Do you have a copy of the police report?"

Hines did. He handed Kirk the thick manila folder labeled "Eckles." "It's all in there. Look through and we can make copies of whatever you need."

"Know anything about this Eckles? If he's been involved in other large claims?"

"I ran his name through the computer like we're supposed

to. It came out clean. I didn't sell him his policy. That was"—
he glanced at his notes—"one Daniel Lakonis. He retired four
or five years ago, before I started to work for the company."

"Do you have Lakonis's address?"

Hines didn't, but he could call the main office and see if it
was on record. Kirk began scanning the papers while Hines
dialed. By the time the rep hung up, he had a small stack of
documents for copying.

Hines handed him a slip of paper. "He's still in the state.
Lives down near Durango now: phone and address."

After making his copies, Kirk thanked the man and said he
would be in touch as soon as he had something. Then he drove
back to his office and began telephoning. The first call was to
set up an appointment with Officer Cappiello, the burglary detective who had investigated the claim for the Jefferson County
Sheriff's Office. Insurance investigators have better rapport with
police agencies than do p.i.'s, and Cappiello invited Kirk to
meet him late in the afternoon at the sheriff's office in Golden.

His second call was to the retired insurance salesman, who
said he did remember selling a policy to Mr. Eckles.

"Real nice man," said Lakonis, voice hearty with a healthy,
outdoorsy retirement and the pleasure of suspecting the company didn't run as well without him. "Worked at the Johns
Manville headquarters. No trouble with his policy, is there?"

"He submitted a claim for burglary loss. We're checking
it out."

"Hey now. I may be retired, but claims aren't investigated
unless there's some good reason. How big a claim?"

"The claim may be a little larger than it should be. Can you
tell me anything about Eckles?"

The long-distance line gave that hollow, muted hiss. "Well,
I guess it's possible. It's always that. But I wouldn't think it
likely of Eckles. He retired from the air force before he went
to work for Manville. A colonel."

"And he's been insured by the company for a long time?"

"I sold him his first policy some, let's see, fifteen, eighteen years ago. And I even sold his sister a policy too. He told her about me. Liked the way I did business."

"She lives in Denver?"

"In Arvada. Basic household coverage with a couple increases over the years."

"Can you tell me her address?"

Lakonis couldn't. But he did spell her name for Kirk and mentioned a company telephone number that would provide the policyholder's current address. In answer to more questions, Lakonis said no, he didn't know of any other relatives or friends Kirk could interview. Yes, he would be happy to call collect if he remembered anything else that might be of use. "Well, Mr. Kirk, I tell you this, though—I'm glad I'm retired and out of all that. The fishing down here's wonderful. Next time you're down this way, give me a call. I'll show you some real trout streams."

Bunch came into the office before Devlin left for his meeting in Golden. He pushed a piece of paper across the desk and tapped it with a wide finger.

"What's this?" asked Kirk.

"License number and owner for that BMW."

Kirk looked at the name. "Columbine Auto Leasing?"

"Yep." Bunch pushed a Xeroxed sheet over to Devlin. It was a copy of a lease agreement.

"You've been busy." Kirk read the name. "Arnold Minz? Where do I know him from?"

"It ain't the men's room."

Kirk searched through the names in his memory, knowing that he should be able to dredge up something. But the thread leading to the tickle was too frail.

Bunch finally helped him. "He's the guy who beat a heavy rap on possession with intent. Two, maybe three years ago."

"A kingpin charge—right! But they couldn't tie him to the cocaine in court."

"That's it. The old chain-of-evidence trick. Bring the guilty s.o.b. in for his fair trial and let him off." Bunch shook his head. "Dave Miller was on that one—he told me about it. When he left the courtroom, Minz looked at Dave and laughed. Hasn't been able to pin anything on Minz since then."

Kirk toyed with the copy of the lease agreement. "Why would Vinny talk with a big-time coke dealer?"

"Who doesn't have a wife to be worried about," added Bunch. "One thing Vinny doesn't have is the money to buy into a deal. And if he snorts at all, he's just a recreational chipper, so Minz wouldn't be his supplier."

"Minz doesn't deal on the street anyway."

"Right. But it could be Vinny's planning on finding a lot of coke soon. So much he'll need somebody like Minz to move it."

Pushing back from the desk, Devlin turned to stare out the arched window and across the flat roofs of the brick warehouses and converted factories. The continual flicker of cars through the distant trees along the South Platte River said that the afternoon rush was building along I-25, and soon the flicker would congeal into the purple haze of a ribbon of smog. "He'd do it, wouldn't he?"

"You're damn right he would," said Bunch. "I think I'll go unscrew his face and plug it in his rectum."

"If it's what we think, then he's made a contact. A good one."

"You're telling me something, partner."

"I'm telling you we let him run with it until he gives us a lead. Maybe put somebody else in to keep an eye on him."

"Who? We can't afford that, and Reznick's not going to pay for it! What, you're going to tell Reznick that our agent—that he's already paying for through the nose—needs another agent to watch him?" Bunch's fist thudded onto the desktop, a deep sound that Devlin could feel in the floorboards. "I say we pull the little bastard and turn him into peanut butter!"

"If we pull him, we lose the whole thing." Devlin shook his head. "Now we know. Now we can make it work for us."

"How?"

That was a good question and one Devlin was asking himself. "We sit on Minz."

"What?"

"We sit on Arnie Minz. If it's what we think, Vinny has to tell him when he's ready to deal. We put remotes on Arnie's phone, bug his car, tap his house. You're the genius of electronic surveillance, Bunch. Start geniusing. Just make damned certain it's nothing that can be traced to us."

Bunch nodded. He didn't want to spend time in a federal pen for the likes of Vinny Landrum either. But it was the kind of challenge he enjoyed. As Devlin left the office for Golden, Bunch was already rummaging through the shelves of the air-conditioned closet that served as his electronic armory. He didn't even hear the rumble of the sculptress's casters overhead.

CHAPTER 14

Detective Cappiello was a balding man of medium height who looked taller because he was built like a Popsicle: narrow at the shoulder, wider at the waist, widest of all at the hips, and with long, skinny legs. The office was a cramped and smoky corner partitioned by a movable blackboard and made smaller by the photographs, notices, bulletins, and posters covering the walls.

"The Eckles burglary?" He settled back onto the worn cushion of his swivel chair. "Yeah—I wondered how long you guys would take to sniff at that one."

Kirk looked up from the burglary report signed by Cappiello. "Why?"

"The place was too neat. That's what struck me about it right off. The victim had been packing up to move. San Diego. He and his wife had the stuff stacked for the movers. The burglars had all night to take what they wanted. But they didn't go through the effects, see? They just grabbed a few things and left."

"You were the only investigating officer?"

"Yeah. There was only two of us in burglary at the time. I took the report, so I caught the investigation."

"It says you found no signs of forcible entry."

"That's right. Now, the door lock could have been picked. The victim said they were away for the night at a motel because the furniture had been taken down. The beds and all, see?"

"Have you had any other burglaries using a lockpick?"

"Funny you should ask. No. Usually they lift a screen and break the window. Or pop out a glass next to the front door. Go in through a garage, something like that." He ran a hand across his shiny scalp and added, "There was no dirt tracked in either. No paint chips around the door. No tool marks."

Devlin read over the list of items claimed: jewelry, rare coin collection, sterling flatware, clothing, stereo components, valuable antique furniture. "Looks like they knew what they wanted."

"They took some big-ticket items, sure. But they left behind a large-screen television and a boat and trailer. Both easy to take and worth a lot of money."

"No suspects?"

Cappiello drew on the crackling cigarette and shook his head. "Lakewood was running a big sting operation. A lot of stuff taken from our area turned up there to be fenced, see? But not one thing from this hit. And none of the burglars we've arrested in the past few weeks have copped to this one."

"How did Eckles behave?"

"You mean, do I think he's guilty of insurance rip-off?"

"Yeah."

"I don't know, Kirk. All I have is the facts, and some of them don't sit so well. He was worried about the loss; he was eager to help if he could. He calls now and then to see if any progress's been made on the case. But like I said, the books were stacked up carefully, the cardboard clothes hangers had been opened without damaging the contents, the boxes that had been packed already were unloaded, not just dumped out. Most careful damned burglars I ever heard of."

"When did Eckles call last?"

"Couple days ago. I told him what I have to tell you: no suspects, no goods."

124 • REX BURNS

"Thanks, Officer."

"No sweat." He inhaled on the cigarette again. "San Diego—a guy needs his boat in San Diego."

In the Healey, Kirk located the address on his Denver regional map and drove slowly through the neighborhood. It was a spacious one, carved into the crest of a long ridge that gave views of the Front Range to the west and, to the east, of Denver in its wide, shallow bowl of prairie. The homes matched the scale of the development—multistoried and sprawling, with heavy shake roofs, snug gables peeking here and there, lots of brick facades and arches, and an emphasis on thick wooden beams. Instant estate.

Eckles's home sat at the end of a wide drive which arced to the three-car garage and was protected from its neighbors by hedges and strategically placed blank walls. The realtor's For Sale sign tilted slightly in the long grass, and the window curtains had the airless look of a locked and empty house. Kirk rang the bell, not surprised that the muffled chimes weren't answered. Then he walked across the wide lawn to the house next door. A woman in her late forties or early fifties—thin, with sculpted and frosted hair—answered.

Devlin showed his identification. "I'm investigating a burglary that took place next door. I wondered if you might remember anything suspicious that happened two weeks ago Wednesday."

"A burglary? At the Eckleses'?"

"Yes ma'am. Did Mr. or Mrs. Eckles say anything about it at the time?"

"Two weeks ago? Well, no! They never told me anything about it." Her brown eyes showed a mixture of alarm and worry. A burglary next door was a burglary very close. "Did they lose much?"

"They were hit pretty hard. This would have been the evening or early morning of the twenty-second. Can you remember anything at all—strangers in the neighborhood, unfamiliar cars parked next door, dogs barking? Anything at all?"

"The twenty-second . . . No, my husband and I were in Santa Fe on the twenty-second. We came back the twenty-fourth. We didn't know a thing about it." She frowned. "That would have been about the time they were packing to move, wouldn't it?"

"Yes ma'am."

"That's all I do remember—the moving vans and all that. They did most of the packing themselves, I think, and rented a motel for a week while the movers came. Is that when it happened? While they were out of the house?"

"Apparently so."

The woman shook her head. "With the turmoil of packing and moving, it's no wonder Sharon didn't mention a burglary. Still—" She had cooked breakfast for them the morning they left. Eckles had loaded his and his wife's cars and then stopped by. Both of them were fine people. He was an ex–air force officer and she was just the sweetest thing. And the house had been vacant since. There had been other people driving up now and then—the realtor, she assumed; people looking at the house. The Eckleses had been trying to sell their home for a long time. "Houses in this price range aren't moving very quickly," she said with some expertise, "and the cost of money is so exorbitant anymore it's a wonder anyone can afford a house." But there was no one at all she remembered who looked like a burglar.

The other neighbors told Kirk much the same thing they'd told Cappiello, though one did recall a dog barking for a long time. It might have been the twenty-second or a day or two either way, he couldn't be certain now. But none had heard of the burglary from Eckles. He hadn't mentioned it to anyone— which, one woman said, was like him. He was very military, you know; self-contained, efficient. When Kirk finally left the last household, the wide streets held only the light traffic of late afternoon, and kids on bicycles began to swoop down the side-walks, burning off the energy pent up all day in school.

———

Bunch, too, had been busy. Now he watched the lowering sun through the office window as it burned the mountains into a black silhouette of ragged peaks. The final rumble of casters had long ago rolled away overhead, and his ear was hot from the rub of the telephone. He cursed Vinny and his greed that caused this extra work, and Vinny's mother for spawning him in the first place. The early afternoon had been spent working on a listening device, the late part on chasing down information about Arnold Minz: home, business, family, frequent contacts, police records—anything that could be combed out of documents or Bunch's acquaintances. Dave Miller would have saved him a lot of time. But then he'd want to know why Kirk and Associates was interested in Minz. Miller always wanted to know about anything involving Minz. As a friend, Bunch would have had to tell him. But they weren't ready yet to alert the Vice and Narcotics detective that they would be poking around one of his favorite people. And violating federal law to do so.

Bunch stretched, fingers brushing the ceiling. He felt the stiff muscles pull against each other. Honesty, Bunch was convinced, was not only the best policy, it was—in the long run—the easiest. But Vinny, who was lazy in every other facet of his life, had never discovered that. Instead, he focused all his energy on the challenging task of looking after himself in the most underhanded ways possible. Not that Bunch didn't have his own degree of self-interest; he didn't know anyone who lacked it. But with Vinny it was a religion: every thought, every move was based on the question What's in it for Vinny? Well, maybe this time the little puke would get something he hadn't been planning on.

"Devlin." Bunch looked up as Kirk came in, spilling a waft of cold air from his jacket as he shrugged it off. "What's the word on Eckles?"

The tall man poured himself a cup of coffee from the hot plate resting on the metal filing cabinet. They were always talking about moving it so if it spilled, it wouldn't drip into the drawers full of papers. But they hadn't done it yet. "There's smoke. Maybe there's fire. Nothing definite yet, but it's worth digging deeper." They talked a bit about how to do that, the leads and possibilities that could be followed up tomorrow when offices were again open for business. Then Kirk asked what his partner had come up with for Minz.

Bunch carefully brought a cluster of wired equipment from his workroom. "Here's a little jewel I kind of modified from an early-model remote infinity listening device."

"Jesus. It looks like a Rube Goldberg bomb."

Bunch held up the small black box with a series of wires leading to a plastic case and a large dry-cell battery. "Better than a bomb—much better. Usually these things run off the power in your telephone wires. That's how you spot them: you get a drain bigger than what you're using. If Minz knows what he's doing—and he hasn't been caught yet—he probably runs a sweep of his lines every day. I can't imagine any big-time dealer not checking his phones. Hell, maybe he has a permanent monitor set up. Anyway, I rigged a self-powered device and added a storage tape on it, too. It doesn't drain power from the telephone lines—it runs off its own batteries. And it only sends when we want it to, which means it can't be picked up too easy by a transmitter detector."

"How's it work?"

"Like an infinity device. It hears everything near a telephone and puts it on the tape. Then what we do is trigger a playback from a remote when we're sure nobody's listening for a transmission except us. Two o'clock in the morning, say." He stared at the awkward collection of wires and units and dry-cell batteries. "Trouble is, it's too damned big."

"Does it work?"

"Hey, where's your confidence?"

"Uh huh. Now tell me we have to plant this monstrosity in his house."

"Well, yeah. That's another problem, all right." Bunch smiled. "But it can't be traced to us—no wires."

The feds were touchy about wiretaps and other illegal electronics. A lot of detective agencies, including Kirk and Associates, turned down bugging jobs a couple times a month for just that reason. But there were those situations when no other type of surveillance was possible. Kirk tended to draw a line—admittedly thin and erratic—between using electronics for someone else and using them only for the agency. He doubted that a federal judge would accept an ancillary plea like that, however, and twenty years was a long time to spend in jail for violating a dope pusher's right to privacy.

"Hey," said Bunch, "we'll be careful. I've been doing a little background on Minz. Here's how we can work it."

Minz's office address and telephone had been on the car lease agreement. His legal occupation was commercial real estate, and his secretary told Bunch he was out showing a property. He would return to the office about six to get any messages. His home number had taken a bit more sleuthing—it was in the telephone book—and Bunch's call to that number had been answered by a tape-recorded message. It was one of those comedy routines complete with the roar of a jet plane and a butler's voice announcing that Arnold Minz had just flown off to Tahiti and would return shortly. Please leave any message with James. Beep. Bunch figured that the real comedy of the message was its expression of Minz's fear—latent or admitted ironically—of being on the run from the police.

The East Jewell address turned out to be a sprawling complex of large and expensive condominiums built around a series of courtyards. Each multibedroom unit was angled for privacy and the least amount of shared wall space. High fences painted gray-green like the rest of the buildings formed secluded little patios attached to each unit. On the west side of the complex, rows of double garages provided parking for residents. Visitors were offered islands of parking around the periphery of the condos. Minz's garages were empty, and no metallic-blue BMW sat near the walk leading to his unit. Devlin backed the newly rented van to the curb and, wearing coveralls, he and Bunch carried large toolboxes to number 8.

Bunch asked again, "He still didn't answer the phone?"

The last call had been from a public telephone two minutes away. "Just his machine." Devlin turned his back to the door and surveyed the network of tall fences and shrubbery that offered privacy—and concealment—to the units' entries. Behind him, half hidden, Bunch quickly worked a pick into the lock.

It clicked and swung open. "It's clear."

Devlin followed him in, noting the unused chain dangling beside the deadbolt lock, another indication that Minz wasn't home.

But just to be certain, they glided through the rooms for quick glimpses at the carpeted and multileveled spaces which looked both warm and open under skylights that punctured the ceilings.

"I'll set it up in the basement," whispered Bunch. "Take about five minutes."

Nodding, Devlin settled in the kitchen, where the windows overlooked the walkway through the patio to the garages. The latex gloves made his fingers squeak on the shiny tile of the countertop, and—emphasizing the silence—a tall clock in the living room steadily counted each second. Whatever Vinny was plotting—even if it had nothing to do with the Advantage case—could mean trouble for Kirk and Associates. A little insurance wouldn't hurt and might help a lot. But if he was arranging some kind of deal that involved Martin and Atencio, it meant Vinny had learned something. He knew when, maybe even where, the next shipment would arrive. It also meant that either Martin had brought Vinny in on the deal or Vinny was planning to force himself in somehow. Maybe the latter, maybe not. Eddie Visser said he went through middlemen to move his cut. But Minz wasn't just a middleman. He was a major source. He was somebody who dealt in large quantities and who took a big bite out of the profits. Vinny could afford a bite like that if he was going to get the whole pie instead of just a sliver.

"Okay, Dev." Bunch had come silently from the basement, and they went quickly to the front door. A woman, passing by with arms full of plastic shopping sacks, glanced their way as the door opened.

Bunch leaned back into the room. "If it gives you any more trouble, Mr. Minz, call us. We take pride in our work!"

"Afternoon." Devlin smiled. The woman smiled back and disappeared around a bend in the brick walk.

Bunch quickly relocked the deadbolt on the door.

CHAPTER 15

The equipment checked out. Bunch called from a pay phone and listened to the recording of the now familiar jet noise followed by the orotund voice stating that Arnold Minz had just taken off for Tahiti. When the message cleared the line, he dialed another number—one the phone company didn't know about—tooted a multitone whistle to activate the tap's transmitter, and listened to the recording play again.

"Where'd you hide it?" asked Devlin.

"Couldn't hide it too well. I put it in a dark corner behind the heater and moved some empty suitcases in front of it." Bunch thought a moment. "Did you look at his telephones for a voice scrambler?"

"I didn't notice any black boxes."

"Me, I was in the dope business, I'd use an encryption unit. Expensive as hell, but so far, they can't be beat. You can tap them but it won't do any good." He shrugged. "Besides, fifteen, twenty thou, that's pocket change for a guy like Minz."

"And now you're going to hit me up for an antiencryption unit? Say, thirty thousand dollars' worth?"

"If they made them that cheap, Dev, I'd do it. But so far, you're safe."

Apparently the phone tap was safe too. For the next couple weeks, either Bunch or Devlin was hauled out of bed at late hours by the clock radio to dial the number on Minz's tap and tweet the whistle that started the playback of his calls and the snatches of conversation that took place within sound of the telephones. These last were few—and, as Bunch said, thank God Minz wasn't the partying type. A couple hours' whooping and hollering would fill the whole reel. One consistent caller was a woman named Louise whom Minz was dating. She would call to tell him about theater tickets or concerts that would be fun, or just to talk about what had happened to her since they'd been together last—usually eight or ten hours ago. Minz's replies gradually grew shorter and his voice more polite as the days passed. Other voices, men and women, ranged from cryptic messages about precise times and vague places to inquiries about commercial real estate. Both Devlin and Bunch suspected that the prices quoted were often for property that wasn't anchored to the earth. There was nothing from Vinny on the telephone tap. And the daily reports Kirk now insisted on having from the man were a constant litany of "Nothing yet, Kirk." Consequently, there was nothing Kirk could tell Reznick when he called the executive.

"Nothing? Jesus H. Christ, Kirk. It's going on a goddamn month and you're telling me you people haven't found out a thing yet?"

"We're dealing with a very sophisticated organization, Mr. Reznick. And a very cautious one—there's a murder charge floating around. They haven't made any moves that we know of, but they haven't closed down their operation either."

"How do you know that?"

"For one reason, the suspects are still working for you. Despite having enough money to live very comfortably."

"Jesus."

"For another, our agent. He's made a contact and he's waiting to hear about the next shipment." It wasn't what Vinny told

Kirk but what he did that provided the slim foundation for that statement. Devlin hoped Reznick wouldn't ask more about it, and was relieved when he didn't.

"How goddamn long's that going to be?"

"That's up to them—it has to be. But my guess is, it can't be much longer. If they take too much time, they're going to start losing customers. People with habits have to get their dope. If a pusher can't supply, they'll shop somewhere else. I think Atencio and Martin will be under pressure from their supplier, too."

"How's that?"

"A lot of dealers work on margin. They don't have the cash to pay up front, so they put money down and pay the rest after they've marketed it. But suppliers don't like to wait too long; trust doesn't go very far in the dope trade."

"All right, all right. I get the picture. You people stay on it, then. But by God, I want to know the instant something happens. The very instant, understand me?"

"You'll know as soon as I do." He didn't tell Reznick that an operation this big and complex probably paid in full at time of delivery. No sense giving the man grounds for more worry. Besides, no matter how restless Reznick and Kirk grew, it was still Martin and Atencio who set the pace.

At least there were other files to service. Bunch had the security bids, Kirk had Eckles, and they both had the evasive Ms. Truman.

"I think it'd be cheaper if we just moved in next to Truman's condo, Dev. Be a hell of a lot more comfortable, too." Bunch twisted his shoulders hard against the stiffness of his spine and felt the vertebrae crackle deep in the muscles of his back. They'd been taking turns again on surveillance, but the only view either had of the woman was once when she limped out of the house in neck brace and walker to wait for a taxi to take her to a doctor's appointment. As she waited she stared down the block to where Bunch lounged low against the seat back and tried to find relief for his cramped legs. And it was possible that, as the taxi pulled to the curb and the driver opened the door for her, she smiled and nodded a brief hello to the white Subaru.

Kirk was having better luck with Eckles. The realtor whose name was on the sign in front of the empty home didn't mind answering any question she could about her client.

"He started out asking far too much for the house." The woman was in her late thirties, smartly tailored, and had red-gold hair whose tight curls spiraled out in a wide aura around a tanned face that smiled a lot. "I tried to talk him out of it, but he insisted. He said he could always lower the price but he'd feel like a fool if someone out there would have paid the higher figure."

"It didn't move, obviously."

"No. And he waited too long to drop the price. Buyers who had been initially interested found other sellers—Denver's a buyer's market right now. And no one new came on the scene."

As with a lot of realtors, the woman's world was divided into three parts: buyers, sellers, and financiers. Kirk asked about the third. "Do you know if Eckles was having any kind of money troubles? Did he tell you why he was selling the house?"

"He was moving to San Diego. A new job, I believe." She picked up the telephone. "I can find out about his payment history, if you want to wait a couple minutes."

He wanted to and did. The realtor talked briskly with a mortgage company in Texas. When she hung up, the smile had been replaced by a frown. "He's delinquent in his payments—six months. He's paid a little each month, but nothing like what he owes. And it's getting worse with the reverse amortization."

"So he's trying to dump the house."

Her blue eyes studied the papers from Eckles's file. "It certainly looks that way, doesn't it?" In the silence, he could see the woman wonder what this development would mean for any sale.

Well, that was her headache. Kirk had his own problems with

Eckles. He stood and thanked her—"Oh, thank *you,* Mr. Kirk. I wouldn't have found out about this if you hadn't come in"— and drove to Arvada, one of the bedroom communities in the northwest suburbs of Denver. Eckles's sister, a Mrs. Sybil Matson, was a short, heavyset woman whose straight gray hair had been clipped into a tight-fitting cap around her head. Her speech was equally no-nonsense.

"You're investigating an insurance claim my brother made? He didn't tell me about any claim."

Kirk showed his identification and the letter of authorization from Security Underwriters. It looked even better attached as it was to the clipboard full of papers with her brother's signature. "I'm authorized to make an inventory of his personal effects, so we can determine the extent of his loss, Mrs. Matson. I wonder if before he moved, he brought any property over here for storage." He smiled. "You know, until he and Sharon got settled into their new place in San Diego."

"Well, as a matter of fact, he did. I guess you know they're in an apartment right now and don't have much room."

"Yes ma'am," Kirk lied. "Mr. Eckles told me. Is it still here?"

"In the storage house out back. Mostly boxes." The hair flipped as she jerked her head to point somewhere behind the house. "I suppose you'll want to look at them."

"Yes ma'am. I'll need to. The inventory should be as complete as possible."

"Well, let's do it then. I'll get the key."

She led him through a living room that was rigorously decorated with dark furniture, family photographs on the walls, and rugs set at precise angles to chairs and doorways. The wooden floor gleamed. The kitchen, small for the rest of the house, was equally at attention. The secluded backyard, with its two apple trees, two peach trees, and two plum trees, had been mowed and clipped from the high hedge on one side to the tall board fence on the other. At the end of a flagstone walk that went past a birdbath sat a small barn-shaped storage building painted and trimmed like the house.

"It's in here. Ralph said it was stuff he didn't want to leave in the rental place."

"What place is that, Mrs. Matson?"

She looked up from the dial of the combination lock. "The storage rental place where he took the other stuff that we couldn't fit in here. My husband helped him unload it."

The door with its Z-shaped brace swung open. The crowded storage barn was lined on one side by racks for tools and garden chemicals, and on the other side by two-by-four framing that held plywood shelves. Half a dozen cardboard boxes were placed on the top shelf.

"Those are the ones. You need to open them up, right?"

"Yes ma'am."

He did. The woman stayed to watch as he inventoried the contents and filled out a list on his clipboard. One of the boxes held the missing sterling flatware and serving bowls, carefully wrapped in felt cloth and packed with small sacks of desiccant. The other boxes contained clothing and stereo components. Kirk finished his notes and resealed the boxes. "Do you know the address of the storage rental your brother used?"

"No, afraid not. My husband might remember, but he's out on the road right now. He's a drug salesman. Not," she added quickly, "the illegal kind. He works for Stuart Pharmaceuticals and sells to the medical profession."

"When will he be back?"

"Tuesday afternoon. You're welcome to call then."

He might not have to. A glance through the Yellow Pages under "Storage—Residential and Commercial" identified a dozen self-storage lots that were within a few miles of Eckles's or his sister's home. He started driving.

He had luck at the fourth address, a series of cinder-block rows painted flamingo pink and marked with white doors. The lot manager, stroking his full beard and finally accepting twenty dollars for his time, read down the list of renters and stopped at Eckles. "Ralph Eckles? That the one, man?" He read an address that was familiar.

Devlin nodded. "What unit?"

"Twenty-seven. But I can't let you in there without a search warrant, man. I mean, you know, I can tell you who rented it, no problem. But you want to go in, you got to have a warrant. That's the law."

"Right you are. And if I need to get in, I'll be back with one."

"No problem, man."

It wasn't until the following morning that Kirk could reach Allen Schute in New York and tell him what he'd discovered.

"Good job, Kirk. Can you run out to San Diego and interview Eckles?"

He glanced at the wall calendar with its cramped writing scattered thinly across the white squares of days. "I think I can fit you in. You want me to squeeze him or just get a statement?"

"If you can shake something out of him, go ahead."

"I'll call you after I talk with him."

Bunch came in as Devlin was about to telephone for plane reservations and a rental car to be held at the San Diego airport.

"You going to make it back by tonight?"

Devlin nodded. "I'll take an overnight bag in case, but I plan to be back on the red-eye. Why?"

"Guess who I got a call from last night?"

Devlin couldn't.

"Mitsuko-san. She and Humphries are eager to see you or me this evening."

"Oh?" Devlin paused with a finger on the telephone's cradle. "Did she say why?"

"No. But she sure as hell sounded worried. And here." Bunch tossed a scrap of tablet paper on the desk. It held a series of brief notations. "Last night's log from Minz's telephone. Nothing very exciting."

Devlin looked it over as he called the airline. Then he hurriedly gathered the Eckles papers into a zippered folder. "See what Humphries wants, Bunch. But make sure he's telling us everything this time. See you in the morning."

Devlin's hurrying footsteps rang on the iron stairs, and Bunch half listened to them as he filed the Minz log and then headed for the tiny Subaru and another stint of staring at Jean Truman's closed front door.

CHAPTER 16

Later, Bunch stopped at the health club for an hour's sweat and strain before driving south to Humphries' home. The exercise shook out the stiffness and boredom of surveillance, and the gyrating, Lycra-clad bodies of after-work secretaries and lady executives brightened his outlook on the world. Funny, though, how—despite pleasing the eye—none of them drew him with the hunger and excitement Susan had. And the few women he'd dated in the couple years since her death had been nice people, good times, and fond memories. But even the warmest moments of lovemaking had not touched that center where, gradually, the hole of emptiness had closed with a scab of acceptance.

He shifted down and angled the Bronco onto the long dirt road leading to the house.

No complaints—he and Susan had some time together. That was a hell of a lot more than a lot of other people ever had. But before knowing Susan, Bunch would have enjoyed a woman and, when the enjoyment ran thin, kissed her off with the usually justified belief that she knew it was coming anyway and was just as tired of him. Now he kissed them off with a sense of waste. Waste of himself, waste of them. Funny . . . Maybe what Dev told him had some truth: he was getting so goddamn sensitive. Bean sprouts for breakfast. Glass of Perrier and a slice of lemon for lunch. Followed by a thrilling evening at the Women's Institute for Unisex Bonding. Bullshit. In time, someone else would come along. It wouldn't be Susan—there had been only one of her—but, in her own way, it could be someone as good. And this time, by God, he would know what to look for. Meantime, as the wailing, nasal song said, "It wasn't love, but it wasn't bad." And that one brunette jogging around the track—the one with long legs and the smooth, strong stride of a natural runner—had given him the big eye. He'd seen her before, and he just might make it a point to see her again.

As Bunch turned out the headlights Humphries peered through the curtained windows, a target shooter's silhouette. God preserve the innocent from their own foolishness. If there was a God and if He gave a damn about preserving anything. Bunch took a deep breath and stood for a few moments, looking. Over the range of mountains, the western sky still held the pale green of long mountain twilight. But in the east, where the yellow of autumnal prairie grass rippled like the hide of some tawny animal, the rim of earth had already rolled beneath the chill of coming night. Scattered distant lights marked the occasional houses and ranches that dotted the broad valley and plains. Carried on the warmer breeze that began to sigh up from the valley came the low of a homewardbound cow. It was nice, Bunch thought. Maybe one day he'd have enough money to live in the country. But right now he couldn't afford it, and he didn't really want to anyway. A week, two weeks, and he'd be bored out of his gourd and sneaking back to the city to find out what was happening along the streets. Not, to judge from Humphries' worried eyes, that everything in the countryside was always so peaceful.

"Evening, Mr. Humphries. How's the security equipment holding up? Everything still work okay?"

"Yes. Please come in." His eyes searched the dusky trees beyond Bunch's wide torso. "My wife's in the living room."

The large windows had been closed off by drapes. A small fire crackled deep in the recess of the moss-rock fireplace that formed one end of the room. It didn't do much to take the chill off the early-autumn air, or the tension from Humphries' quick gestures and nervous stride. Mitsuko Watanabe, feet curled up under her thighs, forced a smile. "Good to see you again."

"You're looking good too. What's the problem? More prowlers?"

The smile disappeared. "Not yet."

"More threats," said Humphries. "No one's showed up yet. But I've received threats."

"What kind?"

The man chewed at a sliver of dry flesh on his lip. "I can't tell you the whole of it. But I'm certain someone's going to try and kill us."

"Why are you so certain, Mr. Humphries?"

"Someone in a good position to know told us."

Bunch sighed and settled into an overstuffed armchair covered with some kind of fuzzy nap. The soft pillows wheezed as he crossed his legs and leaned back. "Look, Mr. Humphries, if you're in trouble, why not tell me about it? All about it. There's not a damn thing I can do to protect you if I don't know the players and the game. Nobody can do it that way."

Humphries chewed again, the ticking of teeth at his lips matched by the tiny crackle from the fireplace.

"Oh, for God's sake, Roland. There's nothing to hide. Certainly not for my sake." The woman scratched at a porcelain lighter and held it to the slightly quivering tip of a cigarette. "Either you tell Mr. Bunchcroft about us or I will."

The man swallowed and sat on the other end of the couch, his knees high and elbows resting on them. "Well—ah—Mitsuko and I, we're not married."

"So?"

"Well, to a lot of people, I suppose it makes no difference. I know that." Nonetheless, his expression said it should; if it was that important to him, it should be important to Bunch. "But to her family, it's an eternal stain. An insult to their ancestors."

"Ancestors are very important to us in Japan, Mr. Bunchcroft. The living generation is the temporary guardian of the family's history and pride. It's our responsibility to go to our ancestors without having besmirched the family name." The cigarette waved and her voice took on a note of bitterness, "We're supposed to live for the dead instead of living for ourselves."

"Mitsuko's far more modern than her family. She doesn't do justice to the intensity of their feelings. But it's strong enough that they . . . they want to kill us for dishonoring the family name."

"They said that?"

"Not directly, no."

"We Japanese seldom do anything directly."

"After Mitsuko first moved in with me here, we were afraid her family would try to find us. Mitsuko said—"

"My father is a very powerful man, Mr. Bunchcroft. He has many acquaintances in America. When I left New York to move out here, I tried to do it quietly. But . . ." The cigarette waved again.

"That's why we wanted your help initially. In case one of her father's acquaintances—or someone hired by her father—tried to find her." Humphries stood and started pacing again, three steps per sentence. "That's what we were afraid of then, but things seemed quiet."

"So there were no prowlers. No brown car."

"No. That was Mitsi's idea—with my approval, of course. We had to be certain no one had followed Mitsi from New York." Three paces. "But there could have been. You have to understand the strength of her father's feelings about Mitsi living with a *gaijin*—a foreigner."

Bunch glanced at the woman sitting with her legs stretched out on the sofa. She stared at the pink dots of her toenails.

"When we couldn't find anyone, you figured you didn't need our services anymore," he said.

"Yes."

"But now something's happened."

"Two days ago, Mitsuko telephoned home. She wanted to talk to her family, see how everything is at home. You understand."

"Filial piety, Mr. Bunchcroft." Her tone belied her smile. "Very important to us Asians."

"Her mother was extremely upset. Somehow they'd found out about us—about where Mitsi was and who she was with. She said Mitsuko's father had gone to Tokyo to talk to some people he knew. Someone who would be able to . . . to take care of the situation."

"How?"

Mitsuko shook her head. "My mother didn't say." She stubbed out the cigarette and stared up at one of the prints on the wall. "She didn't have to. *Yojimbo.*"

"Say, what?"

"*Yojimbo.* Professional warriors who rent their services."

"You mean a samurai?"

"Sort of. The samurai owed allegiance to a lord. The *yojimbo* was a free-lance warrior who sold his services. Usually as a bodyguard." A wry smile. "Like you."

"So your daddy hired a warrior to protect you?"

"That's how they think of themselves." She shrugged. "They're just hired killers, really. Gangsters. The *yojimbo* tradition gives them some . . . respectability." She deepened the ironic tone. "Like geisha—call girls who pretend to follow an old and honored tradition. Customs die hard in Japan. Especially when they can save face."

"Why in hell didn't you tell me this before?"

It was Humphries' turn to shake his head. "I didn't want to embarrass Mitsi. And it didn't seem necessary—your security checks didn't turn up anyone."

"Now someone is really after you."

"Yes."

The woman nervously lit another cigarette and nodded.

Humphries cleared his throat. "What makes it most frightening is the—ah—dedication of a hired Japanese killer, Mr. Bunchcroft. As Mitsuko says, there's a sense of honor in the calling."

"Bushido," said Bunch.

Mitsuko's eyebrows lifted. "You know about them?"

Bunch had seen a few movies on the late-late shows. "If the killer takes the job, he has to finish or lose face with his employer and the other *yojimbo,* that right? And if he loses face, he's supposed to commit suicide." That's what the creaky plots were made of. Here and there maybe somebody believed in that crap. The few hired killers Bunch had run across—Japanese or otherwise—were no different: if they could make the hit without being caught, they would. If not, they passed. "Has the guy been hired yet?"

"Probably." The woman stubbed out the long cigarette. "My father likes to think he's a man who doesn't act idly."

"Is he?"

"In this, I think yes."

Humphries swallowed. "We probably won't know for certain until someone actually tries to kill us."

"Have you told anyone besides me about it? The police?"

"Well, just you. I mean, I went to that policeman a while back when Mitsi first moved out here. I told him of . . . possible threats. But he didn't take me seriously. He said Japan was out of his jurisdiction."

"Yeah, I guess he would. Exactly what do you want me to do, Mr. Humphries?"

"Well, isn't it obvious? I want protection—I want you to keep me and Mitsi alive!"

"You have to figure if somebody's coming all the way from Japan to kill you, it's going to take more than just protection to stop him."

Mitsuko looked up from studying her toes. "What do you mean?"

"I mean," Bunch spelled it out, "if somebody really wants to kill you, nobody—not me, not the police, nobody—can give you enough protection. It'll take what the politicos call a preemptive strike."

Humphries fiddled with his class ring. "You mean you'd have to—ah—do something to the assassin?"

"That's what I mean. And maybe to the next assassin. And the one after that—if Mitsuko's old man has that kind of money."

"I don't know if he would send more than one."

Humphries sank onto the couch again, his head in his hands. "I don't know what else to do! The man could be on his way right now. The killer could already be here in Denver and looking for me and Mitsuko. What are we supposed to do, just wait for him?"

"Mitsuko could go back."

"I don't want her to." Humphries looked at her. "I mean, not if she really doesn't want to."

"We've talked about that, Roland. I don't want to."

"See?"

"Then maybe you should get married right now. Then Papa-san would be killing a member of his own family. Something the old ancestors might get pissed off about."

Humphries shifted on the couch. "Well, we've talked that over, Mr. Bunchcroft. But I can't get married right now—family reasons . . . political in nature . . ."

"Roland doesn't want to marry me, Mr. Bunchcroft."

"That's not entirely true, Mitsi! I've told you how my own family—"

The woman smiled widely. "It's not an option, you see."

"Then split up. Send Mitsuko back to New York."

Humphries' expression shifted from discomfort to stubbornness. "I don't want that, either. Mitsi and I are trying to work out our lives together, and—well—we love each other . . ."

"I don't think that would do us any good now, Mr. Bunch-croft. The family name has already been insulted."

"So your choice is hara-kiri or sushi, that's it?"

Pallid and suddenly sweating, Humphries mumbled something and walked swiftly out of the room.

Mitsuko looked at him with some surprise. "He's going to be sick, isn't he?"

Bunch leaned toward her. "Honey, just what the hell is your game?"

She stared at him a long moment, black eyes calculating and bright in the mask of her face. "My game?" Standing slowly, she stretched her locked hands high above her head and tilted her face to the ceiling. The white clothes outlined a lithe and softly muscular body, and her black hair swept down to tickle the swell of taut buttocks. "My game, Mr. Bunchcroft, is to stay alive. It is my father's wish to kill me. He has the power and the will to do it."

"And you don't have the money to run away from Humphries?"

Another long stare. "You are perceptive. I have a little money, but—as you guess—I've had to rely on my father. Now"—a shrug—"I have to rely on Roland."

"What about your mother? Can't she send you money?"

"No. All the wealth is in my father's name. Women in Japan are owned by men, Mr. Bunchcroft." Sharper bitterness pulled her mouth into a scowl. "Our lives are their property."

"Have you tried to talk to your father?"

She said it once more. "He wants me dead." Then, "Please stand up."

He did. "Why?"

She measured herself against his jacket. "I barely reach as high as your chest, don't I? I've never been with a man that big. Are you so big everywhere?"

He sat again. "Look, Mitsuko, I'm not a congressman. My

services are limited to the security business. Not monkey business."

"But you've thought of monkey business. I've seen you." A laugh briefly replaced the worry in those black eyes. "My God—talk about rabbit-woman and elephant-man!"

"Try a sumo wrestler."

"They're too fat!"

"Well, quit vamping me. It's not going to do you any good."

She strode over to the window and yanked open the drapes. "He could be out there right now. Out there in the dark staring through the window right now, couldn't he? Just waiting." A deep, shaky breath. "Maybe that would be best: just get it over with."

"For God's sake, close the curtain, Mitsi!" Humphries, still pale but no longer sweaty, half ran across the room and tugged the drapes shut. "Don't do that—it's dangerous!"

Bunch eyed the tense man and the woman who tried to hide her own fear with a tinkling laugh. What he should do was walk away from this loony bin. Let Humphries find out for himself what kind of tiger's tail he'd gotten hold of. But the trouble with that was, Humphries' realization could come slightly after the fact—maybe one thousandth of a second after the bullet hit him. Even Francis Macomber did better than that. So he wouldn't walk away. What the hell—people were always telling him he was just a big old softy. Some people were. He thought he remembered somebody telling him that one time. And Devlin would be pissed to lose a client like Humphries. Most important, Bunch was curious, and this gig beat the boredom of sitting in that Subaru watching Jean Truman's silent house. "Mr. Humphries, here's what we do."

The flight to San Diego touched down a little after six, Pacific time. Devlin worked his way through the crowded, small airport located almost in the center of the city. Despite being cramped, it was one of Devlin's favorite airports because of its downtown location. But it would only be a matter of time before real estate interests—hungry to develop the prime land—would convince voters to build a new facility on some miles-distant mesa. The car rental was waiting at the end of a shuttle bus that lurched beneath tall palm trees, and Eckles had answered the telephone, assuring Kirk he would be waiting too. The colonel hadn't been difficult to find. He expected settlement of his claim and had been in touch with the insurance company regularly since the burglary. When Devlin showed up at the sprawl of multileveled stucco and bougainvillea that made up the Wind 'n' Sea Residential Plaza, Eckles was all smiles and anticipation.

Soon dashed. "I need to ask you a few more questions about your claim, Colonel Eckles."

"More questions? Jesus, you people didn't ask so many questions when you wanted my money for premiums." His trimmed gray hair and clipped mustache echoed the note of command in his voice.

"I'm sure that's true, Colonel." Kirk settled onto a rattan couch that faced the small balcony. It had a fine view of San Diego Bay and Point Loma beyond. The man's wife rattled around in the tiny kitchen, clinking ice cubes into glasses. "It's about the household effects you stored at your sister's in Arvada. The sterling silver, the clothes, the stereo components. Are they the same items you've filed a claim on, Colonel?"

The blood drained from the man's tanned face, making his pale blue eyes look twice as large. Then it rushed back in a purple flood. "I—ah—I forgot all about taking that stuff over there!"

"Here's some iced tea. Would you like lemon with it, Mr. Kirk?" Sharon Eckles, nervous as a tuning fork, smiled brightly over the tray of glasses. They were large and squat and had cheery Hawaiian motifs painted on them. The tray was a familiar white and blue and said *Clark Air Force Base, PI—Officers Club.* "Dear? Lemon?"

"Out! Get out!" Crouched in his chair, Eckles whipped his face to the woman in the doorway. "Leave us alone!"

"Ralph, what—"

"Get out, God damn you!"

The kitchen door swung shut behind her. In the ringing silence, Kirk heard the blat of traffic from a freeway nearby. "You forgot you took it over there?"

"Yes—completely—just forgot. With the move and all. And then the burglary . . . I just assumed . . ." He took a deep breath and forced stiff lips up into something like a happy face. "I'm relieved it's been found!"

Kirk nodded and pretended to write something on his clipboard, letting the tension work for him. "Have you had any luck selling your house?"

"No." The purple had ebbed from Eckles's face to leave two bright marks above his cheeks and a film of sweat on his forehead. "Not yet."

"And you're still delinquent in your payments?"

"I don't see that as any of your business, Mr. Kirk. And I'd like to know just what gives you the right to pry into my affairs! A man's entitled to some privacy—"

He tapped the clipboard. "It's your claim, Colonel Eckles. When you file a claim, you authorize investigation into everything pertaining to that claim."

Eckles's lips pressed into a thin line.

Kirk turned back to the clipboard. "The stereo components listed as stolen you say have a value of three thousand dollars. But the ones I found at your sister's house retail routinely for under a thousand."

"I—ah—might have made a mistake. I can't remember the cost of every item I own."

"The value of the silver is listed as quite a bit higher than its actual value too."

"Damn it—"

"It raises questions about the value of other items in your loss report, Colonel. Would you care to make any adjustments to the claim?"

Eckles scraped at the corners of his mouth with thumb and

forefinger and tried to read Kirk's eyes. "Well, certainly, if the statement's not true. I don't want to make a false claim. Even accidentally. You understand, I was guessing at the value of those things." A small laugh came out like a catch of breath. "People always think what they own is worth a lot more than it really is, I suppose." Another laughlike sound. "Anybody who sells a used car goes through that, don't they? Or a house?"

Kirk nodded and doodled some more interlocked boxes on the clipboard. The faint sounds from the kitchen had started again, and from the tenseness behind the door he heard the dry squeak of a cork pulled out of a bottle. Kirk looked up suddenly, nailing the man with a hard stare. "Want to tell me what's in the self-storage unit? The one you rented on Wadsworth Boulevard?"

The shade of gray in Eckles's face didn't change this time. But he sagged slowly against the seat cushions as if something were slowly draining from him.

"You can tell me voluntarily or I can get a warrant."

The man's hands hid his face, and his fingers dug into his scalp and jaw. A wet, muffled sound came from behind them and Kirk saw the colonel's shoulders jerk.

"It's the rest of the stolen goods, isn't it?"

The head nodded.

"I didn't hear you," said Kirk.

"Yes! My God, yes. All of it."

"There was no burglary?"

A long silence as Eckles mastered his breathing and scrubbed at his wrinkled eyes with a knuckle. Then he whispered something.

Kirk leaned forward. "What?"

"I want to withdraw my claim."

Kirk turned off the tape recorder in his vest pocket. "That will be up to the company, Colonel."

CHAPTER 17

On the flight back to Denver, Kirk finished the draft of his report on Eckles. The man had tried again and again to convince him that the claim should be withdrawn, and Kirk had replied again and again that it wasn't his decision to make. Finally, as Kirk tugged himself loose from the grasping fingers, Eckles had begged Kirk not to say anything to his sister about the fraud. Mrs. Eckles never returned from the kitchen to hear him plead.

If Eckles's insurance company followed standard procedures, the colonel was in a lot more trouble than Devlin cared to tell him about. To start with, his name would go on the shitlist and any insurance coverage would be hard to get. More important, and Devlin knew Allen Schute and Security Underwriters would take care of this as soon as the report was received tomorrow, Colonel Eckles's name would be turned over to the FBI for investigation of mail fraud and wire fraud. And that, given Eckles's need for a security clearance to hold his present job at Avionics Instruments, would leave the man stranded. All for the sake of chiseling a few thousand dollars off an insurance policy.

It wasn't satisfaction Kirk felt as he walked the long, almost empty corridors of Stapleton Airport toward the baggage claim. It was a shade of sadness. So far, Eckles had gotten what he deserved. Now that he was caught, the man would learn how impersonally vindictive a righteous insurance company could be. They would make an example of him. Eckles would be pursued through the courts by an army of attorneys whose reputation depended on the amount of blood they squeezed from that particular turnip.

Still the man had brought it on himself. Like any other thief, he wanted something for nothing. How he got it made no difference. Like any other thief, the Colonel had put his own greed ahead of the rights of others, and the only error he perceived was getting caught.

Kirk rode down the escalator past cleaning crews that moved with the contented slowness of people putting in their time. At the luggage carousel, a handful of sleepy passengers waited for their baggage to thump down the ramp onto the broad aluminum apron. Devlin fished his suitcase from the tumbled pile and drove home through cold streets to be greeted by the glow of Mrs. Ottoboni's porch light and the red gleam of the telephone answerer beside the living room phone. He took time to pry off his shoes and open a beer before turning on the tape.

Among the several routine calls was Bunch's voice: "Dev, call me as soon as you get in."

He did, and Bunch woke up quickly to tell Kirk about Humphries and the difference between *yojimbo* and samurai. "I kid you not, Dev—a goddamn *yojimbo*. That's what they're afraid of."

"You think it's true?"

"I really don't know. Mitsuko swears her father would do it. But she's using Humphries. Hell, they're using each other. He's a spoiled rich kid who wants to have his cake and eat it too. She's playing her own game and I can't quite figure it out."

"We can't keep them under surveillance twenty-four hours a day, Bunch. We don't have the people for it."

"Right. I told him. But he's safe enough as long as he's at home. There's plenty of electronics to warn of anybody coming after him there. And I hooked up an automatic nine-one-one to the sheriff's office. All he has to do is flip a switch and the call goes out."

"So what's that give the killer? A half hour to do the job? Come on, Bunch."

"Closer to twenty minutes. I also showed them where to barricade themselves in the house while waiting for the cops. And how to use a thirty-eight—I figure a revolver's better for them than an automatic. Anyway, when they're at home, they'll be warned and armed. It's the best we can do without moving in with them, Dev."

That left Humphries' place of work and the trip back and forth. The office complex had its own security force and clearances, so with a few additional precautions, he'd be safe enough on the job. "What's his transportation setup? Chauffeur or convoy?"

"Convoy. I went ahead and hired Peterson to help out. Humphries didn't want to do it. He wanted to rent a goddamn armored car and drive it himself. But I convinced him it was better to have Peterson convoy two times a day."

That was true—two cars gave an assailant more to worry about than a single one. "Peterson knows what he's facing?"

"I filled him in. And I'll be along too."

That seemed okay to Devlin. Peterson, despite his soft and pudgy appearance, was a competent man for bodyguard work, and Devlin had used him before. "Sounds fine, Bunch."

"Here's topic number two. I checked the tap on Minz about an hour ago."

"And?"

"Well, good ol' Louise is still after the guy. Wants to know if he's trying to avoid her, and if he is, all he has to do is tell her, because she sure as hell isn't going to sit around waiting for any man to call her."

"What's that got to do with anything?"

"Just thought you'd be interested. There were a couple more

messages on so-called real estate deals. And a very familiar voice: your buddy and mine calling to say the shipment from Pensacola's due sometime next week."

"Vinny?"

"Didn't give his name. Didn't have to."

"Pensacola. That's in west Florida. That's where the Advantage Corporation has its East Coast manufacturing plant."

"You suffering too much jet lag to go over and spoil Vinny's beauty sleep?"

Vinny had moved his office into his apartment. It was a suite of rooms on the first floor of a large red stone mansion that had been cut up for rentals. He said that business fell off after one of his clients was found dead in his old office. Besides, this arrangement was better for tax purposes: part of his utilities and rent could be listed as business expenses. And it cut down on commuting time too. The outside lock on the front door of the house took Kirk about two minutes before it squeaked open to a hallway that held permanent odors of boiled cabbage and ineffectual detergents. Bunch said it was bush-league time, and to prove it, picked Vinny's door in one minute, four seconds. The door was bolted from the inside by a safety chain which Bunch snipped with a pair of cutters. They eased into the living room/office, with its mixture of well-worn couch, gray metal desk with crooked drawers, stuffed and sagging armchair with neighboring lamp, filing cabinet, and a scattering of men's and women's clothes strewn in a hasty trail toward an open door.

Vinny and another figure lay tangled in the covers on an oversize waterbed while the dull light of a television screen showed the various pinks and browns of bodies entwined and grunting. Bunch noiselessly shut the windows and pulled the curtains tight. Devlin groped for Vinny's pistol under his pillow and set it across the room near an uneasily burping lava lamp.

"Vinny . . . oh, Vinny . . . Someone here to see you . . ." Bunch rocked the blotchy flesh of the man's shoulder.

He knuckled a gummy eye and snorted. Kirk flipped on the

bedside light and the eye popped open, bloodshot and startled. "What the hell!" Beside him, the woman groaned and pulled the covers over her head.

"What the hell are you people—"

Bunch shut off the panting and gasping VCR. "Can't you do it without a training film, Vinny?"

The sound of a second male voice popped the woman's head out of the covers. "Who are you? Vinny, who are these men? What's going on here?"

Devlin tossed her a grimy towel from the floor. "Scram."

"Better get rid of her, Vinny. We need some privacy."

"You need some privacy! What the hell about me? What the hell do you—"

Bunch sat on him. The bed gurgled, and the big man jammed a hard knuckle into the thin bone under Vinny's nose. "Keep mouthing off, fucker. One more word. Go ahead—one . . . more . . . word."

His eyes, blinking tears of pain, squeezed shut and Vinny quivered his head no.

"Get out," Kirk said to the woman. "Now."

"Well I can't just—"

"Now!"

Gathering the towel around her lumpy body, she backed into the living room and office to grope for her clothes. Her wide eyes watched Kirk and Bunch as she hopped on one foot and jabbed the other at her underwear.

Bunch rose and pulled the covers off Vinny. "Stand up, my man. We talk."

"Let me get my goddamn pants on, Homer!"

He wrapped a wide hand around Vinny's neck and lifted him like a plucked chicken out of the tangle of bedclothes. Vinny's eyes bulged and he made little gack-gack-gack noises as Bunch carried him in one hand to the middle of the bedroom carpet. "What's my name?"

"Gack-gack-gack."

He set the man down. "What's my name?"

"Bu . . . unch . . ." It came out a wheeze but they could understand it.

"And your name is Asshole. Now, Asshole, we want to know about the shipment coming in and we want to know why you didn't tell us."

"What—?"

"Vinny, Vinny, Vinny. Don't fib to us. You'll get a lump of coal in your stocking." Bunch smiled—an unnerving sight—and nodded toward Kirk. "And Devlin there is royally pissed at you. He takes these things personally. I don't know how long I can keep him under control."

Vinny's eyes slanted Kirk's way to see what the grim and weary face was meditating. He hurried to explain. "I didn't know about it until today. Honest to God. I just found out this afternoon."

Behind Kirk, a final zipper yanked and the door closed hurriedly. "You should have called in."

"I was going to—believe me. But this broad, you know, we had a couple beers at the Rocky and got to talking to each other. Man, it wasn't my fault! What the hell would *you* do? She was all over me—"

"The shipment, Vinny. Tell us now."

"There's a shipment. I heard there's a shipment. It's coming from somewhere back east. That's all I know. Honest!"

"Where back east?"

"I don't—"

"He's fibbing again, Dev."

Kirk stepped forward. "That's naughty." Bunch had trained in karate and tae kwon do. He liked the hitting and punching techniques of those styles. Devlin preferred the holds and throws of jujitsu and judo—an affinity growing out of his high school days on the wrestling team and the Secret Service training in how to grapple with assailants. Leverage and body joints, like the wrist that Vinny was lifting to ward him off. You grasped the thumb side of the hand firmly and twisted back to skew the upper body off balance. Then, combining a sweep of the leg at your opponent's feet with a straight pull on the bent wrist and a stiff arm to the opposite shoulder, you could lever your opponent to the ground, where an immobilizing hold could be effected by making use of your knee under his elbow.

"Goddamn! Quit it—that hurts!"

"Where back east?"

"Pensacola. Pensafuckingcola!"

"Stand up, Vinny." Kirk said. "Tell us more. In fact, tell us everything."

"There's a shipment of coke coming in from Pensacola. That's someplace in Florida." He flexed his arm and winced. "It's coming in sometime this week but I don't know the exact day."

"How's it coming?"

"By truck. It's in a bigger shipment of company parts. Martin's got some kind of code so he knows what container it's in."

"What kind of code?"

"I don't know! Honest to God, I don't know that! I got the word from Atencio, not from Martin. He knows what Martin's got set up, but he don't know how it's done. Martin's never told him, so he couldn't tell me."

"You and Atencio real asshole buddies now?"

"No, not real buddies. We talk. I share a joint with him, we talk, that kind of thing. I told him I wanted to make some big money and he asked if I cared how and I said no."

"That, we believe."

"Well, I had to lie, didn't I? I had to get next to him. That's what you wanted me to do, ain't it?"

"We also wanted you to keep us informed."

"I'm doing it! I'm doing it right now. I was going to call you first thing in the morning—all you people had to do was . . . How'd you find out anyway?" His eyes darted to the telephone beside his bed and he massaged his elbow while he thought. "You fuckers got a tap on my phone!"

"We knew your life was venial and boring, Vinny. But it's really depressing to find out just how bad it is."

"Hey, I do all right! You saw that broad I had tonight, didn't you? I do all right, Kirk!"

"If you want to keep doing all right, you do the job we're paying you for."

"I'm doing it. Who the hell found out about the shipment? It wasn't you people. It was me!"

"What about that enforcer—Tony? You hear anything about him yet?"

Vinny, a worried wrinkle between his brows, shrugged. "Not much. I know I don't want to ask nothing about him."

"What'd you hear? Have you seen him? Has he been around?"

"No—far as I know, he's still back east. All I know is, Scotty Martin's scared shitless of the guy."

"Why?"

"No reason I could tell except he's a bad dude. Me, I think he's the organization hit man—something like that. Scotty's never said anything about . . . you know, that Newman kid. But Atencio told me Scotty and somebody from out of town had to take care of a fink, and that was the only time he ever saw Scotty really uptight: when he knew that Tony guy was coming in. Atencio thought that was why Eddie Visser skipped too. He thinks Visser heard what Tony and Scotty did to Newman and cut out."

Bunch tossed him a pair of tangled slacks and Vinny tugged them over his goose-bumped legs. "You call tomorrow after work. You tell us when and where that shipment is coming."

"Hey, I can't—"

"Call, Vinny. Give us no shit about it. Just call."

He hadn't called by afternoon when Kirk brought Reznick up to date. "Shipped from the Pensacola plant?"

"That's what I understand, Mr. Reznick. How many containers usually come in from there?"

"Well, the number of loads varies. But each full trailer holds around a hundred units. And sometimes there are three or four trailer loads." He explained: "They mold the base units at the Pensacola plant and send them to us for assembly with the electrical components from Sunnyvale."

"California?"

"That's right. Then we distribute them to the marketing outlets."

"Can we go through the shipment before it arrives without anyone finding out about it?"

Reznick chewed his lip and shook his head. "It would be tough. The parts are in sealed, pressurized containers." He added, "The higher pressure inside the drum keeps out dust and moisture. They're sealed and loaded at the Pensacola plant onto trailer trucks, piggybacked by rail to Denver, and then trucked from the rail terminal to here." Looking out the window toward the long concrete wing of the assembly plant, he scratched his jaw. "That's another reason we assemble in Denver—the parts come up from sea level, so the pressurization's even more effective. If a container's opened, it loses its pressure and we know it's been contaminated. How big a package are we talking?"

"I'm not sure. It depends on how pure the cocaine is."

"I don't follow."

"The purer it is, the smaller the size. They're usually bagged in one-kilo blocks. But by the time coke gets to the street, ninety percent of the mix may be neutral agents."

"A ten-pound package of pure could make a hundred pounds of street-value coke?"

Kirk nodded. "Or more."

"What's that worth?"

Kirk told him and Reznick's eyes rounded. "No wonder they take the risk!"

With this setup, there wasn't much risk. Sealed containers meant that dogs would be no use. And if anyone opened the container en route, Martin would be tipped off and run.

Reznick had been thinking of other ramifications. "Kirk, I don't see how we can trace the Pensacola end of this thing without letting their management know what's going on."

"If we limit the number of people who know about this, the chance of a leak is reduced."

Reznick jerked on the tangle of gray and black curls that formed his long sideburns. "I appreciate that, Kirk. But I've been thinking . . . This has grown far beyond what I thought it would be. It's a companywide issue now."

And, Kirk saw, along with his second thoughts had come a fear of not being covered. A man could dare and, if successful, collect his laurels. But he could also reap the thorns of failure. Especially if he was out there all alone. "It's your decision, of course. We can restrict the investigation to this plant alone and be satisfied with that," Kirk said, adding, "Unfortunately, that leaves the organization intact elsewhere. And there's no guarantee that—if this is the only cell—they wouldn't infiltrate someone else here later on."

"I know that, Kirk. You've explained that already." Reznick turned from the window and wiped a nervous hand along his cheek. "Well, damn. Decision time, right? Well, by God, that's what I'm paid for, isn't it?" He thought a moment more and then made the decision. "It's time to talk to Stewart. It's his company. He has a right to know. I'll be in touch with you shortly, Kirk." He followed the taller man to the door. "Keep the investigation focused on this plant for now. But don't be surprised if it expands to Pensacola. That's going to be my recommendation to Stew."

Bunch, when Devlin reported Reznick's words, nodded. "He'd be a fool not to go after the whole gang. I bet that's what his boss tells him too."

"You figure it reaches Pensacola directly from South America?"

"That makes sense." Bunch pointed to a map from the office file of charts. With a thick forefinger, he traced a line across the blue of the Gulf of Mexico. "A freighter on the way to New

Orleans or Tampa from Caracas or Panama. It swings near Pensacola and a fishing boat meets it. Or it makes Pensacola Bay a port of call. Then the dope's shipped out here before even being unwrapped. That's the beauty of this little scam, Dev. Our local narcs have no clue that Pensacola's the point of entry, so they can't get to the source. If a local dealer's busted, all he knows is he got it from Atencio or some middleman. They probably guess it comes across through Nogales or LA, so they tighten up security there."

Kirk agreed. He thought it was shipped straight through too. You dump a couple kilos on the local market, it's reflected in street prices and the narcs hear about it. But if there's no big splurge—if it's shipped out—the importer doesn't feel any heat. And the price in Denver was probably a hell of a lot better than in Pensacola or anywhere else in Florida. The farther from a port of entry, the higher the price because of the increased transportation costs and the risks of ferrying it across country.

But no one took risks with these shipments. They just used a delivery system that was a hell of a lot more secure and reliable than the U.S. Postal Service. "A lot depends on Vinny," said Devlin.

"Vinny's health depends on Vinny. And he better remember that."

Humphries' health depended on Devlin and Bunch, as he reminded them with an urgent phone call the next morning. "It was the killer. I know it was."

"Slow down, Mr. Humphries—start from the top." Bunch settled on a corner of the groaning desk and flipped on the telephone speaker so Kirk could hear. "What time did he call?"

"About ten minutes ago. The phone rang and I thought it was Len at work—we have a project that's been giving us some trouble, and Len and I planned to get together early this morning. So I thought it was him, and I—"

"Was it a man or woman?"

"A man. He said something first in Japanese and I didn't catch it. I think he asked who I was, but I wasn't expecting it, so I didn't catch it. Then he spoke English."

"What'd he say?"

"He asked if I was Roland Humphries and I said yes. Then he asked if he could speak to Watanabe Mitsuko. That's when I got suspicious. I asked him why and he got angry. I could hear it in his voice. He got angry and said if I didn't put Mitsuko on, I would be very sorry."

"And?"

"I asked who he was and what he wanted with her. He said it was none of my business. So I said it was too my business and I wasn't going to call her to the telephone unless he answered my questions. Then he said something else in Japanese too fast for me to understand and hung up." Humphries drew a long breath. "It was the killer. I know it. And he's here!"

And if so, he knew for certain that Mitsi Watanabe was, too. "How do you know it was a local call?"

Humphries paused. "Well, it wasn't an overseas call. There wasn't that delay you get with a satellite relay." He added, "But even if he's not right in Denver, he's in the country someplace. It won't take him long to get here."

"All right, Mr. Humphries. Here's what you do. Peterson should be there any minute. Tell him what happened and that you've called me. Tell him that either Mr. Kirk or I will be out there as soon as possible." Bunch glanced at Devlin, who nodded. "Then you and Peterson go on to work just like always. We'll look after things."

"Shouldn't we call the police?"

"It wouldn't do any good, Mr. Humphries. I hate to tell you, but that phone call's just not exciting enough to stir them up."

"But he wants to kill me!"

"And that's why you've hired us, right? Now you just do like I told you, Mr. Humphries. And let us take care of things, okay?"

Bunch hung up and Kirk said, "The call could have come from anywhere. LA, Seattle, San Fran."

"Or Denver." Bunch shrugged into his windbreaker and stared for a long moment through the arched window at the distant mountains. Above the irregular line of peaks, pale traces of clouds drawn long and wispy by high-altitude winds promised a change in the weather. This late in October, the change would be toward colder. "You want to ride shotgun with Peterson this afternoon? I can take care of the house, but he might need some help."

Devlin saw what Bunch meant and agreed. "Yeah. Mitsuko-san should be pretty safe with you there."

Bunch paused at the Mosler and took out the Python .357 magnum that he liked to carry in the holster welded under his Bronco's dash. "I think that spider woman would be pretty safe anywhere, Dev." He twirled the pistol on his finger. "This is to protect me."

Mitsuko was waiting for Bunch by the time he reached the sprawling, single-level home. This time she wore a black outfit: skintight Lycra pants and a sleeveless silk vest that clung to each firm breast as if it were painted on. The glossy black fabric matched her long hair and perhaps her mood. There was a lassitude about her, as if she knew it was only a matter of time before the other shoe fell. "Roland was very worried when he left this morning."

"If that was your *yojimbo* on the phone, Roland was right to be worried."

"You don't really think we're safe here, do you?"

"If he knows where you are, it's as safe a place as any."

"So you're not going to carry me away to some secret place." There was no flirtation in the question; it was just a resigned acknowledgment.

Bunch was tempted to ask what kind of obligation she thought he owed her, but the question could be read as an invitation he didn't want to make. Instead, he shrugged. "How secret was New York? How secret's Denver?"

She looked down and shook her head. "Not very."

"What is it you're really running from, Mitsuko-san?"

"I told you."

"Yeah, I know what you told me."

"You mean you don't believe me."

Bunch sighed and strode to the large windows to look out at the trees and hillside beyond. From the kitchen, Mrs. Lucero's ranchera music made a bouncy noise. "I don't know how much to believe. I still can't see a man wanting to kill his own daughter. Humphries, maybe. But not you."

"You don't understand our Japanese sense of honor."

"Among other things." Bunch gave the electronics controls a quick check, verifying the integrity of the circuits. Then he switched them off to run a leisurely patrol around the property. The exterior units had to be inspected as well, but the real reason for the tour was that it felt better to be outside than prowling through a house where Mitsuko hung around waiting for him to save her from something she would not name.

The sound of shears led him to Mr. Lucero, who was clipping evergreen shrubs back from the base of the house.

"Seen anybody around?" Bunch asked.

The man wore a khaki work shirt with the sleeves rolled up to show wiry arms. "No." The straw hat bobbed toward the driveway. "Mailman come by a little while ago. That's it."

Bunch nodded. He finished the perimeter and, with his binoculars, conned the horizons and the distant glimpses of the few neighboring homes. Then he found a comfortable rest on the pine needles between two ponderosas and settled in the warmth of a hazy sun. From there he could keep an eye on the country road that notched the rise and dipped into the wide valley at his feet.

Devlin arranged to meet Peterson and Humphries around six. The procedure was for Humphries to leave work before or after the main rush hour instead of joining the confusion of cars that spewed onto the highways between four and six. That way, any tail could be spotted more easily, and the random time made it more difficult for an assailant to plan an ambush. Today was a late day, Peterson told him. Kirk used the extra time to swing past the Advantage Corporation's parking lot. He wanted to impress on Vinny once more the importance of his cheerful, willing, and prompt cooperation. Devlin waited down the street as Vinny's smoking Chevrolet chugged past. Landrum had someone riding in the front seat with him. Devlin pulled into traffic, just keeping in view the Chevy's roof with its thin remnant of green cloth and blossoming scabs of rust.

Landrum merged into the tangle of trucks and homeward-bound traffic that choked the I-70/I-25 Mousetrap. Then he shook free long enough to swing onto the off-ramp at Pecos. With some twists and turns, Vinny led through the Chaffee Park neighborhood down to Forty-third Avenue and a frame house at the corner of Navajo. There he pulled to the curb and his rider got out, a dark man of medium height who lifted a hand goodbye. The man disappeared down the driveway to a garage that had been converted into a cottage. Vinny pulled away slowly, turned onto Lipan, and coasted to the curb, where he waited. Kirk parked close behind him, and Vinny got out and walked quickly back to the Healey 3000.

"What the hell's the problem now, Kirk? What the hell you trying to do, get my ass carved up like goddamn Newman?"

"You haven't called us, Vinny."

"Call! What the hell I got to call about yet? You know who that was I give a ride to? Johnny Atencio! Goddamn it, I got Johnny Atencio riding in my fucking car and I look up and see you on my tail. You can blow this whole thing, you know that?"

"Why give Atencio a ride?"

"His car's in the shop, so I told him I'd take him home."

"What about the shipment?"

"I don't know! He don't know. It's sometime this week, but only Martin knows. When it's here, he'll tell us. For Christ's sake, get off my back!"

"I want you to be impressed, Vinny, with how much we value your work. And how disappointed Bunch and I will be if you screw up."

"All right—I'm impressed. But if anybody screws up, it'll be you people because you won't back off. Now, goddamn it, stay away. Don't call me, I'll call you." He spat angrily at the pavement and stalked back to his car, heels jabbing at the ground.

As Bunch had said, he was a righteous little bastard. Devlin watched the smoking car lurch away, left rear fender flapping indignantly. After Vinny was out of sight, he swung around to guide the Healey toward the south side of the city and Peterson.

Kirk shifted positions around Humphries' speeding Mercedes. First he scooted the Healey out among the thinning traffic in front of the man, then pulled off to let Humphries—tracked closely by Peterson—move past. The small radio crackled and popped with the noise of distant transmissions, but neither Devlin nor Peterson made much use of it. They had worked together before.

Today's route, Peterson had told him, would be down I-25 to the 470 loop and across to South Santa Fe. Then south to the small town of Sedalia and onto State 105 as far as the graveled county road that led past Humphries' long driveway. Peterson had mapped a variety of routes, and changed portions of the journey each day in a random pattern. But there were a few intersections and certain stretches of road that couldn't be avoided. The idea was to come at them from different directions and at various times. And—as now—for Kirk to move ahead and scout key junctions for any waiting cars, to watch Humphries' and Peterson's sedans flash past, and then to remain for a few minutes and see if anyone followed.

He angled the Healey under the ragged shade of a hackberry tree that leaned out of the weedy drainage ditch, and killed the engine. Without the throaty hum of the pipes, the sounds of late afternoon drifted on a chill autumn breeze. It swept across the wide valley formed by the Front Range and the low ridges of limestone shelves stepping up to the prairie on the east. Somewhere beyond a weathered barn and across a white-fenced pasture, a cow moaned persistently. Her long, soft grunt rose to a squealing bellow and died away unanswered. In the hazy sky above the dark mountains, a small airplane droned and faded as it changed the pitch of its propeller. Behind him, at the turn from 105, Kirk saw Humphries' Mercedes swing around the corner and come over the bobbing ridges of the narrow strip of road. Following it, less than a car's length back, was Peterson's gray Dodge—a rebuilt Highway Patrol cruiser. They flashed past, tires sizzling on the asphalt, leaving a taint of exhaust on the breeze. Kirk listened for any engines straining to catch the two automobiles. The cow. The dying buzz of the airplane. The cold, dry wind rustling the dark leaves of the hackberry. Then he heard it: a whining rattle that meant motorcycle. An instant later, the black visor of a helmeted rider glanced his way as a Yamaha leaned tightly through the turn and ran up the gears. Kirk pulled out after it, looking in the rearview mirror to see if anyone else was joining them.

The motorcycle, its sharp angles urging the driver forward like a jockey on a racehorse, dropped into high gear. Kirk speed-shifted the Healey and watched the tachometer bob up to the red line. Ahead, appearing and disappearing like bouncing balls, the two automobiles crested the series of ridges and flickered through the trunks of a line of bare Lombardies that marked a gentle curve in the road.

"Pete—motorcycle coming up fast."

The radio crackled but no words came back.

Kirk waited until the gray Dodge was in sight again, pulling a long incline toward the next ridge. "Pete—motorcycle coming up fast. Read me?"

"Got you."

The cars disappeared over the treeless crest, and a moment later, Kirk saw the motorcycle top the rise with a little hop and sink out of sight. He shoved the Healey's gas pedal down to the floor. She answered with a surge that pressed him against the thinly padded seat back, and he blessed the old twin SU carburetors that poured fuel into the screaming cylinders. With a soaring glide, the Healey left the pavement and thumped back down to show the narrow road falling away into another arm of the valley. A string of bright-shirted bicyclists labored up the oncoming lane. Humphries and Peterson, close enough together to be car and trailer, whipped past them. A few seconds later, the Yamaha, slowly closing in on Peterson's Dodge, rapped past the startled line of riders. Then Kirk—their faces angry ovals of unheard shouts. In front of him, the road empty again as it sliced across the grassy fields stretching east and west toward high ground on both sides.

The motorcycle was slowing now and the Healey pulled closer. Kirk got a glimpse of glaring brake lights as the three vehicles topped the next ridge and disappeared again. As Kirk came over the crest he saw the motorcycle pull out to pass Peterson. The Dodge slid even closer to Humphries' bumper to prevent the two-wheeler from cutting between them. The Yamaha hovered a long moment as the road began another gentle climb toward the high ground where the gravel county road branched off toward Humphries' home. Kirk was near enough now to see the rider's arm reach out. The long streak of a weapon, like an accusing finger, aimed at Humphries' car. A flash of smoke blew back from the muzzle. Peterson's Dodge suddenly swung behind the motorcycle and leapt forward. The front bumper lunged for the Yamaha's rear tire, and the motorcycle wobbled as the arm snatched back to grab for the handlebars. Then the motorcycle swerved again, wilder now, as the rider tried to pull it back under control. Humphries slammed on his brakes, to slide sideways into the gravel and tilt through the turn in an explosion of frantic dust. Peterson jammed his vehicle between Humphries and the skidding, bucking motorcycle that squealed past the turn. Kirk slewed the Healey onto the gravel road behind Humphries and rattled through the thick dust and flying stones to follow the fleeing man. In the rearview mirror, the dust closed over the road behind and Kirk saw only the yellow-gray of roiling cloud. A couple minutes later, Humphries turned sharply into his own driveway and twisted up through the pines to skid the Mercedes under the opening door of the garage. The door clattered down quickly over the still-gleaming brake lights and the splintered rear window. Kirk pulled the Healey to a halt behind Bunch's Bronco. He hopped out and peered into the valley, searching for Peterson's gray car.

"Did you see that?" Humphries, hair disheveled and eyes wild, stood in the open front door and pointed toward the highway. "Did you see him? He tried to shoot me! He had a pistol and he shot at me! Look at my car!"

A large arm wrapped around Humphries' chest and half lifted him away from the doorway. "Anybody hurt, Dev?" Bunch's face replaced Humphries'.

On the county road that glided down the hillside into the valley, a single plume of dust moved rapidly and Kirk could see the glint of Peterson's Dodge. "I don't think so. Here comes Pete—he looks okay."

"He tried to kill me! I told you he was here—it was him—he shot at me!"

CHAPTER 19

By the time Peterson's car coasted to a stop on the circle of driveway, a wide-eyed Mitsuko had convinced Humphries to disappear into the back. The hot tub was there, she reminded him, and she would make him a drink and he could tell her all about it. Clucking in Spanish, Mrs. Lucero and her husband opened the garage door to stare at the shattered rear window of the Mercedes. "He got away," said Peterson. "I couldn't keep up with that two-wheeler."

"What the hell was he shooting?" asked Devlin.

"Machine pistol. Looked like a Bushmaster. You know that heavy sleeve they have at the end of the barrel? Thirty-round magazine."

"Little sucker like that can do some damage," said Bunch.

"On full automatic, it can."

Lucero, straw hat in his hands, edged toward Bunch. "This is very bad."

"It ain't good, Elias." He asked Peterson, "You get a look at the rider?"

"Not with that helmet on. Could have been Darth Vader for all I saw."

"He must have been waiting at the 105 junction," said Kirk.

"It had to happen sometime," said Peterson. "We always go through there sooner or later."

"This man, this killer," asked Lucero, "he will come to the house now?"

Bunch looked at the lean man who stood bowlegged and frowning. "I can't say he won't, Elias. But I don't think so."

Lucero considered that. "I think it's too damn dangerous for my wife to work here no more." He put his hat squarely on his head. "I think we get the hell out now."

They watched the two figures close together and walk quickly around a wing of the house. A few seconds later, their rusty pickup truck rattled down the driveway.

Bunch stared after the dust. "I wonder if Mitsi can cook?"

The electric sensors had been turned on and the three men sat in the dark living room. The setting sun turned pink and gray through clouds above the serrated outline of the horizon. In another wing of the house, they heard the occasional thump of heels as Mitsuko walked back and forth busy at something.

"Must be running up and down Humphries' spine in her bare feet," said Bunch. "Give him a little Oriental massage after his hot tub."

"That, on top of an Oriental message," said Kirk.

Peterson squeaked air between two of his front teeth, tongue busy as something stuck there. "He's tested the defenses. Next time he'll be more careful. And maybe aim better."

Kirk nodded. He didn't think the assailant would return tonight. But a wrong guess would spoil everybody's weekend. "You want to stay here?" he asked Bunch.

"Hell no. But I guess I better. Humphries might die of a heart attack, if somebody doesn't kill him first."

They settled on a rotation that would give Humphries and Mitsuko protection around the clock, at least for the next few days. The three made one last patrol of the grounds before Peterson and Kirk left, and they switched on the warning systems. Bunch leaned into the dim glow of the Healey's dash lights as Devlin started his engine.

"We're going to have to do more than just sit and make targets of ourselves, Dev. That bastard means business. I mean a goddamn Bushmaster, after all . . ."

Kirk agreed. "Any ideas?"

"Not yet."

"Well, let's put our minds to it, partner. A couple geniuses like us should come up with something."

Bunch grunted and slapped a hand on the cockpit's rail. "Don't forget to run that tap on Minz's phone tonight. Probably nothing there, but we should clear the tape."

When Kirk got home, he listened to that and to his own answering tape. The only thing on either that held any importance was a brief call from Reznick telling Kirk to telephone him first thing in the morning. Devlin did.

"Kirk? I called Stewart. He thinks you should go to the Pensacola plant as soon as possible and clean up that end of it, too."

"I can, of course. But I should have a better idea of what I'm looking for before I go."

"What's that mean?"

"It means we don't yet have any idea who in the Pensacola plant is shipping the stuff. Or even what division it's coming from. We might be able to get that information after we intercept the next load."

"But won't that alarm the people at the other end? They'll take off!"

"There is that risk. But I don't think it's a big one. I think if we move knowledgeably and fast, we might get away with it."

Kirk could picture Reznick on the other end of the line, thick eyebrows pulling together in a frown. "Kirk, I don't mind telling you, Stewart was damned upset to find out about this. And he wants something done yesterday."

"If we catch Martin and Atencio with their hands dirty, we'll have some leverage. They might make a deal: information for dropping the charges."

"Dropping them! I'll be damned—"

"Or for filing lesser charges. And while they're in custody, we have seventy-two hours to trace out the Pensacola end of the operation before any charges have to be brought."

"That cuts things pretty thin."

"If I go down there knowing who to look for, I can be a lot more effective."

"Yeah. I see that." Silence. "Do you have any word yet about the next delivery?"

"Only what we know already: sometime this week."

Reznick thought. "Well, I can explain that to Stew." And the lean, gray-faced man would probably nod his head with his usual stiffness and tell Reznick to do what Kirk suggested. After all, he had unbent enough to tell Reznick he was doing a good job so far on this thing. "A few days more isn't too long to wait, I guess. But you hear this, Kirk: You by God keep me informed. You have my office number and my home phone, and you call me the instant anything breaks." Because Stewart, in his understated, WASP way, had made it clear that he expected to hear immediately if not sooner about any developments. "I've told my secretary to put you through no matter what. Hear me?"

Kirk heard him. Vinny, when he called that afternoon and found out what Reznick said, hoped no one else heard the man tell his secretary that.

"I mean, shit, Kirk, all some goddamn secretary has to do is whisper about it and my ass is grass!"

"Not even Reznick knows who you are, Vinny."

"He knows I'm the fucking new man in the warehouse crew. How many goddamn new men are there in the warehouse crew?"

"The secretary doesn't know that. And nobody in the front office talks to people on the floor. You know that. Relax."

"Relax? Yeah, relax. I'm out here my balls swinging in the breeze and you tell me relax."

"All right, don't relax. What do you have for me?"

"I got the word to clean out my locker by Thursday."

"Scotty Martin said this?"

"Who else? Christ sake, somebody else knows about it, clue me in!"

"Who's sending the stuff?"

"Don't know. Not asking."

"What are you supposed to look for?"

"Didn't tell me that, either. I mean, Scotty's got a few smarts, you know? I've been carrying one of these little back packs in and out of the plant so the security people get used to seeing it. That's all he told me to do until now."

"So what's your gig Thursday?"

"He ain't told me yet. Not all of it. What I do, I wait for Scotty to give the high sign so me and Johnny can walk the stuff into the locker room and stash it."

"How do you do that?"

"Under our shirts. Scotty wants us to wear work shirts Thursday. Not just T-shirts."

"Then what?"

"I'm not sure. I don't know whether we leave it in the lockers or take it out. He hasn't said nothing about that yet."

"If it gets taken out, do you meet to divvy it then?"

"I don't know."

"Insist on it."

"What?"

"Insist on getting your share that afternoon. You don't know Scotty. He might take the whole stash and run. You make goddamn sure that if the load goes out of the plant, you ride with it to the divvy."

"Yeah. All right."

"Any idea how much is coming in?"

"No. I figure a lot of kilos, though. We split ten percent of whatever comes through, and Scotty's acting like we're going to be fucking millionaires or something. And he gave me and Johnny some of these plastic garbage bags to wrap the stuff in when we handle it. Big bags. I figure it's a big shipment."

Kirk figured so too. It would probably include everything that had been in the pipeline since they closed down operations so many weeks ago. "What time?"

"I don't know, Kirk. Look, Scotty's not going to tell me what's going down. He'll tell me where to be and when and that's it. I mean, it's not like he's dealing in grapes and bananas, you know?"

Devlin knew, and he wasn't surprised at Vinny's lack of information. Martin would tell the other two only what was necessary, not just for security reasons but also because information was leverage. "Has Martin met with anybody lately?"

"Not while I been with him. Anybody like who?"

"Like Tony."

"Tony? Oh—the one who . . ." The phone went silent. "I hope not. I hope to shit not."

"Okay, Vinny. I'll catch your act on Thursday."

"Hey, wait a minute! What's going down, man? I mean, what you going to be doing that I better know about?"

"We'll handle it. Don't worry."

"Yeah. Right. You clowns, and I shouldn't worry. Just remember, you don't know me, right? You pull any bust or something, you fucking well do not know me at all. Right?"

"That's exactly the way we want it."

"Well, just remember! All's I need's this Tony whosis on my ass for being a snitch."

Although the next few trips were uneventful, Humphries' escort service had lost its sense of the routine. Humphries had insisted on an armored car to ride in, but it would take at least a week to ship one up from Texas. In the meantime, they varied the vehicles' drivers. Once, Peterson led in the Mercedes and kept an eye on the rearview mirror that showed—through the newly replaced back window—Humphries crouched over the steering wheel of the Dodge. Another time, Bunch drove a convoy car and Peterson was in the cover car. But aside from a couple of nervous moments when an unmarked panel truck tailed them for a few miles before turning off, Humphries was delivered safely to work and home. Though the extent of his safety at home was problematic, Bunch told Devlin.

"You know what that Mitsuko broad said to me, Dev?" Bunch settled into the desk chair and stretched out legs whose thighs mashed against the chair's arm braces.

"That she's madly in love with you and wants to be your sex slave."

"I mean besides that. You know when Humphries got shot at? She says she made him screw her half the night. Says she couldn't keep her hands or whatever off him because of the idea that might be the last piece either of them got."

"Why'd she tell you that?"

Bunch stretched and yawned and on the back of his eyelids could still see the woman's slightly puffy face framed by loose, straight hair. A bedroom face. And her eyes—black, shiny with still-unslaked lust—staring at him hungrily. "She thought it would sex me up. Did, too."

"Hey, you didn't—"

"Naw. God knows I wanted it. She did too—you know that smell broads get when they're fuck-happy?"

Kirk didn't, but he nodded.

"All over her. But aside from not screwing the clientele, I just don't need to be tangled up with a nut case." He heaved himself up in the chair and reached for the telephone. "Maybe the Japanese way of loving is a bit different. She's always talking about showing me her geisha prints. Or maybe she's a hundred percent certifiable. Either way, I don't want to slip my dong into that mess." He punched a series of buttons and, when someone answered, asked for Detective Miller. "Time to bring in Vice and Narcotics," he said to Kirk, his hand over the mouthpiece.

"Dave? This is Bunchcroft. Remember that sample you let

us borrow? Yeah—it's all right. We got it locked up. . . . No, it paid off. . . . Yeah—"

Kirk half listened as Bunch explained about the expected shipment. His own job was to draft an operations and equipment sheet to make certain nothing went wrong.

"Okay, Dev. Miller says he'll be standing by with a backup team when we leave the plant."

Reznick might not have been happy that the police were called in, but neither Bunch nor Devlin wanted to pull any kind of citizen's arrest without the cops around. In fact, the preferred way for most parties concerned was to let the police make the bust. Reznick would order a locker room shakedown on Thursday, and that way, Martin's tipster in the plant security force would warn him about it. That, Kirk hoped, would force Martin and company to take the drugs off Advantage property and into police jurisdiction. The idea was to trace Martin to wherever the divvy took place, and then call Miller in for the arrest. The only time the Advantage Corporation's name would make the news would be if the defendants went to trial. And given the popularity of plea bargaining or even—in good cases—a guilty plea to some lesser charge, the means of shipping the drugs might never be publicized. Besides, they'd promised Miller the glory, and that would make up for the quarter-ounce or so missing from the sample.

They went over the details one more time, checking the plan against eventualities, and then drove south to baby-sit Humphries again.

CHAPTER 20

Vinny squawked about wearing a wire to work.

"What you do, Vinny, is make sure Martin doesn't put his hands all over you. Why the hell are you letting him feel you up anyway?"

"He doesn't feel me up, Homer! But you goddamn well know he could spot it. I'll be wearing the thing all fucking day."

Bunch finished taping the transmitter to the inside of Vinny's skinny shin and started dropping the microphone wire down his shirt collar. "He won't spot it. His mind's on bigger things. Just keep your pants leg pulled down."

Vinny studied his profile in the washroom mirror. "These things never work anyway."

"Sure they do. Besides, if you have to call for help, you want someone to hear, don't you?"

That gave him food for thought and provided Bunch and Devlin with a couple minutes' relief. Bunch pinned the tiny microphone inside Vinny's T-shirt and plugged the other end of the wire into the AR-8 transmitter on his shin. Vinny, sweating about someone coming into the gas station toilet where they were working, tugged his shirt back on and urged Bunch to hurry up. "If I'm late, Scotty's going to nose something, Homer. Finish up!"

Vinny was right about the limitations of body transmitters. They could only work on line of sight and at a maximum distance of two hundred feet. And they picked up every sound: Vinny's excited breathing, the static of his shirt rubbing across the mike, background noises. Moreover, it wasn't unknown for a transmission to be broadcast over a neighboring television set, much to the embarrassment of the undercover agent. But Vinny was assured that this unit checked out, and that Bunch and Devlin would be close enough to catch his transmissions. Then they sent him on his way into the morning traffic while Bunch and Devlin followed in the rental van.

"I screened the tap on Arnie's phone last night, Dev. Vinny hasn't called him yet."

"Well, he won't have anything to sell Minz anyway."

"Yeah. The little shit." Then, "Good thing we didn't tell Miller about that. Now he won't be disappointed."

"Right."

They pulled into the visitor's lot just after the day shift punched in. Reznick waited for them in the warehouse manager's small office, which looked down through a series of windows into the cavernous warehouse. Bunch slid open one of the windows to make radio transmission a little easier for Vinny's body pack; Devlin turned on the manager's desk lamp to make the place seem normal. Then he and Reznick moved back into the shadows away from the glass while Bunch set up a chair as a rest for his telephoto lens and peeked over the lower sill into the dim alleys of cartons and dark gray barrel-like canisters. Hague, the warehouse manager, tried to work at his desk as if nothing were going on.

"This is really the payoff?" Reznick's excitement showed in his tense whisper and the way his fingers fidgeted continually with the monogrammed pewter buttons on his blazer.

"It'll be a while yet, Mr. Reznick. These things get pretty boring before they get exciting."

Reznick laughed nervously and tried to settle back into the

folding chair Hague had bustled around to find for him. The warehouse manager had been both surprised and worried when Reznick led them in, and the man's eager compliance was meant to show he had nothing to do with whatever it was the three men were investigating. He also made it clear that he had noticed nothing out of the ordinary or he would have reported it.

"It's all right, Hague," said Reznick. "None of us noticed."

On the floor beside Bunch, the receiver popped into static and mechanical noises. The open-reel tape recorder began turning slowly. Bunch quickly damped the volume to a murmur and scanned the warehouse floor with his binoculars.

"That's Vinny. He's driving the forklift."

The morning dragged into noon, then through the lunch hour. They saw Vinny cross the parking lot to his car in the long, sun-glinted rows of vehicles. Then he came back. The radio was silent. Reznick's early enthusiasm shifted into bored yawns, and finally he said he had work piling up in his office and told Hague to call him the moment something happened. Bunch and Devlin were glad to see the man go.

"Roast beef or ham?" Bunch lifted cellophane-covered sandwiches from cardboard boxes and tossed one to Devlin. He had enough photographs of Martin and Atencio for identification purposes, and only occasionally now did he follow the men through the binoculars. Vinny's conversations with the suspects revealed nothing except that Atencio liked blondes with big tits and Martin had a thing for girls with short hair and tight buns.

"Christ, it's getting near quitting time, Dev. You think that little fart had the wrong scoop?"

"It wouldn't be the first time." And it wouldn't be the first time a surveillance failed to pay off.

Hague's telephone rang and he covered the mouthpiece. "It's Mr. Reznick again. What should I tell him?"

"Tell him we're still waiting—hold it . . ." Bunch leaned to the tape recorder and turned up the sound. Vinny's voice came faint but clear: "How do you know which one it is?"

A second voice answered, "Got a stenciled code on it."

Bunch, straining through the binoculars, muttered, "There they are. They're going down aisle four."

Devlin crept to his side and peered through the lenses while Bunch set up the camera. Aisle 4 was lined with shipping drums stacked three high toward the dim ceiling. Each unit was six feet tall, and the towering walls broke up Vinny's transmission as he tried to pump Martin about the method of identifying the right drum.

"Don't worry about it, Vinny. I know what to look for. You just—" The transmission faded again. Then came the clatter of something hard banging on the microphone and muffled grunting and static. "Okay, Johnny. Here."

Through the binoculars, Devlin saw the three men wrestle one of the drums toward an empty corner of the quiet warehouse. Behind him, the door opened quickly and Reznick's hot breath stirred against the back of his neck.

"Is this it? Are they getting it?"

"They're taking it out now." Bunch's camera clicked rapidly. "There goes Atencio."

They watched the man stroll casually down a cross aisle to act as a lookout.

"How many kilos we got, Scotty?" It was Vinny's voice.

"Twenty, man."

"Jesus!"

"I told you it'd be a big mother. But don't get excited—it ain't all ours. We hold five; the rest gets shipped out later."

"Where we stashing it?"

"We stash it where I say, so don't worry about that, man."

A third voice said, "All clear. You ready?"

"Yeah."

Vinny, equally casual, walked toward the door leading off to the locker rooms. His voice came softly over the receiver. "I hope you can hear me, Kirk. It's twenty kilos. The drum's number is 488244-88220. We're taking the stuff out after work. I'm the mule. Scotty wouldn't—" A door cut his voice off. A couple minutes later, Atencio wandered toward the doorway. They came back for their next load from Martin, who stood guard by the drum.

"What do we do now?" asked Reznick.

"Wait," Devlin said. "When they punch out after work, I'll secure the canister. Bunch will wait for me outside and we'll follow them."

"Can they escape?"

"Not likely," said Bunch. "I put a bumper bug on Vinny's car. We can sit a mile off and know where he is."

An electric bell rang the end of the workday and almost immediately men started for their cars. Hague and Devlin trotted down the metal stairs to the warehouse floor while Bunch packed the electronics gear. The drum had been moved into a line of other empties but it wasn't hard to locate. It was the last in the row and had an additional line of digits in white paint below the stenciled invoice codes.

"I'll be damned," said Hague. "I never noticed something like that. Somebody looking for it would see it, maybe. But nobody else."

"That's the idea," said Kirk.

He and Hague tipped the barrel on edge and rolled it aside. He wrote his initials on its lip and asked Hague to lock it in a safe place. Then he found Bunch waiting in the van, engine idling, as he tuned the locater on the receiver.

"Got him?"

"Yeah. He's still waiting to clear the gate."

"You think they had Vinny carry it because he's the new man?"

"Makes sense—if somebody gets popped, it won't be them. But you can bet your grandma's teeth they're following him."

They fell into the traffic that slowly drained from the parking lot onto the streets surrounding the plant. Ahead, Vinny's car was only one of many roofs edging forward, and somewhere on each side of him the automobiles of Atencio and Martin must be standing guard. Bunch, his borrowed GE radio pack on the prearranged police channel, asked, "Dave, can you read me?"

"Four by four," came the terse answer. Miller and his people would join them when they passed through the gate. Devlin operated the locater and they were finally off and running.

The small convoy led west on I-70 and then north on the Valley Highway a short distance to the Forty-ninth Avenue exit.

"Where's he at, Dev?"

"He turned again. South—must be heading for Forty-eighth." That was one of the few streets that crossed the Valley Highway. "Yeah. Going west now. Has to be Forty-eighth."

Bunch relayed the information to Miller, and in the side mirror Devlin saw an unmarked car slowly turn to follow them.

"He's stopping, Bunch."

Heavy traffic choked the artery as Bunch slowed. They saw two cars on the shoulder: Vinny's Chevy and Martin's metallic-blue Pontiac Firebird.

"Drop off, Dave. They've stopped to check for tails. We'll pass them and stop down the block."

"Ten-four."

Devlin stared straight ahead into traffic as the van rolled past the two parked cars. Atencio's dented Mustang was missing. "Keep going, Bunch. I think they're leapfrogging."

"I don't want to get too far out of range." Bunch pulled into the parking lot of a convenience store and coasted toward the outdoor telephone. A few minutes later, the locater began moving again, and in a short time Devlin saw Atencio's Mustang go by with Vinny following three or four cars back. Martin was gone.

A static-fractured voice came over the receiver: ". . . following Johnny now. Scotty's on his . . ."

"Damn," muttered Bunch. Then into the radio pack, "Dave, sit tight. Martin's gone somewhere. Probably checking their backside. Target's still headed west on Forty-eighth."

"Ten-four."

"Let's go, Bunch. Signal's getting weak."

BODY GUARD · 185

They followed them to Pecos and then south. There they sat out of sight while Atencio led Vinny in a series of repeated loops around a residential block in the Chaffee Park neighborhood until he was satisfied there was no tail. Then they took Forty-fourth Avenue straight to Federal and turned north.

"They're headed for it now, wherever the hell it is." Bunch fed the information to Miller, and dropping back into heavy traffic, they followed the straight signals from the locater as Atencio steered north on Federal for a couple miles. Just beyond Sixty-fourth, Vinny's car made a right turn, then a left, and halted.

Bunch and Kirk turned and drove past the spot far enough so the signal weakened. They swung onto a parallel street and moved back.

"I bet it's that storage lot," said Bunch.

Over the low roofs of scattered small homes and cinder-block buildings that housed generator-repair shops, distributing companies, novelties wholesalers, was a sign for U-Rent-M Self Storage.

"Dave, two of them are at the U-Rent-M just off Federal north of Sixty-fourth. We can't see the main man."

"You want us to move in now?"

"Not yet. We're going closer. Maybe we can pick up something from our man's wire."

"Ten-four."

Martin was smart enough to delay his arrival, figuring that if Atencio and Vinny were going to be busted, they'd get hit just after they stopped at the storage bin.

"Pull into the parking lot of that RV place, Bunch." The locater bug hadn't moved and they could see both Vinny's Chevrolet and Atencio's Mustang parked at the end of one of the rows of garage doors that opened to the storage bins. Bunch fiddled with the antenna of the receiving unit while Devlin watched in the rearview mirrors. Vinny and Atencio began loading something from the trunk of Vinny's car into the open bin.

"I got him," said Bunch.

Vinny's voice came thinly out of the speaker. "When the hell's he supposed to get here?"

"Don't worry, man, he'll be here. Let's get this crap inside—we ain't got much time."

The voices gave way to the rustling crackle of hands busy at something. Then Vinny's voice again: "That it? You done?"

"Yeah. Pull that up there."

Silence.

"He's taking his fucking time."

Atencio's voice laughed something indecipherable.

"I just want to get it over with."

"Chill out. He's not going to leave this crap alone for long."

"Here comes the fucker. You set?"

"Yeah."

Bunch radioed Miller. "He's pulling in now. There's only one gate. You ready to move?"

"We're on our way."

"Remember, Dave, cover our man."

"I remember."

It happened quickly. Martin's Firebird crackled across the gravel as he coasted through the gate toward the two waiting cars. It stopped and the man got out and they heard Martin's voice distant on the speaker: "Everything okay?" Then Miller's unmarked sedan squealed through the gate, tires spraying dust and gravel in a hard slide to block the cars. Someone said, "Jesus Christ!" and Vinny's voice came loud: "What the hell! What the hell, Scotty—they followed your ass!" Four plainclothes officers leapt out of the rocking vehicle, guns drawn, as another voice shouted excitedly, "Get 'em up! Lift 'em, God damn you, or you're dog meat!"

Kirk and Bunch watched as the officers separated the three men and spread them over the hoods of the cars. Vinny's voice came again. "Take it easy, shitbird—ow!" The transmitter went dead and the three, arms shackled behind, were hustled into the police car. Then the vehicles pulled away and Bunch, too, drove to the station.

Miller was waiting in the Vice and Narcotics offices. "I put them in separate rooms, Bunch. There's the stuff." He pointed to the stack of plastic-wrapped bundles on a desk. One of them was open, and a small pile of white powder sat on waxed paper beside a bottle of liquid and an eyedropper. Behind it, covering two walls, rows of identification photographs pictured arrested prostitutes. One section was for women, another for female impersonators. Additional photographs showed the impersonators stripped of their disguises. A third panel was for homosexual prostitutes. Here and there red marker pen over a photo spelled *AIDS*.

"Any trouble?"

"Naw. It was sitting out waiting for us. It tests positive; it's a good bust."

Bunch eyed the stack of bags and whistled. "All that ninety percent?"

Miller, too, was impressed with the quantity. He should have been—it was one of the biggest hauls in V and N history. The swing of his leg as he sat on the corner of the desk and stared at the packets matched the satisfied nod of his head. "The lab will give us a breakout tomorrow. But I bet my badge we got us a kingpin. And we got him by the balls!"

"How's my man?"

"Uh? Oh, he's okay." The detective fished in his pocket. "Here's the wire. I pulled it when I patted him down. You know, sitting cheek-to-cheek in the same car with the others . . ."

"Thanks. We talk to him?"

Miller led them to the holding cells. Vinny, like the other two, was in isolation. He stood up from the single metal bench bolted to the bare wall. "It's about goddamn time. They get the stuff checked yet?"

188 · REX BURNS

"It's positive," said Miller.

"No shit, Dick Tracy. Where's Martin and Atencio?"

"Down the hall," said Bunch.

"You'll let Atencio go, right? That's the deal, right?"

Miller cocked an eye at Bunch.

"That's what I promised him, Dave. Atencio's only a mule. Martin's the one behind it all. Vinny thinks if we let both of them go, Martin won't know which one snitched."

Vinny nodded quickly. "Johnny'll turn state's, too. He told me. And he's not the one you want anyway."

Miller grunted. "He'll have to testify. You too."

"Yeah, he knows that. It's okay with me, too. Better cover."

"All right. I'll book the both of you and take statements—go through the motions, like." He led Vinny away to an empty desk and started filling in the paperwork. Another detective had already begun marking and registering the unopened packages.

Martin, alone in his cubicle, was handcuffed to an eyebolt anchored into the wall. He said nothing as Bunch and Devlin entered and told him who they were.

"You're facing twenty to thirty, Martin."

He shrugged as best he could against the pull of the cuffs. "We'll see. We'll see what my lawyer says."

"He'll say Kingpin Statute, Scotty. Twenty to thirty."

"Uh huh. Now I got something for you: I know who snitched. You tell Vinny he's dead meat."

Bunch pulled a locater transmitter from his pocket and held it up. "Here's your snitch, Scotty. A bug. Your car's been bugged for the last three weeks." The big man smiled widely. "You led the cops to it yourself."

The man stared hotly at Bunch, his straight hair hanging raggedly down over his collar and forehead.

"The cops are going to offer Vinny and Johnny a deal," Devlin said. "All they have to do is tell the truth and they both walk."

"Bullshit."

"Think they won't do that? What do they owe you?"

"They won't fink! They know what'll happen if they fink!"

Bunch snorted a laugh. "Yeah. They know. Here's what'll happen: You go to Canon City, they go on probation. The cops want you, Scotty, not them. They're just mules. The cops are willing to trade for testimony against you."

"You're all on your lonesome," agreed Devlin. "Unless you've got something to trade, too."

His eyes, a kind of muddy green, narrowed. "Like what?"

"Information."

"Screw that."

Bunch said, "We don't work for the cops. We work for Advantage Corporation. But the cops will listen to us on the charges. Maybe, with Mr. Reznick's help, the charges can be reduced."

"Who the hell is Reznick?"

"Your boss. The plant manager."

The eyes studied Bunch and Devlin. Finally Martin said, "Reduced to what? It's only possession."

"No. It's possession with intent to sell. No jury'll believe you brought in twenty kilos of ninety percent pure for your own recreational use, Scotty. You're under the Kingpin Statute, and Miller's hungry for your ass." Bunch smiled. "How's it feel to be a genuine kingpin?"

"And maybe," said Devlin, "the charges will be increased. Remember the kid who was murdered? What's your alibi for that night, Martin?"

"No you don't—"

"Yes, you son of a bitch, I do. Visser threatened us, and you and Tony carried out that threat. You two killed that boy, Scotty. Just like you said you would. Remember Visser? He swore out a deposition that you brought in Tony and you both went over there and killed the kid. Premeditated murder one, with aggravating circumstances. That's a death charge, Scotty. That's the big one."

"Hey, I didn't do that. I don't know nothing about that!"

"Cut the bullshit, Martin."

"I didn't—"

Bunch's large hands grabbed Martin's ears and lifted him to the end of the short chain and thudded the back of his head against the white concrete wall. He leaned over the grunting man. "You shit-for-brains, you're getting a deal! You're getting a fucking deal and you better take it!"

"You can't hurt me like this—I got rights! Guard!"

Bunch picked him up again. "We're not cops. You got no rights with us." He bounced the man again.

"Ow!"

"Everything all right in here?" A uniformed officer leaned through the door to look suspiciously at the three men.

"Tell the man, Martin. Tell him it's not all right. Tell him you want to talk to somebody in homicide."

Martin stared at the black policeman, his eyes wide and mouth open. But no sound came. Instead, he took a deep breath and chewed his lower lip and nodded. "It's fine. Fine."

Bunch smiled at the officer. "We're from down the hall in Vice and Narcotics."

The policeman grunted. "Getting pretty noisy out here."

"Thanks," Devlin said. "It'll be quiet now."

The heavy door with its rivets and tiny Plexiglas window closed again. Kirk gazed down at Martin, and he seemed to be a long distance away, as if bracketed in the sights of a rifle. "I don't want to give you a deal, Martin. I want you to fry. I want to hear your goddamn skin crackle like bacon." The man's eyes gazed hollowly back at Kirk. "A premeditated torture murder. There's no way you'll beat the death sentence on that, Scotty."

"It wasn't me!"

"We've got the deposition. As an accessory, you'll be just as dead."

Martin's Adam's apple bobbed. "What kind of deal?"

"We want Tony and the names of the people in the Pensacola

plant. You give them to us and maybe—just maybe—I'll talk to Reznick about lowering the charges."

A long minute. "What about—ah . . . the other. You know." He swallowed again. "I'm telling you the truth—it wasn't me!"

"Then you by God tell us who it was."

CHAPTER 21

Eventually, he did; in his eyes, justice was a series of deals, and what helped Martin was what was just. He repeated several times that he had not been the one to kill Newman, that he didn't know that's what Tony was going to do. "He said he was going to thump the guy a little. Nothing heavy, just a few thumps to find out what he knew. Me, I was lookout. Outside the door. We went over, the guy sees me through the peephole and opens the door, then Tony steps in. Next thing I hear is the music go loud."

"You didn't hear any screams?"

Martin shook his head, and his eyes moved away from Kirk's stare. "Later, Tony opened the door and told me to come in and help clean up. He'd taped the guy's mouth so he couldn't scream too loud. And there was all this fucking music real loud . . ."

Neither Kirk nor Bunch believed the man, but there was no evidence otherwise. When they got Tony, that scumbag might tell a different version and it would be up to the prosecutors to decide which was the best story to bring into court.

"Why'd he kill the kid? He didn't have to do that."

One of Martin's shoulders bobbed. "I don't know. Maybe

he flipped. Tony's got this thing about hurting people, I don't know. He did hard time in Joliet and some other place."

Tony was one of the Pensacola people, and Martin thought he was the one who put the organization together. He was also the one Martin telephoned after Chris came in with the story about selling cocaine in the factory. "An emergency number, you know? Something comes up, I call this number, somebody calls back, finds out what's the hang-up. Tony maybe takes care of it. Anyway, I told him about this guy wants to sell cocaine in the plant. Tony didn't believe it, but he says he'll come and scope it out because it was bad news anyway. Set up a meet, he told me, use a front, and he'd go along to look things over. So I told Eddie to meet with you people. Eddie and Tony. I never met the guy in person before. I don't know if that's his real name, even. Anyway, he goes along as driver. After the meet, we went over to talk to the guy. Newman. Find out what kind of scam is really going down."

"And you found out."

"Tony came out of the room and said you was company dicks and there wasn't nothing to worry about. We'd just lay low for a while. Keep our eyes open."

"And he said Chris was dead."

Martin looked down at his dusty work boots. "No. Not exactly. He just told me to come in and help clean up." He looked up. "I was along but I didn't know what was going down."

Bunch snorted. "And if you did, you'd have stopped it, right?"

Martin thought about that, then shook his head. "I don't think so. I don't think I could've." A deep breath. "You people going after him? You two?"

"Yeah."

The man shook his head. "Company dicks. You ain't got a chance."

The trick would be to grab Tony before he slid away. Martin would help them do that, though he didn't know it yet.

The Pensacola team was made up of three people. One was

a man Martin did time with in Menard, Illinois—the one who had brought him in on the deal, Stan Schuler. The second was somebody who worked with Schuler in the Pensacola plant, but Martin didn't know his name. The third was Tony, who had the contacts in Colombia or Panama and who ran the organization. "He's got three falls, so he stays behind things. But it's his scam, you know? His contacts and all."

"What about the dope on this end? Where do you send it?" Devlin asked.

Martin chewed at his lip. "You people haven't given me the Miranda, you know? You can't use none of this."

"I told you, we're not cops. But you help us, we help you. You don't help us, only God can help you." Bunch let a drop of spit fall to the concrete between his large shoes. "And He don't really give a shit, does He?"

"What do you do with the dope?" Devlin asked again.

"Take our cut and ship the rest on. We get ten percent of everything we sell, split it with Johnny and Vinny. Johnny gets three, Vinny gets two because he's the new guy. I keep five. We send the rest of the money back to Tony, and the rest of the dope we ship out to other Advantage docks. You know, the distribution points."

"You put it in canisters and send it that way?"

"Yeah."

"To who?"

"I don't know."

"Come on!"

"I don't. The only one who knows the whole layout is Tony. He set it up that way for security. He don't want nobody asking questions about the operation. I don't know who gets it. They don't know who sends it. All they know is a barrel comes in with the mark, they got a shipment in the bracing."

"What mark?"

"A number code. An extra line of numbers we stencil on the canister. They block it out when they get it and the canister goes back to Pensacola or wherever."

"How many points do you ship to?"

"Five docks. The number code I get tells me how to divide it up. Each dock has a number too, and however many times the number shows up, that's how many kilos I send."

Bunch looked at his notebook. "Dock eight gets four kilos from this load?"

Martin looked too. "Eight. A double number means double the kilos."

"Where's dock eight?"

"San Jose."

Devlin asked, "Are you the only people doing this?"

"Working for Tony, you mean? Yeah. There's only one shipping crew in the warehouse. Nobody else handles the canisters."

Bunch propped a foot on the metal bench. "The vice dicks'll want to have the names of the people you sell to around here. We don't give a damn, but they'll want them. You'll help your case by telling Miller all about them. Hear me?"

"I hear."

He heard something else, too: what would happen to him if he in any way tried to warn the people in Pensacola about Devlin and Bunch. Then they turned him over to Dave Miller for the paperwork and stopped at the Brewery Bar for dinner and a couple beers. And to talk over who would make the trip to Pensacola.

It was Devlin. Bunch's job was to sit on Martin and make certain he did his part. Besides, he had Humphries and Mitsuko to watch over, too. Dave Miller gave Kirk a contact in the Pensacola Police Department's vice and narcotics section if he needed it, and Devlin telephoned Reznick at home to bring him up to date. The manager was happy to hear that Martin had been taken out. But he wanted to be certain the company name didn't get splashed in the press. "You'll be working undercover in Pensacola, too?"

"No. We don't have time for that." Even if Martin kept quiet, the word on his bust would get there in a few days at most.

"Well, listen, Kirk. Stewart's adamant that none of this reflect ill on the company—"

"I understand. I'll try to pick them up off company property. Just as we did with Martin."

Reznick told Devlin the name of the plant director—Malcolm Colby—and offered to call first thing in the morning to tell him that Kirk was on his way.

Bunch explained to Miller what he wanted Martin to do. The cop wasn't all that eager to let Bunch violate procedures with his prize catch, but finally agreed on condition that Martin wasn't to go anywhere without a guard. "I can fix it with the chief," Miller said. "But you got to give me a couple hours' lead."

"I won't be able to, Dave. Kirk's on the other end and he'll set up the call for whenever he can. It's not like he'll be calling the shots. You know that."

Miller leaned back and looked at Bunch across the glass top of his gray metal desk. Its surface hadn't been wiped in a long time, and circles of old coffee stains and shreds of eraser and cigarette ash showed up against the family photographs, lists of telephone numbers, and emergency procedures pressed flat by the glass. "You want to keep him the full seventy-two, that it?"

"Hey, it'll save the county money." Bunch added, "And this is a big operation. You saw that. Twenty kilos of pure every shipment, maybe more. You know and I know the chief'll want to break something like that."

Miller stared at his desk and then nodded. The pink scalp on top of his head showed through his lank blond hair. He'd already asked Bunch if his hair looked thinner since the last time they talked. Bunch lied and said no and asked him who wanted fat hair anyway. "We still have to use an escort. I know Chief Pozner's going to insist on that."

"No problem. That way, I can take care of my other chores."

The result was that Martin was moved into his own apartment

under guard, sleeping on a couch shoved against one wall of the tiny living room where they could keep an eye on him. Any of the small rooms he went into, he went accompanied. And when he went to the bathroom, the door was always open to the sound of his stream or to his pink, bony knees. He ate things that came out of cardboard boxes.

If Scotty wasn't happy, neither were the cops who rotated every eight hours to guard the prisoner while they waited for Devlin's telephone call from Florida. At least everyone was equally unhappy, and what was more democratic than that? Bunch was reminded of when he had worn a uniform and guarded prisoners and had wondered what the difference really was between the restraint the criminals were under and that of the cop. The answer once again reinforced his decision to leave the department.

The "other chores" Bunch had mentioned to Miller included sporadic surveillance on Truman and protection for Humphries. The Truman case had to wait—along with the cramped Subaru—because there were only so many slices of himself to go around. Besides, it might be better to let that foxy lady think they'd dropped the case. Humphries, on the other hand, wouldn't wait. Miss Watanabe called the next morning.

"I don't know how he got so close to the house, Mr. Bunchcroft. It came through the front room window. I called Roland and he told me to lock myself in the bathroom and call you right away. He wants you to please come right now."

"Do you have your revolver?"

"Yes." She added in a small voice, "I'm afraid, Mr. Bunchcroft."

"Call 911 and tell the police what happened. I'm on my way out."

He gave the officer guarding Martin his mobile phone number in case he needed it. Scotty asked if Bunch would bring back a *TV Guide* so he could keep up with what was happening on the tube. "I mean, at least in jail they got a dayroom with a newspaper and maybe *People* magazine. Here it's just the god-damn TV, and all I can find is reruns."

"You want a woman, too?"

"Hey, I'm trying to help you people out. A lousy magazine ain't too much to ask, you know!"

"You're trying to help yourself out, Martin. I'll see if I remember."

The day officer, leather belts creaking with boredom, added, "Try hard."

When Bunch sidled cautiously through the front door of Humphries' house, he listened for any sounds. There was the faint warble of a meadowlark beyond the tree line and the sigh of wind through the screened windows. He called out Mitsuko's name but got no answer. With weapon drawn, he inspected the rooms until he came to the master bedroom. He knocked on the closed bathroom door. "Mitsuko? It's me—Bunch."

The door clicked and, clutching the pistol in the white fingers of both hands, she came out. "Is he here?"

"Nobody's here, Mitsi. The sheriff's officers haven't come yet?"

"No."

Bunch carefully set the pistol aside and called in to cancel the 911 alert. "Show me what happened."

She took him to the living room. A trail of glass led from the broken window and glistened across the long white couch and onto the carpet with its raised geometrical border and Chinese characters carved in the center. A smooth rock about the size of a fist lay near the characters. It had scratched the leg of the low coffee table when it hit. Aiming back through the window, Bunch could see the thicket of pine where the man could have stood to throw it.

"The sensor field wasn't on?"

"No. Roland only turns it on at night."

"And you didn't see anyone?"

"No. I was in the kitchen and heard the noise. I came out

here and saw the broken window and the rock. I ran to the bedroom and got the pistol and locked myself in the bathroom."

"Did you hear any noises? Prowler?"

"No. Only when you came." She held out a wrinkled piece of paper. "This was with the rock."

Bunch opened it up. "It's Japanese. I can't read it."

"It says, 'Do what is right before it is too late for you.' "

He looked at the small woman, whose eyes were still on the slightly grimy slip of paper. "What's it mean?"

She shrugged. "I am to go back to Japan. Or be killed."

"It's from the *yojimbo?*"

"Oh yes."

"Your father wants you to come back or he's going to have you killed, that it?"

"Yes. My father."

"And despite that, you don't want to go back."

"No."

"What happens when Humphries gets tired of all this?"

Her head shook once, almost a spasmodic twitch, and she took a deep breath and straightened up. "He's not tired of me yet."

"I wish I knew what your game was."

"As I told you before—to stay alive."

CHAPTER 22

As the plane's ventilation system started pumping local air and the passengers crowded the aisle to disembark, an unfamiliar humidity wrapped around Kirk like flannel. Outside the aircraft too, the air felt sticky under a sun that had nothing of autumn or high altitude in it. But Kirk's strongest impression was of the flat earth paralleling the horizons, a lush, gently rolling green to the north, and on the south the line of the Gulf against a sky burned pale with glare. While the plane circled for its landing Devlin had made out strips of barrier islands off the Gulf shore and a stubby freighter riding at anchor in the brown water of Pensacola Bay. But now there was little chance to rubberneck. The traffic surrounding the airport was heavy, and the roads he'd marked on the Triple A map turned out to be a lot easier to follow on paper than they were in fact. Twelfth Avenue to Fairfield to Pace. Then south a few miles to the industrial area near the shipyards. When he finally turned the rental car into the grid of short streets serving the factories and chemical tanks, his shirt was damp with sweat despite the car's air conditioning, and the industrial fumes that stung his sinuses seemed to leave an oily film on his skin.

This Advantage plant was a series of sharp roof peaks marching like a saw blade across half a city block. A railroad spur holding a line of tank cars ran down the foot of the corrugated-steel walls. A large pair of smokestacks rose toward spongy cumulus clouds whose shadow occasionally lifted the weight of sun but carried the heft of rain. Mr. Colby's office was in a corner of the third and topmost floor and had a view across a point of pine-and oak-shaded houses to the bay and Santa Rosa Island. Out over the Gulf, the sky was dotted with airplanes from the Naval Air Station. If he craned to look past Colby, Kirk could make out the massive gray shadow of an aircraft carrier looming over pale yellow buildings on another point of land.

"I have the employment records of the man Mr. Reznick mentioned, Mr. Kirk. I find it extremely hard to believe this sort of thing is going on in my plant."

"Three people at the other end were arrested yesterday afternoon, Mr. Colby. That's the name one of them gave us."

"Yes, of course. There's no arguing with that fact. Still, my plant security . . ." Colby stood taller than Kirk but weighed only half as much. His head seemed mostly bony jaw and large nose. Devlin took a few seconds to realize that the man's blue eyes goggled not from surprise but because of the thick lenses in his horn-rimmed glasses. "What do you propose to do about all this?"

"You can have him arrested on a warrant from Colorado. That, however, involves the police and a lot of legal paperwork and might bring the company name into the papers—something I've been instructed to avoid if at all possible."

"Yes. Certainly. We don't want that." His long fingers played with an ornate medallion which served as a paperweight and said something about a Fiesta of Five Flags Award. A row of photographs reminded him that he had a wife and four children.

"The quietest way would be to fire him," said Devlin.

"Would that be punishment enough? After all, Schuler is a criminal."

Kirk agreed. "I suspect he and his partner have a good-size nest egg tucked away. So losing their jobs wouldn't hurt them. It would protect you, however."

"Well, it just doesn't seem right to almost condone . . ." Colby's eyes glanced at the photographs and he said earnestly, "Drugs are a very serious problem for the youth of this nation, Mr. Kirk."

Tell me about it, thought Kirk. "Why don't you let me pick up Schuler and his partner and talk to them off company grounds? I'll try to find out if they're working alone or if there's a larger organization behind them. Then we can turn them over to the Drug Enforcement Agency. That way, we can find out what we need to know, and even if there's not enough for a case against them, they'll have a record with the feds. Frankly, Mr. Colby, I think that's the best we'll be able to do and still keep the company name out of the press."

Colby knew how Stewart felt about the company name. And he also knew that Stewart liked to give his plant managers plenty of slack to run their operations. Enough slack, even, to hang themselves. He sighed. This was the kind of problem Colby hated: the ones that came in already so tangled that he couldn't pick the threads up at the beginning. How many times had he told his staff, "Come to me at the first sign of trouble"? It was so much easier to correct problems early on.

Pushing one of the buttons on a metal panel made to look like burled wood, he said, "Mrs. Swearingen, will you have Mr. Mills come up to my office right away, please?" He explained to Kirk, "Randy Mills is our head of security. He'll go with you to pick up Schuler."

He was an ex–sheriff's officer, Mills told Kirk, who had been turned out in a past election when the office changed hands. Devlin was to call him Randy. "I made the mistake of being ambitious, you know? Became the old sheriff's number-one sidekick. New sheriff said he couldn't trust me, so here I am— getting rich in the private sector." He, too, was tall, with straight black hair and skin dark less from the sun than from a trace of

Cherokee or Seminole. He waited until they were off the executive floor before pumping Kirk. "So what you after down here, Devlin?"

Kirk told the man as much as he needed to know.

"Gawd damn! Right here in my plant?" His forefinger scratched at the corner of his mouth where a small scar made a pale line. "Old lady Colby just about pissed on his shoelaces when you told him, didn't he?"

"He wasn't happy."

"Probably thinks I'm not worth shit at this job now." Mills glanced at Kirk.

"We found the other end by accident. We were looking for a guy selling grass and came up with this operation."

"Yeah, well, still it don't make me look good. I'm supposed to know what goes on in this place and take care of it. Colby don't like no trouble at all."

That was Mills's worry. "I'd like to do this quietly—nothing for the newspapers to get hold of. And I want to talk to them before we bring in the DEA."

"Oh, yeah. We'll do that, all right. And I damn well plan to talk to the security guards for that section, too."

"Not until after we're through, though, right?"

The man glanced at him again, understanding. "Right." Another worry that was all his: possible leaks and collusion in his own section. Mills lengthened his stride, a red tinge marking the back of his neck. They clanked down a metal staircase and through a fire door to the main floor of a vast shipping room. Pallets of boxed goods were stacked almost to the ceiling, and a forklift ground back and forth in the shadowy aisles. Its backup horn was an intermittent, shrill tweet. Mills called to a black man in tan overalls. "Heyo, Johnson—where's Schuler at?"

"Coffee break."

The employee lounge for this corner of the sprawling factory was recessed from the main floor and marked by a pair of worn Naugahyde couches and a coldly lit line of vending machines. Half a dozen men in tan coveralls sat and drank coffee and talked. They fell silent and wary when Mills and Kirk walked up.

"Schuler, I see you a minute? Fella got emergency message for you."

A short man with cropped, graying hair set down his steaming Styrofoam cup and stood, eyes widening slightly as he looked from Mills to Devlin. Quiet and frowning, he followed them away from the lounge and around the corner into an alley between boxes.

Equally silent, almost lazily, Mills turned on his heel and drove a fist into the older man's middle. He doubled over with a whoosh of coffee-smelling breath. Quickly Mills twisted Schuler's arm behind his back and yanked up to lever the man's shoulder against his neck. "You and Mr. Kirk, here, going to have a talk, Schuler. You going to tell him all about your little cocaine delivery service. Ain't you?"

"Ahhh—I—"

He yanked again. "Who else you working with, Schuler? Name 'em!"

"I don't—"

That was as far as he got before Mills levered the shoulder again.

Schuler's voice was a strangled, hurting whine. "Hall . . . shipping . . . Keith Hall . . ."

Mills shoved the man toward Kirk and nodded his head at the wide door leading into the yard. "I know that little butterball. You take this piece of shit on out, Devlin. Blue van out there. Says 'Security.' I'll fetch Hall."

Schuler didn't speak until he and Kirk were in the windowless back of the van and squatting on the narrow folding bench that ran down one side. "You—ah . . . you with the police?"

"Company security."

He massaged the twisted muscles in his shoulder. "What you and him going to do?"

"It's not what we're going to do, Schuler. It's what you're going to do: talk to us."

A salt-and-pepper scatter of whiskers showed up darkly against the paleness of his face and he probed his tongue at the corner of his dry mouth.

"We've already got Scotty Martin. That's how we found out about you."

"Oh."

Kirk let him think about that. The sound of boots on gravel came up to the van, and the back door burst open. A fat-faced man sprawled across the metal floor, and Mills followed, yanking savagely at the man's collar to jam him on the end of the bench.

"You keep your fucking mouth shut, Hall—I heard enough from you!" Handcuffs clicked into place as Hall and Schuler were locked to a strut. Mills told Kirk to sit between the two and keep them apart. "I'll drive, Devlin. Either one these shitheads opens his mouth you close it hard." He jerked a nod at Hall. "Especially that there fat turd."

They swung out of the factory compound and across a small bridge, taking a wide avenue bordered by stubby palm trees and the green of a well-kept golf course. Traffic lights periodically halted them among a tangle of hot cars. In the closed van, Kirk felt sweat start to run in little trickles down his back as the humidity began to stifle him. After almost half an hour, Mills turned the van off the highway onto a sandy road that ran in two gray ruts among pin oak and scrawny slash pines. They passed a tar-paper shack where two white-haired children—a boy and a girl—looked up from playing in a patch of shady sand to watch the van rattle by. Then they branched again into denser growth thickened by clumps of palmetto. Kirk smelled the rankness of old grass mixed with the odor of brackish water. The van stopped. Mills went around to the back doors. They opened to a narrow arm of still, dark water and a marshy shore covered with tall grass and tree snags bearded with Spanish moss. Beneath the grass, the gray sand merged imperceptibly with the water. The abandoned clearing had been used as a dump, and Kirk could see bedsprings and tin cans rusting to a dull red and shreds of cloth and stuffing ground into dark blotches of old oil. A jaybird squawked loudly and flew across the bayou—a flutter of iridescent blue against the silent, hot green.

"Well, Devlin, which one you want to start with?"

"Schuler."

Mills tossed Kirk a key for the cuffs. "Right. We'll be back for you, Hall. Wait for us, hear?"

Schuler's first words were, "You can't do this!"

Mills hit him in the stomach. "Hell, boy, it's already done!" He winked at Kirk over the sweat-stained back of the doubled and gasping man. "I got friends in the s.o. and PPD. They ain't going to believe shit he says." As soon as Schuler began to breathe more regularly, he hit him again. "Did this all the time in the sheriff's office. Got downright old after a while." Schuler stayed down this time—knees to chest, and arms trying to hide his paper-white face. Mills hauled him up by the shirt. "We got all day. All night, too. Whenever you're ready, just start singing."

He hit him again, harder, this time digging the blade of his knuckles up under the older man's ribs at the side of his soft paunch. Schuler doubled over again and heaved a lump of puke and skittered around in the dirt and sandspurs hunting for his breath. Mills sat on a fallen tree trunk to watch him. "It'll take a few minutes," he told Kirk. "I should have thought to stop and buy us some soda pop." He looked over his shoulder at the fat-faced man who peered from the dark of the van door. "You watching this, Hall? Good—you just sit tight. We'll get to you, okay?"

"Can you hear me, Schuler?" asked Kirk.

The gray and black stubble of hair jerked a nod.

"Who's Tony?"

The head froze and the man's grunting paused.

"Mr. Kirk here asked you a question, Schuler."

"He'll . . . he'll kill me."

"Gawd damn! Gawd Jesus damn!" Mills pulled the man up by the pectorals and jammed his face against Schuler's eyes. "He'll kill you? He'll kill you! Gawd damn you, boy, you more afraid of somebody else than you are of me? You that goddamn dumb?" Schuler's fist plunged wrist-deep under the man's ribs and Mills dropped him to stand with a boot on the cuffed wrists and strike again at the man's stomach. "You really that god-damned dumb?"

"Tell us about it, Schuler. Everything."

The head jerked.

Mills snorted and leaned over him waiting. His shadow fell across Schuler like a dark threat and the curled man clenched tighter. "Well shit, man, you want to talk or not? Get up and talk!"

Schuler scuttled back and flopped to his knees and, wincing against the pain of his ribs, grunted himself upright. "I can't . . . He'll—"

Mills's boot caught him under the jaw and snapped his head back in a short jab. A thread of bloody spittle swung in a bright, crimson arc through the sunlight. Across the bayou, the jay squawked twice and was silent.

Mills's tense voice was gentle now, almost pleading as he bent over the moaning figure. "It's hot out here, Schuler. And I'm starting to get pissed. You don't want to get me pissed, Schuler. You really don't want that, now."

The man said something.

"What? Talk up, boy!"

"Pierson. Tony Pierson."

Mills sighed and leaned back from him. "All right. That's good. Now you just let it all hang out."

He did, words mushy and slurred through the bloody spittle. Once, a shard of tooth hung on his lip, a pink speck of bone, before dropping into the sandy weeds. Three of them were in on it at this end. They didn't want to split the money any more than that. Pierson had started them off by borrowing from Schuler to invest in a sure thing, a load of coke that one of his—Tony's—contacts was eager to sell. Schuler came up with the idea of shipping the dope out to his buddy in Denver, Scotty Martin. He was a cellmate from the medium-security prison up in Menard. Pierson liked the idea and improved on it.

He had the contacts. He made arrangements for delivery, usually from a freighter coming into Pensacola, Mobile, or New Orleans. Schuler didn't know, but he thought it was usually brought in aboard sealed cargo carriers, the kind that customs agents had trouble searching. "That's what gave me the idea about shipping it to Denver to sell. There's so much stuff around here that the price is bad. Out there, an eight-hundred-dollar ounce goes for fourteen, sixteen hundred. And we don't have to worry about all the heat that goes with selling it." At first, Scotty marketed it all, but he didn't want to move as much as Tony wanted to send. So they came up with the idea of opening up markets in other Advantage sites. "Low profile, like. Cops don't get too excited that way. So we spread it around and each guy's got a quota to sell and gets a cut. Nothing too big but everything steady, you know? It adds up." Gradually, the organization expanded as Pierson and Schuler made contacts in other Advantage locations. Hall was brought in because he ran the crew inspecting the factory's sealed drums. All they had to do was put it inside the Styrofoam bracing on a particular unit, pressurize the drum, and seal it. Then they stenciled it with a number code that said how many kilos were enclosed—just like the accounting office. Then they shipped it.

"What grade is it when it leaves here?"

"Pure. Sometimes eighty, sometimes ninety percent. It changes, so I don't know for sure. Tony's the one who knows, but it's pretty pure."

"Where's it shipped to from Denver?"

"Seven, eight places. It depends on the market. Tony set that up, too. He went around the country to the other Advantage shipping points and got some of his buddies hired on. Took a year, maybe more, but he got his people in the shipping rooms."

"For ten percent of the dope?"

"Yeah. Ten percent of whatever they're supposed to sell."

"Where's he now?"

"Tony? I don't know. Home, I guess. We don't meet too often except on business."

"Where's home?"

"Santa Rosa Island—just down from Pensacola Beach."

"How do I get there?"

He shook his head. "Tony don't meet people there. I never been there, even."

"Where do you meet?"

"Here and there. Bars. You know. Sometimes old Fort Pickens. He likes that place."

"I want him for murder."

"He killed somebody?" Schuler didn't sound surprised.

"Yeah. I want him and you're going to help me."

Kirk thought it might take some more convincing, but Schuler was broken. He only nodded and looked sicker. They dragged him back to the van and pulled Hall out. The front of his pants grew dark and he said, "Please don't please don't please don't," until Mills hit him. He told Kirk it was just to let Hall know it wasn't so bad—"Might help make a man out of him instead of a fucking crawdad." Hall, once his breathing was back, told them everything fast before Mills could hit him again. It corroborated Schuler's story.

The ride back was hot and silent and weary.

They stopped at a pay phone in a shopping center before reaching the factory. Schuler called Pierson to tell him he had a visitor from Denver who claimed he intercepted the last shipment. This man wanted to cut himself in on the operation and had given him—Schuler—one hour to make up his mind. If it was a no, the man said that would be the last shipment anybody sent through the Advantage network. So what should he tell the man?

Schuler tilted the earpiece so Kirk could listen. The line was silent, and in the hot telephone hood, Kirk smelled the sour odor of Schuler's vomit. Finally a tinny voice, stalling for time to think, told Schuler to bring the man to the Sandcrab Bar at six tonight. Shaking his head, Kirk whispered the reply.

"He says he'll meet only with me. Alone and in a quiet place."

Another silence. "How do we know he's got the goddamn shipment?"

Schuler swallowed. "He found out about me, he says. And he says to call Martin."

"Why the hell didn't that son of a bitch Martin call me?"

"He can't. Somebody's sitting on him in Denver, this fella says. If the deal don't go through, he says, Martin's history and so's our organization."

"Shit!" The voice came back. "I can't call Martin before seven to check this out—there's an hour's difference." Another silence. "You tell that son of a bitch you'll meet him at Fort Pickens at eight tonight. You know where?"

"By the old part? Where the wall's broken down?"

"Yeah. Same place. Eight o'clock. You tell that fucker to be there at eight. And then you stay the hell away." The telephone clicked dead.

CHAPTER 23

Bunch had forgotten about Devlin's call to Yoshi Kamakura until he heard the man's heavily accented voice, delayed by a couple million miles of satellite relay. "Watanabe Hiroge—the man is very rich. Very important."

Kamakura was being formal, the way he usually got when he made a report. Bunch, glancing at the wall clock and antsy to get over to Martin's apartment, silently urged the Japanese private investigator to hurry. But of course he didn't; it would have been impolite. "He is a very respected businessman. Also active in politics."

Yoshi was odd that way. Bunch still remembered the World Association of Detectives convention in Singapore. In the ornate hotel's gymnasium, the little man had taught him a couple of nice moves, complete with a formal apology for knocking Bunch on his ass. Yoshi was a good drinker, too—he would get totally shitfaced with you at night and then the next morning act like it never happened. Devlin shrugged it off and said it was part of the Japanese culture. But Bunch tended to be a little irritated by all those manners, and he couldn't help letting the irritation slip into his voice. "I know that, Yoshi. What I don't know—and what I'm trying to find out—is about his daughter. Watanabe Mitsuko. Is her old man really trying to make a hit on her and her round-eye boyfriend?"

"Her father is not so very old, yes? All the more remarkable that he is so successful and has moved upwards in his company so quickly, Bunch-u. Almost making bad manners. But he is very intelligent, so it is okay."

Bunch sighed. Yoshi would make his report the way Yoshi made reports: detailed and in order. There followed a brief lecture on the stately progression of corporate careers in Japan and the honored social position successful businessmen held in the national consciousness. "Very much like famous generals from the war time, yes?" Yoshi was an Okinawan whose attitude toward the purer Japanese shifted between ironic criticism and genuine awe. Finally he mentioned, almost in passing, that Watanabe Mitsuko was safe and sound and attending a university in Tokyo.

"What's that? She's in Tokyo?"

"He has only one daughter. Mitsuko. She is a student of marine biology."

"But there's a woman here who claims she's Watanabe Mitsuko."

Yoshi was too polite to contradict Bunch. But he did repeat what his agent discovered: "The daughter of Watanabe-san is presently enrolled at Tokyo University. She has no serious boyfriend, Occidental or otherwise. She is attending classes. She has not left Tokyo."

"Well, who the hell could this be? She's Japanese, she talks a lot about Watanabe, she claims to be his daughter, and she says Watanabe wants to kill her for shacking up with a round-eye. And by God, someone sure as hell has been trying to kill them!"

A few seconds of silence. "Let me see what I can discover, Bunch-u. I will call back quickly, yes?"

How long that would be, Bunch couldn't guess. But the case of Mitsi whoever had to be kept on hold while he sat on Scotty Martin and they waited for Devlin's call. When his beeper finally told him he had an incoming call, he used Martin's telephone to dial the answering service. Martin and the uniformed officer, sucking on a can of beer while he watched afternoon cartoons on television, both looked up. Devlin's voice sounded slightly fuzzy as he told Bunch to expect to hear from Pierson in an hour or so. "How's Martin holding up?"

"He can't play cribbage worth a damn," said Bunch. "He's almost as bad as you."

"He understands what to say?"

Bunch glanced at Martin, who was staring at him. "He knows what he'd better say. This Pierson guy going for it?"

"We have a meet for after he talks to Martin. If he believes Martin, he'll show up. If not, we stand a good chance of losing him."

Bunch spoke loudly enough for the staring man to hear clearly. "If Martin doesn't convince him—if we lose the son of a bitch because Martin doesn't convince him—then we hang the murder rap on him. It's his ass or Pierson's." Bunch added more quietly, "Watch your back, pardner."

"Thanks."

Bunch eyed the man wearing the county's wrinkled orange jumpsuit. "You heard that, Scotty? I told him you'll do your part."

"I said I'd do it."

The cop belched and crumpled the beer can, banking it into the trash basket. "When's the call coming?"

"When does he usually call you?"

Martin's shoulders bobbed. "Five forty-five, six. It's after I get home from work. But it's always Schuler. I don't hear from Tony. Just Schuler."

"It'll be Tony this time. Don't fuck up, Scotty."

"I know the story!"

They waited, Bunch looking from time to time at the officer's watch. The cartoon figures gave way to the bright and cheery chatter of the early local news and a row of faces that took turns smiling at the cameras across a wide desk. Weather had just smiled at Sports, who was saying something about the Bronco injury report, when the telephone rang. Bunch turned the set down and motioned for Martin to answer.

"Yeah? Yeah, that's me." Martin nodded and started to turn away, but Bunch's large hand steered his shoulders around to face the two waiting men. "Yeah, he's right. No, the guy's right here, Tony. No, he ain't kidding . . . I don't know, man. All I know is here they are . . ." He put his hand over the phone. "He wants to talk to you. I think the crazy fucker thinks I'm trying to rip him off."

Bunch took the telephone. "We got your shit, Tony baby. And you heard the deal. Now hear this. . . ."

He held up the telephone and squeezed Martin's neck so he could gurgle into the mouthpiece, "Tony—do it—"

"I better hear the right thing from my man, Tony. You know what I mean?"

The line stayed open for a long couple of seconds and then clicked into silence.

"Jesus, you didn't have to squeeze so hard!" Martin rubbed at the red patches on his neck.

Bunch gathered up his jacket and started turning off lights. "You were convincing, Scotty. A real actor." The cop drained another beer and tried a hook shot that missed the trash basket. They left the can lying there as they led Martin back to county jail.

Schuler gave Pierson's address to Devlin: a street called Ensenada Siete on the gulf side of the island. Mills dropped Kirk off at his car before taking Schuler and Hall back.

"Can you keep these two out of sight until after eight tonight?"

"Hell, I can keep these two out of sight forever if I have to. Right, boys?"

Their worried silence and Mills's barking laugh were carried away in the van.

Devlin had a slight headache and several hours to enjoy it

before meeting Pierson. The headache was a reminder that his stomach was on Denver time and his only meal of the day had been the miniaturized, minced, and microwaved breakfast served on the airplane. With that thought, he found interest in the restaurant signs beside the highway: Holmes Plantation House, the Bar-B-Q Pit, Tahitian House, Marina Restaurant. Swinging onto the bridge that spanned the flat waters of Pensacola Bay, Kirk let the stop-and-go traffic pulse him across to Gulf Breeze and more signs for seafood. Below the newer concrete spans ran the old bridge, now a fishing pier. Even this late in the season, scattered figures stared down into the cloudy waters, their fishing rods tilted at ready angles. At the end of the Bay Bridge, a sign for Flounder's Chowder and Ale House pulled him out of traffic and into the dim, air-conditioned odor of frying fish. Colorado had a lot of fine things: mountains, skiing, unbounded prairies and high, narrow valleys. It even had Denver, both John and the city. But it didn't have seafood. If this was going to be his last meal, he might as well pig out on something he couldn't get back home. But it wasn't going to be his last meal. That was only a joke, he told himself. Sick, maybe, but a joke nonetheless. And looking over the menu, Kirk found that his appetite wasn't the least threatened by that thought.

Freshly caught flounder, mullet, red snapper; crab cakes, oysters, fillets of pompano and red drum . . . As he slowly drove away from the restaurant Devlin formed vague thoughts of opening a branch office of Kirk and Associates somewhere on the Gulf Coast. But if he was here all the time, perhaps even the seafood would become stale. And it was too good for that to happen.

A toll bridge led across Santa Rosa Sound to the barrier island itself. Devlin was surprised to see the patches of oak trees and scattered pines rooted on the sound side of the narrow strip of sand. The Gulf Beach, when he finally glimpsed it, stung his eyes. An endless line of brilliant white faded into hazy glare shot with the gleam of surf from blue-green water. The highway branched east and west, the latter toward Fort Pickens and the former to Navarre Beach. He turned that way past a series of streets with Spanish names. The land quickly became dunes anchored with sea oats and palmetto. Ahead, the road surface seemed to sink beneath water as heat waves erased the distance. Lining the gulf side, stark condominiums shimmered in the glare and taunted the next big hurricane.

Ensenada Siete was a small cul de sac leading through the dunes almost to the Gulf. Pierson's address was one of a cluster of condos that overlooked the white sand and crashing surf beyond. Kirk slowly turned past, trying to locate a place for surveillance. But everything was open to sun and wind and eyes. A battery of signs warned tourists that all this was private property. Across the island on the sound side, he found a place to pull off, then strolled over to the gleaming white gulf side and along surf-packed sand until he spotted Pierson's house. Trying to look touristy in an open shirt and rolled-up pants, Devlin sat and studied the restless waters of the Gulf with binoculars. The sun, low as it was in the sky, began to burn his skin red. Occasionally, he aimed the binoculars at the house, but saw nothing. It was as if the building were empty and the large windows, covered with drapes, already closed for winter. Strollers passed, searching for glinting shells in the ebb of surf or racing happy dogs through ropes of sea spume. Others, isolated in the crash of waves and the hiss of foam, simply stared out to sea. The constant wind, hot at first, began to chill as his skin burned, and the humid smell of salt spray in the air mingled with the occasional rank whiff of a dead pelican tossed somewhere beyond one of the grassy dunes.

Looking back at the house, Kirk noticed that one of the curtains had been drawn open. His binoculars showed a light and airy living room and the corner of a rattan couch. A blur moved quickly across the lens and disappeared: Pierson or someone walking back and forth. A moment later, a girl stood briefly in the doorway and gazed through the screen at the water. Early to mid twenties, blond, tanned, wearing a burnt-orange bikini bra and flowered wrap around her legs. Then she turned and disappeared.

Devlin walked slowly up the dunes and paused at the top to put on his shoes and survey the condo. The garage, now open, showed a flame-orange Buick convertible and a new black motorcycle detailed with orange pinstriping. At the end of the street, he took a couple of telephoto shots of the vehicles and their license plates. Then he drove west into the lowering sun.

Fort Pickens is part of the Gulf Islands National Seashore. A small entrance building rises lonely beside the flat tar road. A sign posts the hours that the facilities are open and states that the entrance fee is three dollars. But no gate closed the road, and since it was after hours, no fee was collected. Dunes of white sand lifted a few feet above the wind-flattened grasses. Larger clumps of sculpted brush here and there marked both the old World War II artillery bunkers and the direction of the prevailing winds. Occasional wooden signs identified landmarks and recreation areas—"Battery 234 W W II Six-Inch Shield Gun," "Camp Ground Store," "Amphitheater," "Park Head-quarters." The Civil War fort itself was a sprawl of blocks and angles that seemed to seek protection from the ceaseless wind by shouldering itself down into the loose white sand. A pair of bottle-shaped cannons marked the main walk from the parking lot, and a crumbling corner of dark red brick walls rose stark and barren from the empty, treeless flats. In the late sunlight, the walls seemed sharply etched against the sky. The wind sighed vacantly across black gunports. Devlin's tourist brochure said the fort had been built in the early 1830s as one of a cluster of gun sites guarding the entrance to Pensacola Bay. The Army Corps of Engineers erected it using some twenty-one million bricks and an uncounted number of contracted slaves. Devlin figured that made it something of a model for pork barrel projects. Under fire during the Civil War, the fort was later used as a prison for Geronimo and his family, and occupied by coastal gunners during World War II. Now it entertained tourists. And served as a meeting place for a killer.

Schuler had described the corner of the fort where Pierson wanted to meet. Kirk traced it out on the self-guided tour map. The channel side away from the parking lot was hidden by the mass of the fort itself from the visitor information center and museum, both closed for the night. Across a ripple of sand and carefully tended sea pines, the main road circled toward a cluster of modern buildings that held the snack bar and public toilets. Beyond that, darkening with late-afternoon shadows, lay the channel between bay and gulf, the next island, and the low, rolling woods of the mainland beyond. He could feel the day's trapped heat radiate from the crumbly, stained brick, and somewhere in the distance an outboard motor droned mosquito-like over a lull in the wind. One, two silhouetted figures, tiny and still, watched their surf rods and the pattern of currents that wrinkled the channel's waters. But the fort itself—the block of inner buildings and the brick outer walls—and the low, scrubby wind-sculpted pines near it were deserted.

Pierson would most likely come from the parking lot up the concrete walk. It led past the brick casemates with their roped-off sections and signs warning Danger. Devlin walked the area, familiarizing himself with it and listening to his steps echo from the low, ovenlike casemates and the newer gray concrete superstructure that once housed the mortars and cannons mounted for the Spanish-American War. The cool shade of rifle bays and living quarters gaped darkly on a parade ground packed by feet long dead. Sandy paths worn through the sparse grass showed where living feet toured the silent walls. Kirk finally nosed out an angle of grainy and pitted brick that sheltered him from the wind, and settled down to wait.

The sun, barred with a streak of clouds blowing in from the Gulf, was a finger span above the horizon when he heard the clatter of a stone kicked by a shoe. Pierson hadn't come the way Devlin thought he would. Instead, he apparently circled the long way around the battery foundation in the center of the fort, surveying the area, trying to find out if only one man waited for him. Kirk couldn't see him, but he sensed the man search the shadows and angles of the parapet. Devlin moved into the open and waited. A figure picked its way across the low domes of the brick casemates, occasionally looking over the wall and down the twenty or so feet to the sand and marsh grass below. Then it turned toward the bastion where Kirk stood.

"Pierson?"

The man halted and stared. He was clean-shaven, but thick sideburns dropped well below his ears, and his hair lifted long and straight in the wind. "You know me?" Lean, with narrow hips and wide shoulders, he wore denims and burnt-orange deck shoes stained with oil. A dark T-shirt showed both muscle and tan and made it hard to conceal a weapon.

"Schuler told me about you."

"I see." He waited, thirty feet away across the sandy and glass-clumped surface of the bastion. Behind him, gliding into the calm waters of the bay, the lights of a fishing boat glowed red and green and white. "What do I call you?"

"How about Ishmael."

"What?"

"Call me what you will. It doesn't make any difference."

Pierson didn't answer.

"You talked to Martin?"

"Yeah."

"Then we've got some business." Martin would have told Pierson that Kirk had, indeed, hijacked that last shipment and knew all about their setup. And that it was a shakedown: either they cut Kirk in or no more shipments.

"What kind of cut you sons of bitches thinking about?"

"Fifty-fifty."

"Go to hell." Pierson stepped closer, anger tightening his shoulders.

"It's either half of something or all of nothing." Devlin added, "Besides, we can help you expand your market. We can handle all you bring in."

"Shit—who can't?" Pierson had gradually been closing the distance between them, almost casually stepping first to one side, then the other. Which was fine with Devlin—he wanted to get his hands on the man. Behind him, the sun was halfway down behind the ragged shadows of the distant wood line. Close overhead, pelicans lifted heavily into the offshore wind and beat landward. Higher above the pelicans, still glinting in the sun, a few gulls wheeled.

"I don't want to expand. I don't want you in it. And I sure as hell ain't paying protection."

Devlin was close enough now to see the scar on the man's left cheek, a knife-thin semicircle of whitened flesh. "You've got no choice, Pierson."

"Bullshit!" His right arm darted behind his back, and as Kirk lunged for him he saw the handle of a pistol.

Devlin hit Pierson's elbow with the heel of his hand and drove a shoulder hard into his chest. It tumbled the man back against the gritty brick parapet. The pistol wavered in the sky above Kirk's head and he knifed an elbow into Pierson's lower ribs to bend him choking. He brought the weapon down across Devlin's shoulder; the steel thudded hard against his clavicle, tingling the length of his arm. Then Pierson raised it for another blow. Reaching behind his upper arm, Kirk grabbed Pierson's wrist and pulled down, rotating the man's shoulder backward and slamming him into the brick ledge. Pierson beat at Devlin's head and neck with his free fist while a knee jabbed hard against Kirk's thigh. He raked the sole of his shoe down Pierson's shin to crush his instep. Pierson grunted slurs about Devlin's ancestry and twisted to pull his arm free. Strong—his muscles weren't all for definition and posing in front of that blonde. But like a lot of body builders, he was slow. Devlin leaned his bulk against Pierson's arm and saw his whitened fingers loosen their grip on the pistol as the ragged lip of a brick cut into his flesh.

"You fuckg—"

Writhing and pushing, he heaved Kirk off his arm as the pistol bounced and clattered across the stone. Devlin shoved hard, trying to knock it off the barbette into the courtyard below. Pierson groped with his free hand for something else hidden behind him, and Kirk swung him hard into the wall. The pistol was a couple inches from the lip and Devlin reached, Pierson's hand matching his, and for a long moment, the two sets of fingers wriggled in tandem toward the weapon. Then he grabbed Devlin's hair and pulled backward, wrenching him around and away from the weapon. Devlin's fingers sought his eyes. He saw the pistol drop over the edge, and Pierson, twisting away from Devlin's hand, saw it too. His grip relaxed momentarily. Kneeing him with his whole weight, Kirk knocked Pierson's hand away from his hair and jabbed the blade of his knuckles into Pierson's throat. The blow sent him gagging backward away from Devlin and off the bastion onto the parapet.

For a moment they stared at each other, gasping, waiting for the other to commit to a move.

"Without me—" He coughed and spit something. "Without me, you ain't got shit!"

"I came for you. You are shit."

Beneath the glaring rage, something else stirred. "Why? Why you want me?"

"You know why."

Pierson was as winded as Kirk, and as willing to talk. "Bullshit—I don't even know who you are."

"Remember the kid you left hanging in a sack? The kid in Denver?"

It took him a moment. "That's who you are? Fucking company dick? That's who?" Pierson's bleeding lips stretched into a grin of some kind of triumph. "And you're going to be the big hero? Take me back?"

"Take you back. Leave you here. Either way."

"Shit!" A small skinning knife appeared in his hand from somewhere behind him, and Devlin figured he must be wearing an entire arsenal back there. He crouched and circled toward Kirk on the balls of his feet, legs wide to sidle either way with Devlin's dodging. He held the blade low as if he knew what to do with it. Kirk wasn't sure what to do with it, but something would have to be done in the next few seconds. Somewhere in the back of his mind came one of those stray and irrelevant thoughts, as if Devlin were looking over his own shoulder: the sardonic awareness that all his college texts and lectures on deconstruction and the shibboleth that "all we have is language" boiled down to facing a man with a knife. There was no way in the world Kirk was going to rearrange that fact by rearranging his word order. Pierson feinted with one shoulder and lunged with the blade. Devlin swung past its glinting tip to swipe at Pierson's face with the side of his hand. The next thrust was toward Devlin's stomach and up, pulling back quickly before Kirk could grasp his wrist. But Pierson would have to do better than that. Have to come in closer than that. They circled in the dusk, moving down the parapet. On one side was the outer wall, on the other a line of posts and cables and signs that warned tourists away from the ledge above the parade ground. Past Pierson's shoulder, Devlin saw a full moon—gigantic and orange—lift from the other side of the earth. Beautiful, and as distant and unmoved as the old bricks they slid across.

Pierson lunged again, the narrow blade a silver blur, and Devlin felt it catch this time. Its pressure was an oily, hot sting along his ribs as he rolled away and grappled. He trapped Pierson's arm in the bend of his own and levered his forearm under Pierson's elbow. Then he squatted and fell back and jabbed his knee hard into the tumbling man's groin. Pierson gurgled something as they flipped, and Kirk heard his head whack against the parapet. Something gave in Pierson's arm as it crumpled beneath their combined weight. Still grunting with pain, Pierson twisted and writhed and groped for the knife in the black of the wall's shadow. As hard as he could, Devlin drove the heel of his hand under the blur that was Pierson's jaw. The head snapped back solidly and he went limp.

They lay there, tangled like savage lovers. Devlin pumped air into his aching lungs and tried to make his flesh tell him how deeply it was cut. Untwisting his arms and legs from Pierson's, Kirk started to stand. Pierson exploded in fists and elbows and feet, shoving him back and stunning him with a solid hit on the temple. When Kirk shook the whirling sparks out of his eyes, Pierson was a running, panting shadow disappearing down the barbette toward the uneven steps formed by the crumbling wall.

Devlin staggered after him. Groping fingers along his ribs, he was relieved to find only a narrow slit in the blood-slick flesh. No deep and pulsing hole, no wide flap of flayed skin. It would be sore—it already ached—but it wasn't fatal and nothing below the skin was cut.

He heard more than saw Pierson scramble down the loose stone where the wall of the fort had been breached and weathered into grit. A bounding silhouette against the white of moon-washed plaster and drifted sand, Pierson turned at the foot of the wall. Racing back, feet muffled in the clumped grass of the parade ground, Pierson sprinted for the pistol that had been knocked over the ledge. Devlin rolled over the parapet and dangled from the rusty guard cable. He dropped to tumble across soft earth and stretch his legs after the man. A series of squat arches formed by the casemates and the massive brick groins echoed their panting. The shadow bent and bobbed and groped along the ground. As Devlin rushed up it turned to fire a red jab of flame and then another, the blue of the round's gases flashing with a *thoomp* from the chamber. Devlin leapt, both feet clubbing the shape. He landed heavily against Pierson's torso, knocking the man to the sandy ground. Pierson rolled into the shadow of a casemate and scrambled brokenly to his feet. He dodged toward the mass of a thick pier. The pistol lay in the grass and Devlin picked it up by its hot barrel. Sprinting through the flickering semicircles of moonlight that fell in a line through the casemate arches, he ran after Pierson. The man would have to double back around the concrete gun emplacement; his car would have to be near Kirk's on the asphalt parking apron. Devlin cut across to head him off when he doubled back.

But Pierson didn't. Running and halting to listen, Devlin lost him in the maze of doors and tunnels that led toward the quarters area. Then he glimpsed Pierson limping over the shoulder of an earthen apron piled against the battery housing. The shadow disappeared like a rat into another tunnel. Before Kirk could reach the dark entrance, Pierson swung out onto one of the triangular walls of a bastion and crawled over its face to hang a moment against the rough brick. Then he was gone.

Devlin made it to the top in time to see him still running with that tilted, broken sway through the bright glow of moonlight toward the fishing pier. By the time Devlin found a way to follow him, the throb of a heavy motor fired. A moment later, the silver water of the bay split with the spreading wake of a speeding boat.

CHAPTER 24

Bunch squinted, as if that could help him better understand
Yoshi Kamakura's English. From what he could figure out, the
Japanese investigator said that Mitsuko's last name wasn't Watanabe but Saito, and she was not the big man's daughter but
his mistress. "But not so much mistress anymore, Bunch-u. Now
his once-mistress."

"Ex-mistress?"

"Yes. 'Ecces.' But also a . . . how you say, bond-gift to
yakuza."

"Yakuza? What's the Japanese Mafia have to do with this?"

"I told you, Bunch-u. Watanabe-san is active in politics. This
means he has dealings with yakuza. The Kobayashi gang. Pay-
offs, you understand?"

"You mean Watanabe owed Kobayashi a favor and Saito
Mitsuko was the favor?"

"Yes. But it was not to Kobayashi. It was to one of his
lieutenants. But Saito did not accept this, yes? Not like the old
days, this woman is Westernized, yes? Or maybe it's because
the man she was given to is a Korean. Kim Soon." Yoshi's voice
dropped with embarrassment. "Much loss of face for her to be
given to a Korean."

"Yeah. I guess that'd upset anybody. So what happened?"

"She ran away. Flew to New York. Very embarrassing to Kim Soon. A lot of people know about it now and laugh at Kim Soon, yes? A yakuza who cannot control a woman. What kind of yakuza is that?"

"Aw, yeah. He's got my sympathy. But Saito's not in New York, Yoshi. She's here in Denver."

"So? Not Big Apple?" A muttered Japanese phrase, something apologetic with *okudusai* in it. "My worthless operative was told she was in New York."

"She was there. Now she's here, and someone has tried to kill her American boyfriend."

"Ah so. Yes. Of course. Kim Soon."

"It's him? You're sure?"

"Yes. Certainly. Who else? He has to kill her boyfriend and bring Saito back. Or kill her, too, and bring back her head." Yoshi laughed with embarrassment. "Much loss of face to have a round-eye copulating with your woman. Even for a Korean."

Bunch thanked him and started to hang up, but the Japanese detective had one more thing to add. "*Aksamio!* You be very careful for the nine-fingered man, okay?"

"What nine-fingered man?"

"The yakuza. They have nine fingers, most of them. They cut off one of their fingers to show loyalty and . . . Bushido . . . obedience, courage."

"I will. *Domo arigato gozaimas,* Yoshi."

"*Genke pali pali,* Bunch-u."

Bunch played the tape recording of their conversation and leaned back in the desk chair, feet on the iron rail, to listen and to stare at the mountains in the distance. An early snow had dropped a light film of white on the mountains' dry east flanks. Heavier pockets of it still marked the blue-shadowed folds that led up into the cap of thick clouds leveling the horizon. Above the clinging layer of cloud, the sky was clear and blue and marked here and there by scratches of contrail. On cue, the rumble of casters, like a jet overhead, crossed the ceiling and punctuated his conclusions.

He made a few notes to himself and sighed and heaved out of the gasping chair. It was time to protect Miss Humphries/Watanabe/Saito.

Bunch's inspection of the house's perimeter defenses was perfunctory and routine. He had other things on his mind. Gleaming and fluid in a silver spandex exercise suit, Mitsuko was taking advantage of the warm October sun. On a corner of the brick patio outside the sliding glass doors of the dining room, she bent and stretched and twisted. Bunch settled on an empty chaise longue to watch.

"You've got some nice moves, Watanabe-san."

The full lips curved in a smile and she made a gliding, rolling motion with her pelvis. "That's one I learned in Hawaii. It's good for the spine."

Bunch figured it was good for two spines: hers and the guy riding. "Humphries is a surprising man."

"Why?"

"He doesn't look like a great lover. But he must have something." He watched the spandex divide into legs as she bent and reached her arms between them. "Is it his money?"

A dark eye tilted toward him. "Jealous?"

"Nah. Just curious. The guy doesn't seem like an imaginative bed partner."

She exhaled and stood slowly, inhaling all the way, and then held the pose for a long count before sighing her breath out. "He doesn't have to be. Besides, he's learning."

"A little different from screwing a yakuza?"

She looked up from a deep bend that pressed the curves of her torso against a straight leg. "A who?"

"Yakuza. Kim Soon. The man who wants to kill Humphries and take you back."

Slowly, she straightened, surprise slacking her face and rounding her eyes. "How—? What do you know—?"

Bunch shrugged. "I'm a detective. I detect, remember? Now why don't you just tell me what the hell's going on?"

She stared without answering.

"Was the guy on the motorcycle Kim Soon?"

A nod. A shrug. "I think so."

"And the note was from him too."

Another shrug.

"And you're not Watanabe's daughter but his ex-mistress."

This time she said nothing; her eyes said it all.

Bunch leaned forward. "You still think Humphries is going to marry you?"

"I don't know. I hope so. No . . . maybe—"

"But he thinks you're Watanabe's daughter."

"Yes."

"And if he finds out you're not, you're out on your sweet ass?"

"Please don't tell him, Mr. Bunchcroft."

"But that was your plan, right?"

"Yes. He would never marry a . . . geisha. But perhaps if he thought I was someone important . . . From a family even more important than his own . . ."

"Kim Soon found out you were in New York?"

"It was only a matter of time. He searched—he discovered what flight I took." A sigh. "I called my sister. To let her know I was alive. Kim Soon visited her. He threatened her and her husband and children if she didn't tell him where I was."

"That's who you called when you told Humphries you telephoned home?"

"Yes."

"But New York's a big place. You could've hid there."

She shook her head. "Not for a Japanese national. And there are yakuza in New York."

"So you met Humphries."

"He was at a cocktail party. I was there with Lawrence and I remembered meeting him in Japan when I was with Watanabe-san." She smiled slightly. "Roland assumed I was his daughter. Watanabe said I was. He didn't want to lose face with Roland.

Roland didn't understand that in Japan a gentleman's wife or daughters don't go to that kind of public conference."

"And then came Kim Soon."

She looked at the ground, her shoulders sagging slightly. "Watanabe owed Kim Soon. I was what he wanted."

"But not what you wanted."

When she looked up, the hurt had been replaced by anger. "The woman of a gangster? I, who had been first mistress to one of Japan's most powerful men, given like a dog to that man!"

So she ran, skating on the thin ice of hope and lies and terror. She was tough, and Bunch admired that. "Suppose Humphries does marry you? He still thinks you're Watanabe's daughter. How're you going to keep up that role?"

She shrugged. "I would be a daughter Watanabe refuses to acknowledge. One who could never go home again."

Bunch grunted. "And he wouldn't ever want to see Humphries, either."

"Yes."

Bunch sighed. It might work; it was a long shot, but it looked like the only shot she had. "So where's Kim Soon?"

"What?"

"Kim Soon. He gave you a note, said you should do what's right. He must have told you how to get in touch with him so you could do it."

Her black eyes stared at Bunch. "If you go to him, Roland will find out everything."

"If I don't go to him, you and Roland are both dead. Mitsi— Is that your real name, Mitsi?"

"Yes. That much is true."

"Mitsi, we can't keep you safe against that guy forever. We've got to change his mind about what he wants to do."

"No." She shook her head. "He won't. He can't, now."

"What about Humphries paying the guy off? He's got plenty of money." Bunch smiled. "Call it a new kind of head tax."

Her head shook again. "Money won't be enough now. He's made a public gesture."

"You mean by coming to the States?"

"Yes. Bushido. He must return with his vengeance satisfied."

Bunch whistled a crooked little tune between his teeth. "I think I better talk to him anyway."

The woman's eyes widened in fear. "He is a very dangerous man, Mr. Bunchcroft. A hired killer!"

"Yeah, you told me: *yojimbo.*"

"A trained warrior, Mr. Bunchcroft. A professional. That's the reason he's here!"

Bunch smiled. "Sounds like my kind of guy. Now where do I find him?"

"I still don't see how you let him get away."

Bunch drove and Devlin tried to keep still against the pull of stiff, hot flesh beneath its gauze pad. He'd telephoned ahead to let Bunch know when the flight would arrive from Pensacola and to give him the bad news. "Maybe you could have done better, Bunch."

"I didn't say that." He added, "But then I don't have to."

"I gave his name and description to the DEA before I left. They weren't all that excited about it—you know how those people are. But they did pick up Hall and Schuler and said they might put Pierson on their hot list."

"Might?"

"Might. Hall and Schuler they have confessions from, so DEA didn't have to work. Pierson calls for a little effort on their behalf. So 'might.' "

"You know he's got a getaway stash somewhere. He's probably on the Riviera or down in Argentina by now."

Devlin winced as Bunch swerved to avoid a pothole and angled onto Martin Luther King Boulevard. It led across the sprawling residential section of north Denver toward their office in lower downtown. "But he's an ex-con," added Bunch. "Maybe he couldn't get a passport."

"Maybe."

"Then again, maybe he'll come looking for you. Scotty Martin thought he was crazy enough to do something like that."

Devlin grunted. "Fine. I'd like another shot at him."

The Bronco jolted and rattled past the black neighborhoods and Devlin watched a handful of kids chase each other through the rainbow arc of a water sprinkler on somebody's front yard. Their wet, dark bodies glittered in an afternoon sun that was unseasonably warm for late October. As they ran and jumped he tried to remember what it felt like to find that much excitement and joy in the simple act of motion and in the shock of cold water on sun-heated skin.

"I turned Scotty over to Sergeant Kiefer in homicide," said Bunch. "He sent a request to Florida for the arrest of Pierson on that charge." He sighed. "Kiefer was really happy."

Kiefer was happy. Reznick was happy. Even the Pensacola DEA office had been a little bit happy to have a solved case complete with confessions dropped in their laps to enhance their statistics. Devlin wasn't happy. He wanted Pierson and had missed his chance. Despite the official termination of the case, it still didn't seem finished with Pierson off and running. The guilty memory of Chris Newman's body dangling in that bloody bag hadn't been satisfied by merely fighting with his killer and then letting him escape. But life had a lot of loose threads. Devlin knew. And he was beginning to learn that sometimes a standoff was the best one could expect. "Did Kiefer say what the chances are of finding Pierson?"

"Kiefer doesn't know about it yet. I talked to him last night when you thought you had the bastard wrapped and delivered to the Pensacola PD." Bunch shook his head. "I'll call him when we get to the office, and tell him to put Pierson on the FBI wire. He won't like it, but there's not much else to do now."

They pulled into the parking lot behind the office and Devlin stifled a grunt and slid stiffly out of the Bronco's high front seat.

"What's the matter, Dev? You move like you're pregnant."

On the way upstairs, he told Bunch about the knife.

"Jesus—guns and knives, both. You keep this up, your insurance'll be out of sight and we'll both have to listen to Uncle Wyn preach to us."

"We don't tell him. There's no sense worrying him over nothing."

"Okay by me." Bunch picked up the telephone and punched in a number from memory. After a few seconds, he asked for Sergeant Kiefer. "Dave? Bunchcroft here. I got some sad, bad news."

He told the homicide detective about Pierson's escape, holding the receiver off his ear as it squawked angrily. "No, if he'd brought in the local cops, the guy wouldn't have showed at all. You know that, so quit your bitching. It was a good try, and a pretty good fight, too. And I got to tell you, old Dev's pretty cut up over it." He winked happily at Kirk. "No, my guess is he's either out of the country or holed up so deep he might as well be. Maybe the FBI can come up with something. . . . Yeah, yeah, I know how much help they are. But what else do we have? . . . Okay, let us know." He hung up the receiver and shook his head. "Pissed, Dev. The good sergeant is really steamed."

"I don't give a damn if he's parboiled." The cut along Devlin's ribs was throbbing slightly, a sign that infection hadn't been entirely overcome by the doctor's swab and a needleful of antitetanus serum. "I'm going to figure Reznick's bill and then I'm going home to sleep."

"Uh, Dev, as long as you're feeling so depressed and all . . ."

"What?"

"We're off the Jean Truman case. Allen Schute called—he says he can't afford to lose any more money on her."

"Is he getting another agency?"

"He didn't say that exactly. Just that he was surprised to see Kirk and Associates outsmarted."

"Crap."

"Hey, look on the bright side: no more squatting in that Subaru."

"Probably no more insurance cases, either."

"Nah, Schute wasn't all that pissed. He'll just make sure we get the dumb ones from now on." Bunch began pulling on his jacket as Devlin punched up the Advantage file. "I'll see you in the morning, Dev."

"Where are you headed?"

"Got a date. My busy social life."

CHAPTER 25

It wasn't exactly a social date, but Devlin didn't have to know that. He looked tired enough to fall asleep up against the computer screen, but if he knew where Bunch was headed, he'd insist on coming along. And that was all Bunch needed: someone else to look after if things got sticky with the *yojimbo*.

Mitsuko hadn't wanted to give him the address. Her face held a mixture of hope and fear. The hope, of course, was that Bunch could somehow convince the Korean to return to Japan without either killing Humphries or telling him about Mitsuko's real relationship to Watanabe. The fear was that Bunch would fail. And even, she said softly, that he would be killed.

"Kim Soon has earned high respect in Japan. For being one of the best of the yakuza."

"Was respected."

"He wants that back."

"He can lie. He can tell his buddies he took care of both of you and go home with a lot of Humphries' money too."

She thought about that. "It's possible. It might work."

"Then tell me where he is."

She told him, and when Humphries, baggy-eyed and nervous, was convoyed home, Bunch, leaving out some details, told him the plan.

"You think he'll do it?" Humphries looked first at Bunch and then at Mitsuko. "I'm willing, if you think it'll work."

"Can't hurt to try. He can tell Watanabe he killed his daughter and take home a few bucks too."

"It sounds so bizarre—so . . ."

"Hey, having the guy after you is bizarre, right? This is a way to end it without hurting anybody."

"But, Mitsi—you'll have to give up your family! They'll think you're dead."

"My father wants me dead, doesn't he?" She shrugged. "And I don't want to go back."

Humphries looked at her for a long moment, studying the downcast face, the body whose touch he never seemed to get enough of. Maybe it would work. God, what a sacrifice she was making for him. While he . . . He turned to the big man who waited patiently. "You really think it has a chance?"

"Sure. Give it a try—it's just money."

And compared to what Mitsi was surrendering, compared to the Japanese reverence for ancestors and family, fifty thousand wasn't much. "Okay." He went to his desk.

Bunch cruised past the motel a couple times before pulling out of traffic onto the trashy shoulder of the busy highway. It was one of those old-fashioned collections of look-alike cottages that used to line the dirt sides of South Santa Fe before that road was supplanted by I-25 a few decades ago. Bunch couldn't count the times he'd driven this stretch of road, but he'd never noticed this cluster of brown, flat-roofed units. They were pinched between a salesroom for hot tubs and a rug dealer whose Day-Glo orange sign screamed Factory Outlet. The motel had a name—Mesa Land Oasis—and it looked like something out of one of those black-and-white movies where the lovely blonde in trouble picks up a tough but honest hitchhiker who falls in love with her. And they drive away in a '38 Mercury convertible with bulbous fenders.

Cars were parked here and there on the dusty gravel that

formed a quiet square back from the busy thoroughfare. Most of the cars looked as if they had coasted to a final rest at the Mesa Land Oasis, and in their weary silence seemed grateful for the shelter provided by the surrounding cottages. A semi's tractor, dark and bulky, loomed like a powerful sleeping animal. Bunch walked past it to the unit whose tiny porch caught the glare of passing headlights. Under the unlit Mesa Land Oasis sign, a smaller sign said "Office." It, too, was faded and the paint cracked. Above a doorbell someone had penciled the word "Manager." Above that, "Weekly and Monthly Rates Available. Ask Within."

Bunch expected the manager to match the decor. But instead of a wizened and suspicious old man, the girl—possibly as old as twenty—could have been pretty if her face hadn't been pale and lined with weariness. And if her hair hadn't hung in lifeless ropes to frame that drawn face. From somewhere behind her came the thin, sickly wail of a baby exhausted from long crying. The odor of dirty diapers floated into the cool air through the open door. "Yes?"

"You're the manager?"

"His wife. You looking for a room? All we got's one without a kitchenette. All the kitchenettes been taken."

"I'm looking for one of your roomers. Korean guy named Soon." He showed a corner of the envelope. "I got a letter for him."

"Korean? I thought he was Chinese or something. You a police officer? That a summons?"

Bunch shook his head. "It's a letter I'm supposed to give him personally."

"You look like a policeman."

"Well, I'm not. What cabin's he in?"

The baby's howl rose. "Five. Down on your left." She closed the door while her hand fumbled at her blouse. A moment later, the fitful crying stopped.

Bunch's shoes crunched in the gravel as he passed a rusty station wagon with a slab of cardboard in place of one of the rear windows. An equally battered bumper sticker announced, "I Voted for Reagan When I Was Rich."

Cabin 5 was half hidden beneath a towering cottonwood tree whose dry leaves clattered in the evening breeze like a small stream. In the twilight, Bunch saw the flicker of a television set through the window of cabin 3. As he passed, the loud noise of the set drowned out the chatter of leaves, and a silhouette of three heads—one adult, two children—made bumps of darkness against the pale glow. The only light from cabin 5 was a faint yellow fringe around a tightly pulled blind. Bunch knocked on the doorframe.

"Kim Soon? We need to talk." He knocked again. A few curls of green paint spiraled down.

No answer.

He tried the doorknob. The fragile lock gave with a metallic twang and the door sagged inward. Another flake of paint settled on the back of his hand like a warning touch.

"Soon?"

Through the partly open door, he glimpsed a corner of the room crowded with a rumpled bed and lit dimly by a lamp. Bunch pushed the door slowly wider to show the empty bed. A small end table held the lamp and a telephone. A sagging upholstered chair was jammed close to a dark bureau. He glanced through the crack between the door hinges. The dark behind the door was empty. *"Konichi-wa?"* He stepped in carefully and closed it behind him. On a folding stand rested a suitcase, shut but not locked. From behind a closed door came the faint sigh of a running shower. Bunch eased across the room to listen at the dark wood. Then he turned the handle slowly.

He opened the door to a wisp of steam and the louder rush of water. The tiny shower stall billowed hot mist over the top of a plastic curtain, and the wetness beaded on his jacket and swirled across his eyes. Bunch stepped past the bulge of a toilet to rap on the fiberglass wall. He wasn't sure if it was a sound or a tiny flicker of motion beneath the fogged glass of the mirror or just the feeling on the back of his neck, but he wheeled in time to see a gleaming arc of silver swing toward him through the hazy air: a sword.

A squat, barrel-chested man wearing black pants and a white undershirt lunged from the recess beside the shower stall. Both hands swung a samurai sword in a chopping curve toward the base of Bunch's neck. He fell back to shove against the toilet with all his strength and felt the porcelain stool tip and rock as he pulled the door hard against the falling blade. It caught in the wood with a solid chop, biting a deep slice into the door's edge. It stopped at Bunch's ear and sent a spray of splinters prickling his cheek. Soon wrenched the blade free and jabbed, a two-handed thrust that pierced the loose fold of Bunch's coat and sliced upward, reaching for his clutching stomach and lungs. Grabbing the man's wrists, Bunch shoved. The blade ripped clear of his coat to clang against the shower stall and dig a furry gap in the fiberglass wall. The Korean, a round face with black eyes squeezed almost shut by high cheekbones and the effort to push against Bunch's strength, grunted something and aimed a sudden knee at Bunch's crotch. The big man swiveled to take the thudding blow on his hip and drove the point of his elbow into Soon's solar plexus. A burst of garlic-smelling air, and Bunch followed with a hard chop up under the Korean's chin. He aimed for the throat but half missed as Soon saw it coming and twisted away to try a jabbing kick to Bunch's face. It glanced off his shoulder. He wrenched the Korean's hands and drove the heel of his own hand against the back of Soon's elbow. The gristle squealed and popped and the Korean's lipless mouth, a slash of agony across his face, opened in a strangled howl.

The sword pulled free of Soon's hands and quivered in the wall of the shower stall. Bunch twisted again, squeezing both the man's wrists together like dried sticks. He drove a knee into his ribs to fold him backward into the steam and spewing water and thud his skull against the sagging sink. Another chopping blow with the side of his hand low against the man's neck, and Soon grunted and sagged, not quite out. But he was numbed and boneless in Bunch's fists.

Panting, Bunch dragged the man from the tiny, wrecked bathroom. He dropped him on his back in the middle of the grimy carpet and pulled the gleaming sword from the shower stall. Soon began to make rasping sounds and to dig his heels into the carpet. He tried to roll onto hands and knees. Bunch thudded the side of his fist against the man's skull and he lay quiet.

"You speak English?"

No answer.

Bunch jabbed the Korean's ribs with his shoe and held the sword's blunt tip just under his chin. "*Yo, jimbo,* I asked you: You speak English?"

Soon's round face twitched and one of his eyes blinked. The other was already swollen shut. His mouth was a clamped, soundless line.

Bunch, keeping his face and the sword toward the man, clicked on a floor lamp whose chain tinkled briefly against its ornate brass stand. Then he groped through the suitcase's elastic pockets until he found what he wanted—a passport case and its booklet. The photograph matched the silent Korean, and the name beneath it, in both Japanese and English, said Soon Kim. Bunch studied the man on the carpet. The wiry muscles showed a lot of exercise. Dark scrolls of tattoos covered his arms and torso wherever it showed beneath the sleeveless undershirt. The left hand, lying splayed on the floor, was missing the last knuckle of its little finger. The single eye studied him in return, and all the grogginess was gone.

Bunch swung the sword in a long arc. Its blade made a deep hum in the quiet room. "I came here to talk. You willing to talk about all this Bushido crap?"

The eye glittered.

Bunch felt through his sliced jacket and drew out the envelope to lay on the suitcase. "Money—a lot of it. And a plane ticket for a direct flight to Tokyo. Leaves at nine forty-seven tonight. Be on it." He waited, but Kim said nothing. "Mitsuko says go home. She ficky-fick round-eye now."

"Son of bitch!"

"Ah. We've established communications." Bunch sat on the side of the bed, which sank dangerously and squealed. "Your boss, Kobayashi-san, know you're in America?"

No answer.

"Take the money and go. Tell Kobayashi you killed Saito and her boyfriend. Nobody knows the difference—you save face and get rich too."

"Son of bitch!"

"You said that already." Bunch picked up the telephone from the small table. It had a rotary dial, the kind Bunch hadn't seen in years. "Mr. Humphries? No—not yet. Can I talk to Mitsuko, please?"

In a moment, she answered, voice breathless. "Yes?"

"I don't know if I'm getting through to the guy. Tell him in Japanese, will you?" He held out the phone to the glaring man and gestured for him to take it.

Kim, eyes on Bunch, held the receiver to his ear. *"Anone!"*

The telephone buzzed, and every now and then Kim grunted. His one good eye focused on Bunch as he listened. Finally, *"Ieh! Ieh!"* Then, *"Hai!"* Scornfully, the man yanked the wire out of the receiver and tossed it on the bed.

Bunch shook his head. "I sure hope you listened, Kim baby." He stared for a dozen seconds at the man still sprawled on the grimy carpet. Its threads showed through in large gray patches beside the bed and in front of the bathroom door. "But I bet you didn't." He wiped again at the tickle on his neck and looked with surprise at the blood that gleamed on his fingers. The Korean's thin lips tightened in the trace of a smile.

"By God, you nicked me, didn't you?" Bunch touched the top of his ear where a flap of loose skin stung under his fingers. He tapped the sword on the floor and listened to its clear ring. "Good steel—I didn't even feel it."

Kim said nothing. Bunch saw that his arms and feet had gathered together into springing position.

He sighed and shook his head. "You'd try it, wouldn't you? You didn't listen to a goddamn thing Mitsuko-san said, did you?" He tossed the sword on the bed. Kim's eye followed it. "Okay. Let's get this over with."

He reached for the man. Kim flopped quickly to hands and feet and lunged for the sword. He jabbed a side-kick at Bunch's knees as he moved. Bunch caught a foot under Soon's thigh and lifted, turning him in the air and grabbing his left arm to fold it back and around his body in a kink that froze the Korean in an arc of pain. "This is going to hurt you more than it does me."

The bone gave a muffled crackle like something crunchy under a shoe. Bunch saw beads of sweat spring out on Kim Soon's wrinkled forehead. A strangled grunt came from his pinched lips but he made no other sound.

"Now the other arm."

He tried to struggle. A swat across the broken arm took the fight out of the Korean, and Bunch bent the man's right arm until a bone snapped.

"Nothing personal, right? Strictly business, Japanese style."

The Korean's face, a sick color that made his shaven whiskers stand out darkly against the wet flesh, stared back at Bunch. He made no sound. If there was any hunger for revenge in the eye, it had been washed out by pain. Bunch pulled a shirt and shoes from the suitcase and a jacket from the closet and tossed them to the hunched man. Then he locked the luggage and set it by the door. Kim Soon, his breath a loud whistle in his nose as the shirtsleeves pressed against his swelling arms, struggled into the clothes. Picking up the suitcase and sword, Bunch opened the door for the man, who walked in his untied shoes as if he were slightly drunk. Removing the cash from the envelope, he riffled the money under Kim's nose and then stuffed it and the airplane ticket into Kim's jacket pocket. Bunch would escort the Korean to the plane and watch it take off. When it landed, Kim could explain the money and the two broken arms to Japanese immigration. And then to Kobayashi and his *yojimbo*.

CHAPTER 26

Kirk didn't remember going to sleep. He did remember half waking a couple times to swig down some water from the glass by the bed; the infection had made him thirsty as well as sore. He remembered hearing the telephone ring a time or two before the answerer took over, and he remembered that he hadn't cleared the calls when he came in. When he woke in the morning, it was with that odd feeling of dreams that were intense enough to cling beyond sleep. He sensed they had been replays of his fight with Pierson because of the lingering images of fortress walls and gunports and rushing, threatening shapes that hung at the edge of recall. But despite that unease, he woke feeling better. The damp sheets told him that the fever had broken, and his ribs, though touchy, no longer held the heat of infection. He could even stretch a bit, torso still cramped from airplane seats that, even in the first-class section that Advantage Corporation paid for, were never big enough to support his spine or let his legs unfold all the way.

As he shaved, he listened to his telephone tape. A deal on carpet cleaning was spaced between silent gaps indicating the caller had hung up. By the time he limped into the office, the early-afternoon sunlight was already carving an arc on the rug. He rewound the answering machine there and listened to those messages while he cranked open one of the panels in the window. There was nothing from Bunch, and Kirk wondered vaguely what his partner was up to. He should have asked Bunch for a report on the Humphries file, but he had been too tired to follow the thought when it crossed his mind yesterday. A series of blank spots was on this tape too. A call had come in at 11:18 A.M. from Dave Miller, DPD Vice and Narcotics. He asked Bunch or Kirk to get in touch with him as soon as possible, and left a series of telephone numbers to try. Miller himself answered the second number on the list and told Kirk that there was a little problem with the Scott Martin drug bust. "The dope tested out at only two or three percent. That's street-level, Kirk. That means Martin doesn't come under the Kingpin Statute. So the most we can get him for is being a street pusher. The son of a bitch'll get a slap on the wrist and that's about it."

"Three percent? The shipper on the other end—Schuler— said it left there at around ninety percent!"

"Hey, I don't give a shit what he says or what you say. The lab report says it's between two and three percent. You told me this was a first-rate bust, Kirk. The high end of a big operation. We let that other asshole go—Atencio—to cover your man Landrum. Now it looks like this whole thing's going to fall apart, and all we're left with is another street-level pusher. Big fucking deal, Kirk." He asked, "Did you run a test on the stuff when it came out of the sealed shipping container?"

"No. There was no way to do that."

"Did you keep your eye on the stuff all the way? Any possibility they split it at the factory?"

"We saw them take it out of the sealed container and go to the locker room. They came out a few minutes later and went to work. I don't see how they had time to cut the stuff then. Right after work, they carried it from the locker room to their cars. We followed the cars to the storage lot where you ran the bust."

"So you can't even swear to a chain of possession?"

"Only presumptive. Only to what we saw."

"Well, your man Landrum can testify. He carried the god-damn stuff."

"As far as I know, he never opened the packages. So he can't swear to what was inside them, let alone to what grade it was." And his testimony would bring Advantage Corporation's name into the courtroom, something Reznick had been told would not happen.

"He can goddamn well say he saw the bastards cutting it!"

"It would be a lie and he'd be torn apart by the defense. You know that. All we can swear to is what we actually saw, and I can't even do that much if Reznick doesn't agree to it."

"Who the hell's Reznick?"

"The CEO of the plant. He wants to keep the company name out of it."

"Hey, Kirk, this is a felony! The DA can slap a subpoena on you sons of bitches. I don't care what he wants!"

"Let me call him. I'll get back to you."

Kirk did, and the answer was predictable.

"No way, Kirk. No way do I want the company name dragged into a court trial!"

"As it stands now, Mr. Reznick, the most he'll get is a year, eighteen months, after time off for good behavior."

"I don't give a damn! You told me this thing was over—you told me Advantage Corporation came out of it clean, and that's what I reported to Stewart. Now you tell me we have to go to court and reveal that the company's entire shipping network served as a carrier service for a major drug ring? That this plant—my plant—was the place where they diluted their drugs? I'm not going to do it!"

"I didn't say you had to."

"You said the district attorney could subpoena you and make you testify! You said the conspiracy charge was their only shot at the . . . whatever it is, Kingpin whatever."

"I don't know if the DA wants to go to all that trouble. It's shaky evidence. Maybe Vice can scare Martin into a plea bargain."

"Well, you figure a way to convince them to do that, Kirk. You were paid to keep the company name clean, and by God paid a lot. And I'm by God not going to authorize any court hearings involving the Advantage Corporation if I can help it! And one more thing—Porter's fired as of now. No police, no criminal charges. I'm just firing his butt!"

Devlin relayed some of what Reznick said back to Miller. The result was another of those inconclusive loose ends—first Pierson disappearing into the sunset, now Scott Martin getting a tap on the knuckles. "I know you don't like it, Miller. Neither do I. But Reznick won't volunteer to testify about the shipping arrangements. He wants to keep the company name out of it. And he's yelling corporate lawyers. You know as well as I do what the defense is going to do with circumstantial evidence and a weak chain of possession. You can ask him, but I bet the DA won't think it's worth the hassle. Especially for street-level stuff."

"Shit."

Kirk's sentiments exactly. "Can you work a plea bargain? Scare Martin into bargaining for a heavier sentence than he might get otherwise?"

"I know my fucking job, Kirk. What I don't know is whether or not I ever want to trust you bastards again. We'll see what the DA says and maybe we'll see you in court. Corporate fucking lawyers or no."

The telephone clicked dead and Devlin set it lightly on its cradle. No sense jarring it into another explosion. Street-level percentage. The dope that Martin was arrested with should have been the same grade as that sealed and sent from Pensacola— the almost pure grade that Schuler said he sent. Unless Schuler was lying. But why would he? The lower grade would have worked in his favor when he was busted, but he never said a word about it.

246 · REX BURNS

The puzzle began to stir ugly suspicions at the back of Kirk's mind, and he sat and stared out the arched window at the mountains until he heard the heavy thud of Bunch's feet on the iron stairs.

"Dev—you look only half dead now. Feeling okay?"

"Like the Russian army crept in, crapped, and crept out. What's with Humphries and the spider lady?"

Bunch told Devlin about Mitsuko and her name changes, as well as about Kim Soon, the yakuza.

"She was Watanabe's mistress? She was given to that Korean?"

Bunch had telephoned Humphries after Kim Soon's flight had cleared the runway, and this morning he'd made a last trip out to their house. Mitsuko had met him wearing a wide smile and a very demure dress. Humphries had been there too, wearing an air of smug, if slightly dazed, happiness.

"I called my mother this morning. I told her Mitsi and I are going to be married."

Bunch glanced at the woman, who gazed modestly at the rug. "She doesn't mind that Mitsi's Japanese?"

"Well, I explained—I mean, after all, the Watanabe family . . . And I told her about Mitsi's father literally casting her off. She—my mother—thinks it's quite romantic! It's a true legend, she says, to add to the family name!"

"I think you're very fortunate, Mr. Humphries. And best wishes, Watanabe-san."

"Thank you, Mr. Bunchcroft."

Kirk, leaning back in the chair, grinned. "So you left the two lovebirds standing in the doorway?"

"Waving and smiling as I drove into the sunset." Bunch tossed an envelope on the desk. "Humphries' check. Said he put in a little extra to thank us."

Kirk looked at it. "Nice." Then, "I hope he doesn't want it back sometime."

"I don't think he will. He got a hell of a lot better woman than he deserved, and I think he knows that."

"Think she'll be happy with him?"

Bunch's shoulders rose and fell. "She'll be loyal to him—Bushido, *ne?*"

"*Hai.*" Kirk logged the check into the computerized account books and addressed a bank envelope. "What happened to your ear?"

Bunch brushed a finger across the soggy, red Band-Aid. "Styled by Kim Soon."

"Oh yeah?" Devlin winced as he twisted around from the keyboard. "What happened?"

Bunch shrugged. "He missed." It wasn't the first time somebody had gone after him armed with a weapon and intent. It wasn't something you got used to, exactly, but you learned not to worry about the ones that missed. Apparently Devlin understood, because Bunch saw him wag his head once and turn back to business.

"Do we still have that tap on Arnie Minz's telephone?" Kirk asked.

"Yeah. We better pull that out of there."

"Let's wait a little."

"Why's that?"

Devlin told him about Miller's call and the street-level cocaine found at Vinny's bust. "Now Miller's pissed off at us," said Kirk. "Maybe we'd do better in the matchmaking business."

"You know what I'm thinking, Dev." Bunch glanced at a telephone number in his small notebook and then dialed it. Kirk flipped on the telephone speaker. They listened to the click and hum of the tape and finally the pinched words. Minz's voice was a constant, but several different females crowded the tape and added up to a variety of woman problems. Early among the number of unidentified male voices came Vinny's: "My phone's been tapped. Don't call me there no more. Run a check on yours, too. I'll be in touch." Much farther down the jumble of messages and pleas, it came again: "It's here, man, and we're clear. Meet me in an hour."

"The little bastard did it, didn't he?"

Kirk nodded. "But when—and how?"

Bunch cracked the knuckles of one fist deep inside the other. "Let's find out."

Vinny's door was locked, which slowed them about two seconds, and his living room / office had the stale feel of disuse. Bunch poked through a bedroom almost as littered as the last time they'd seen it. Only almost because this time there were no figures sprawled half under the wadded sheets. Kirk scouted the kitchen and the small alcove that led to a door and the back landing outside.

"I think he's skipped, Dev."

Kirk was already going through the desk, looking for any paper trail. "He was traveling light, if he did. Maybe he's out on a job."

"Twenty pounds of pure is all the luggage he'd need."

"Any clothes missing?"

"How in hell can anybody tell? The laundry bag's got some dirty socks and crap in it, but the stuff in the drawers is just as dirty. I think he up and left."

"Let's shake the place out anyway."

It took a good two hours to do the right kind of search: room by room, going over first the furniture and then the floors and walls and ceilings. Kirk had the bathroom and started with the toilet bowl and under the old four-legged tub—spaces that could hold the packages of cocaine or a bundle of illicit cash. Bunch started in the bedroom. Each time they heard footsteps on the creaking stairs outside, they paused, waiting for the door to open on a startled Vinny. But it never did. By the time they finished, empty-handed, the apartment looked only slightly more disheveled than when they started.

"It's not here, Bunch." Kirk retightened the trap on the sink drain and rinsed his hands.

"So what now?"

"Johnny Atencio?"

The drive over was slowed by the tail end of rush hour traffic.

Most of the cars had their headlights on against the smoky dusk of the chill early-November evening. The sun had dropped below the ragged black mountains west of town. But lingering daylight—purple with haze on the horizons—gave enough glow to see the street signs.

"Ol' Vinny's going to be ticked when he finds his waterbed emptied," said Bunch.

"He's not going to be worried about his waterbed when we find him."

"If we find him."

Atencio's home was a small rebuilt garage sitting at the end of an unused driveway. Two strips of pitted concrete straddled a weedy alley of grass and led to a front door where the garage door used to be. As they walked past the wall of the main house and along a high fence bordering the property, a woman's face hovered momentarily in a window to stare at them. When Devlin looked up, the face disappeared behind the sudden jerk of white gauze curtain.

In the lower corner of the garage's picture window, the pink glow of a lamp shone. And behind the fence, the scuffle of clawed feet and a throaty growl said the neighbor's dog watched tensely as Bunch knocked.

"No answer. Want to go in?"

Devlin nodded and came back from the corner of the building where he'd been watching the back. There was only the one door, but all of the windows were at ground level. The screens remained undisturbed.

A spring lock held the door and Bunch had it open quickly with a plastic card. An unforgettable, heavy odor filled the dimly lit cubicle that served as a living room. "Don't touch anything, Dev."

He followed Bunch in and paused to let his eyes adjust. "Yeah."

It was the smell of blood turning stale—a lot of it—and Kirk remembered the last time he had found that odor. "See anything?"

Bunch gestured toward the bulge of a recliner chair that filled most of the tiny space. In front of it sat a portable television set, silent and black, and in it sprawled Atencio. His head was tilted back at an uncomfortable angle and his mouth gaped darkly at the ceiling. But it didn't gape as widely as his throat. Blood had pumped down his shirt and ribs and was congealed in the soggy nap of the worn throw rug under the chair. His eyes were half open and the soft glow of the small table lamp glinted under his dark lashes.

Hands jammed in his pockets to keep from accidentally touching any surface. Bunch bent to peer at the wound. "Somebody got him from behind. Stood behind the chair, and *zzzzzk*." He nodded at a scar on the glossy pad of the leatherette chair. "Tip of the knife dug in here when he started."

"Think Vinny didn't want to split the take?"

"He's the first one I'd ask," said Bunch.

Devlin, hands also in pockets, leaned a shoulder against a door to push it open. It led to an equally tiny cubicle that was the bedroom. "Somebody went through the place."

Bunch's voice answered from around a corner. "Kitchen's torn up too. It could have been Vinny looking for the other half." It made sense. Nobody had gone through Vinny's apartment, and only Vinny knew if Atencio had helped with the rip-off. And the man had disappeared. "We better call the cops," said Devlin. "Kiefer's got another one."

CHAPTER 27

They could have made the call an anonymous one. Maybe, despite the face that had watched closely when they walked down the drive, they should have. But Devlin talked Bunch into going by the rules, and Bunch didn't let him forget it as they stood waiting to answer the same questions one more time from one more officer with one more clipboard. Even when you understood the stages of police procedure and had some interest in watching the technicians work a crime scene, a sense of lost time and boredom set in early—reinforced by orders to "just stand over there out of the way, Kirk—we'll get to you in a while."

They had managed to interview the woman in the window before the first policeman arrived. Bunch delayed the call to the cops while Devlin asked her if she'd seen anybody else come down the drive earlier.

"There was this Anglo. He went and knocked and went in."

"Atencio let him in?"

"I guess. I didn't see for sure, though. I mean, I wasn't looking all that hard, you know?" The woman was somewhere between thirty and forty and apparently spent most of her time in the crowded rooms that made up the main house. One wall of the overfurnished living room was filled with framed photographs of smiling faces: family members of all ages. Her husband, beer resting on a roll of stomach, sat in front of the television and occasionally glanced up to catch what Kirk or Bunchcroft asked. He said nothing. Apparently, having his next-door neighbor murdered was less interesting than filling in the clichés on *Wheel of Fortune*. But then his wife had taken the news pretty calmly too, being more interested in Devlin's report of any damage to the furnishings than in her renter's sudden absence of health.

"Can you tell me what he looked like? Any facial hair?"

"He didn't have no beard or mustache I saw. Kind of long hair, maybe. Blond. Down over his collar in back. I remember seeing that."

"What was he wearing?"

She shrugged. "Clothes. Nothing special I could see. Had on a raincoat or something . . . what do you call it? A topcoat? I remember that because it wasn't all that cold yet. But he was wearing one."

"Any idea how tall he was?"

"Not as big as you." She shrugged again. "I don't know, average height maybe."

The vague description fit Vinny Landrum. "How long did he stay at Atencio's?"

"I don't know. I didn't see him come out. I just happened to be looking out the window when he came in, is all."

"Do you know what time it was?"

"Couple hours ago, I guess. Just before my husband come home from work."

"Did Atencio have many visitors?"

She shook her head, dark curls wagging stiffly. "He was real quiet. A good renter—paid up every month. I seen him around in the daytime last few days, though. Thought maybe he got fired or laid off or something. He didn't say nothing about it, though."

"Did he ever talk about any friends?"

"No. Just paid the rent and went to work as far as I could

see. How long's it going to take for the police to get here? I'm
going to have to clean that place."

It didn't take long once Bunch called. There were always
patrol cars cruising that corner of northwest Denver. When the
uniforms arrived, Bunch and Kirk made their statements to an
officer while they waited for the homicide and forensics teams
to get there. Then they said the same things all over again to
Sergeant Kiefer. He also wanted to learn a lot more about what
Kirk and Bunch knew of Atencio's role in the Advantage case,
why they just happened to come by for a visit, and why—as
with Chris Newman—the people they visited just happened to
be dead.

Devlin said, "We wanted to ask him some questions, that's
all. We thought he might know something more about the people at the other end of the operation."

"All right, Kirk. Wait over there. I'll get back to you."

It was almost ten when the crime scene was finally buttoned
up and Kiefer, yawning and rubbing bloodshot eyes, finally
closed his notebook. He tucked it into a pocket of his dark blue
blazer. "You give a set of your prints to forensics?"

"Yeah. But we didn't touch anything except the door."

"Which was unlocked? Same as the Newman case?"

Bunch lied. "Like I told you."

"And of course you've got no idea who that person was Mrs.
Ramirez saw."

Both men shook their heads. "When you find out," said
Devlin, "let us know."

"Yeah. Right." Kiefer sealed the door with a police lock and
a Day-Glo orange sticker. "What happened to your ear, Bunchcroft? Girlfriend cross her legs?"

"Naw, your wife bit me. You know how excited she gets.
Then again, maybe you don't."

"Funny son of a bitch, ain't you?" He paused at the door of
his unmarked sedan. "You people know more than you're telling me. If it turns out to be accessory after or obstruction, I'm
going to have your asses."

"Hey, Kief!" Bunch raised both hands, palms out. "We wouldn't lie to you. Would we, Dev?"

"No way."

They waited until the police officer's white car turned out of sight, its exhaust a plume of steam in the cold air.

"I think we talk to Arnie Minz," said Devlin.

"Yeah. He's all we got left, now."

Arnie wasn't happy to be pulled out of bed to answer the door. He was even unhappier to hear the name Vinny Landrum.

"I don't know him." He kept his arm across the doorway and spoke through a short length of chain.

Bunch tilted a photograph and pushed it through the slot. It showed two men sitting together on a park bench, heads bent in conversation. "That's Vinny on the left. The one he's talking to is you."

"You people cops?"

"No. We people are looking for Vinny."

"I don't know where he is. I mean that."

"Have you talked to him today or yesterday?"

Minz hesitated. Beneath the ragged fringe of mustache that made up for the thinning hair over his eyebrows, the tip of his tongue slid pinkly across his lip.

"He owes us something, Arnie. We're looking only for him."

"Who are you guys? Who you with?"

"We're not cops. Just leave it at that, okay?" Bunch put both hands inside the crack of the door and sucked in a deep breath. His expanding chest popped the chain and stumbled Minz back into his living room, where the single floor lamp made circles of light, one on the beige carpet, another on the canted ceiling with its rectangle of dark skylight.

"Hey—no rough stuff, now! I told you I don't know where Landrum is. That's the truth. I'm not looking for trouble with you."

"Good. We're not looking for trouble either. Just Vinny

Landrum." Devlin closed the door quietly behind them. "When did he call you?"

"This morning. Maybe about eleven. He—ah—wanted to know about a business deal we had going."

"Tell us about it."

"Well, that's all there is—a business deal. It went down yesterday and I sent the money like he told me: a post office box over in Littleton. It should of got there this afternoon. Like I told him." Minz repeated, "It was a one-shot deal—we did our business and he got his share like he asked. That's all I know about the guy."

"Did he ever mention a Johnny Atencio?"

Minz shook his head, pulling his silk robe tighter around his neck. "I know he had some other people working with him. But he didn't say who. We didn't mention names."

"When did you do your part of the deal?" asked Devlin.

Minz hesitated; Bunch leaned forward.

"Couple days ago. It was all set up and went down real smooth. A one-shot deal. Look, if he got the stuff from you guys, I didn't know about it. I swear! He told me his connection back east somewhere was shipping it in. That's all he told me."

"And you don't know where he is?"

"I don't! I swear to that."

Devlin asked, "Was he worried when he talked to you earlier?"

"No. Didn't seem to be, anyway. Just wanted to know if the money had been mailed, and I told him it had and he said thanks, nice to do business. That's it."

Back in Bunch's Bronco, they sat a few moments before he started the engine. "Sounds to me like he was telling the truth, Dev."

Devlin nodded. "Vinny's holed up somewhere."

"Yeah." Bunch pulled into the empty street toward a distant red light that gleamed icily. "Either because he killed Atencio or because he thinks somebody's after him."

"I don't figure it's Minz."

Devlin shifted uncomfortably on the seat. "Maybe somebody Minz knows—somebody who heard about the deal and wants a slice of it."

Bunch glided the car toward a glowing telephone hood. "Let's check the tap. Minz'll be on the phone right now if he's involved."

Devlin waited. A few minutes later, Bunch came back and started the car. "Line wasn't busy—no recent calls about us."

Devlin twisted his torso again. "That leaves the post office box."

"Right. That scratch bothering you?"

"It's getting sore again."

Bunch yawned, his breath fogging the windshield momentarily. "Cuts'll do that. My ear's starting to hurt too. Well, screw it—we can't try the post office until tomorrow. A good night's sleep and things'll look better, right?"

"Maybe."

CHAPTER 28

The porch light over Mrs. Ottoboni's front door was burned out and a weary Devlin Kirk, his sore ribs stiffening his movements, made a mental note to replace it in the morning. He locked his car and crossed the worn concrete of the old sidewalk which had heaved like a string of uneven dominoes from the pressure of tree roots. His shoe scraped on one of the slabs, loud in the silence of the cold street, and the porch boards creaked as he fumbled a moment at the lock before swinging the door open. The only light in his living room came from the faint glow of streetlights filtered through the tall curtained windows, and from the gleams of his telephone answerer: faint green for *On,* a hot red for *Message waiting.* He closed the door and flicked the wall switch that lit a small table lamp near the television. In the soft glow, tilted against the wall on a kitchen chair, a wide-eyed Vinny Landrum waited rigidly. He was still wearing the tan trench coat Mrs. Ramirez had described. His mouth—a lipless slit—stretched in a kind of smile.

"Well, Vinny! What'd you do, come in the back door?"

Landrum nodded stiffly.

"We've been looking all over for you."

Kirk saw the man's Adam's apple bob. The words, when they

finally came out, sounded rusty, as if his voice had been unused for a long time. "You see Johnny Atencio?"

"That's one of the reasons we've been looking. Homicide's looking too."

"For me? I didn't kill him."

Devlin gingerly slipped his jacket off and tossed it over the back of the lounge chair beside the black fireplace. Somewhere across town near the Gates Rubber plant, a diesel train honked a crossing—long, long, short, long. The small sound carried far and seemed to make the night emptier.

"You switched the dope, Vinny. You and Johnny. You sold the pure to Arnie Minz, and when Johnny wanted his share, you got greedy."

Vinny didn't bother to shake his head. "I didn't kill him."

"You made the switch just before the bust, didn't you? When you and Johnny were waiting for Scotty Martin to get to the storage locker. You had a two percent mix ready—Arnie Minz's part of the scam—and hid the real stuff somewhere in your car. Right?"

Vinny's voice was flat. "In my locker. Safer. I brought in the mix that morning. When we drove out to the bust, I took that instead of the pure. Next day we went back and got the good stuff. Minz took it off our hands."

"That's why you were so eager to spring Johnny. He'd spill if you didn't get him out. What'd he do, Vinny? Threaten you for a bigger cut?"

"I already told you." He sounded tired of the repetition. "I didn't kill him."

"Who else had motive, Vinny? That's what Dave Kiefer'll want to know."

The man, still unmoving except for the writhing line of his mouth, glanced past Kirk toward the door of the small study. Devlin heard the familiar sigh of the swinging hinge and turned. A bulky shadow stepped from the blackness of the room.

Tony Pierson.

"It was me, Kirk. I had motive."

The man held a revolver whose long, awkward barrel bore a silencer.

"I cut the little fucker's throat, didn't I, Vinny?" Pierson motioned Kirk toward the wall with a wag of the revolver. "Vinny watched." He winked at Devlin. "Almost crapped his pants when old Johnny started singing through his neck. Didn't you, Vinny?"

Vinny made some kind of little noise and pressed into the chair back. His toes lifted from the carpet as he dug his heels against the floor.

"Why?"

"He ripped me off. Him and shithead here. But he led me to Vinny first. Now Vinny's led me to you—and guess who's going to kill each other?"

"I thought you'd be out of the country by now."

Pierson nodded, the motion bringing into the lamplight a swollen, purple lump along the man's cheekbone. "Figured you might. Maybe I will, later. Maybe I'll set up another organization. It was a good operation, Kirk. Made me a lot of money before you fucked it over."

"Now you're getting rid of loose ends?"

Pierson shrugged and tried to hide a wince. "Now I'm getting even. I don't like being fucked over. Now you're the fuckee. Let's see how you like it." The long, heavy barrel lifted slightly and the man's eyes said he was through talking. Kirk, his spine rubbing the wall switch, watched the tendons rise on the back of the man's gun hand. Then he dropped to douse the lamp and in the sudden blackness roll left and low. His head and shoulders curved across the hard floor, sending a fiery rip of pain down his ribs. The spurt of the revolver jabbed toward him, and he smelled the acrid gunpowder and somewhere behind him heard a thud like a light hammer blow. Vinny's chair clattered as a thicker shadow scrambled crablike along the wall. Kirk lunged for the weapon. A second flare of orange and blue showed a glimpse of Pierson's face, then Kirk had the man's wrist and lifted. His knees drove hard up into flesh as his other hand gouged for Pierson's eyes. His fingers dug into something hairy; a heavy fist thudded against Kirk's nape and jarred orange and red fireworks across the black of his vision. He wrenched the pistol arm down, smelling the chemically sweet odor of men's cologne. Pierson tried to twist sideways, his other arm groping for something behind him. Kirk swung blindly, the edge of his hand trying for the neck, the bridge of the nose, the eyes. Something that would stun the man. It bounced off a bristly part of his face, and his breath burst hot and wet at Kirk's knuckles.

"Vinny—light!"

No answer except Pierson's grunting effort to reach whatever he groped for. Kirk tangled a leg behind the man's knee and shoved, tilting him over and down hard and through a table that splintered with a high-pitched crackle. This time Devlin caught a glimpse of the face above him and jammed up with his head to butt hard against the jaw, pale in the window light. The impact thudded loudly in Kirk's ears and numbed his forehead. He felt Pierson go soft. He shook the pistol arm hard and the weapon clattered somewhere. Its heavy barrel skidded off the carpet onto the wooden floor by a wall. Then Pierson began swinging again. A fist caught Devlin on the clavicle and sent an electric fire down his arm. Another pounded at his ribs, where the ripping cut clenched the breath from his lungs and froze him momentarily in airless agony. Pierson felt him sag and twisted hard to roll on top of Devlin and try to pin his arms with his knees.

"Vinny—pistol—get the pistol!"

Pierson's arm lifted and Kirk saw the glitter of steel. He drove a desperate fist with all his strength up into the stomach that stretched above him. A whoosh of air as the knife came down and Kirk rolled, bucking the man over enough to let Kirk wrap a leg around his neck and draw tight. His other leg clamped in a figure-four choke hold.

"Vinny! Where the hell are you? Get the pistol!"

The knife hand swung wildly and Kirk caught the man's sleeve and wrenched the cloth tightly against the wrist to hold the hungry blade from his body.

"Vinny! Turn on the goddamn light and get the pistol!"

No answer. Kirk, sweat burning into his blinking eyes, stretched against Pierson's desperate writhing and tightened his legs. A muffled nasal sound, and the man tried to twist and clamp his teeth into Devlin's thigh. Devlin squeezed harder. Pierson began to choke with a heavy flop of his torso. The flesh along Devlin's ribs tore wider from the strain. Pierson finally gave a convulsive twist and lay still, but Devlin kept the pressure tight across the man's throat. In the silence, he heard his own harsh breath and, he thought, another gasping pant from a dim corner.

"Vinny . . . if you're here . . . and if you don't turn on that light . . . I'll kill you myself!"

The lamp bulb popped with a white flash, and a moment later, Vinny found another switch that lit up the kitchen and spilled glare into the broken living room and on the tangle of two bodies still stretched tautly against each other. Kirk had Pierson's head tightly clamped in the bend of his knee. Both hands pressed against the knife arm in a wrist lock that bent Pierson's elbow at an unnatural angle. Pierson's free arm was wrapped in the sogginess of Kirk's bloody shirt, the fist clutched deep in the red wetness. Vinny, his dry mouth sour with the foretaste of vomit, grabbed the fallen table lamp and swung hard at the back of Pierson's head. The solid thud tingled his hands, and Pierson's arm flailed and dropped to leave Kirk gasping loudly and making some kind of wheezing, hurting noise as he slowly untangled from the limp man's body.

CHAPTER 29

In the kitchen, Mrs. Ottoboni had the teakettle whistling and they could hear her rattle unfamiliarly through Kirk's counters for rags and cups and whatever it was she thought Devlin needed. Pierson, pale and still unconscious but breathing, lay half propped with his hands tied behind him and his head slightly raised to ease the effects of any concussion. Kirk was in the lounge chair panting lightly against the hurt of his ribs. Vinny walked back and forth between Kirk and Pierson and wiped nervously at the corners of his mouth.

"I saved your life, Kirk. You owe me."

"Who saved—ouch—who?"

Vinny glanced toward the kitchen and whispered hoarsely: "Me! If it hadn't been for me hitting that bastard over the head, you'd be fucking buzzard bait now. I saved your life!"

Somewhere in the distance, the growing wail of a siren worked its way across empty intersections toward the house and the injured men and the weapons that were out of reach on the mantel.

"You say nothing about the dope, we call it even. I mean, what's your life worth, Kirk? The dope's gone anyway. Arnie— My contact's already got rid of it, so you can't pin a goddamn thing on me. I mean, it's my word against yours that I switched the crap, ain't it?"

"Pierson heard you."

Vinny chewed his lip. "I was lying to protect you—keep you alive a little longer. I saved your goddamn life—you owe me!"

"I owe you a swat in the scrotum. You made me look goddamn bad with Dave Miller."

The siren was closer now. Probably the ambulance. Sergeant Kiefer would ride cold through the light traffic.

"Well, it's your fault as much as mine, damn you! I mean, you set up a deal like that and shoved it under my nose, Kirk. What the hell did you expect? Now I just saved your sorry life! You don't want to feel grateful, that's okay with me, man—it just tells me what kind of asshole you really are. You ungrateful son of a bitch!"

The siren shut off but was still growling as the emergency vehicle slowed in the street outside. Devlin levered himself up on one elbow and tried to breathe through the grip of pain in his side. "You hear me, Vinny: Bunch wants to put you in a blender, piece by piece. And there's not one thing in this world that can stop him. Not you. Not me. Not God Himself. Unless . . ."

Vinny envisioned Bunch and didn't like what he saw. "Unless what?"

"Unless you make a couple people happy."

"Who?"

"Kiefer and Miller. That'll make Bunch happy."

"Hand Miller my ass so he'll be kissy-face with you again? No fucking way, José!"

"Not yours. Arnie Minz. Miller's been after him for a long time. In a few weeks, you tell Minz you have another shipment—you set him up for a buy and bust." Devlin added, "Miller will pay a pretty good snitch fee, too."

Vinny thought it over as hurrying boots thudded across the lawn and up the front steps. "What about Kiefer?"

"Tell him you saw Pierson kill Atencio."

"Just tell the truth?"

"I know it'll be hard."

The clatter at the front door was followed by the bulky shapes of the ambulance attendants. One started asking questions about the still-unconscious Pierson. The other began testing his pulse and blood pressure. Vinny told them the man fell and hit his head while struggling with Kirk. Another car skidded to a halt out front and Sergeant Kiefer, coming in without knocking, stared down at the unconscious man.

"This him? Pierson?"

Devlin shifted so the EMT could get a clearer look at his sliced flesh. "Yeah. And Scotty Martin'll turn state's when you tell him Pierson's caught. He's a witness to Newman's killing."

Kiefer ran a palm down the red sweater that peeked from under his dark sport coat. "State's or not, he'll do time."

Kirk grunted. "Fine with me." The EMT—a young man with cropped red hair and wire-rim glasses—was saying something about avoiding infection and seeing a doctor first thing in the morning. A pair of uniformed policemen, jingling and creaking with equipment, came from their cruiser and crowded into the room to talk with Kiefer.

"Kirk." Vinny leaned down as the EMT turned to help load Pierson onto a gurney. "It's a deal—about Miller and Kiefer, I mean. And you won't—ah—I mean, you'll forget all about that little thing with Atencio and me, right?"

"If you get Minz. But if you cross us, Vinny, there's nowhere on God's green earth you can hide."

"Hey, trust me!" Vinny held out a hand. "Shake."

Mrs. Ottoboni, a tray of hot tea balanced on thin wrists and the evening's excitement still in the sprigs of wiry gray hair escaping from her kerchief, edged past the standing officers toward Kirk. "My! The victors shake hands!"